THE

ACTIVIST'S

DAUGHTER

ELLYN BACHE

THE
ACTIVIST'S
DAUGHTER

ELLYN BACHE

Spinsters Ink
Duluth, Minnesota

First edition
10-9-8-7-6-5-4-3-2

Spinsters Ink
32 E. First St., #330
Duluth, MN 55802-2002, USA

Cover photo by Barbara Stitzer
Cover photo enhanced by Denise Burge, Brutal Gift Design
Cover design by Gail Wallinga

Production: Helen Dooley   Ryan Petersen
                  Joan Drury   Kim Riordan
                  Emily Gould   Amy Strasheim
                  Marian Hunstiger   Erika Thorne
                  Kelly Kager   Liz Tufte
                  Claire Kirch   Nancy Walker
                  Lori Loughney

Library of Congress Cataloging-in-Publication Data
Bache, Ellyn.
   The activist's daughter / Ellyn Bache.
      p.   cm.
   ISBN 1-883523-18-4 (alk. paper)
   I. Title.
PS3563.A845A65   1997
813'.54–dc21   97–1159
                                          CIP

Printed on recycled paper with soy-based inks

In loving memory of the Winik family:

Anna and Hyman Winik
Irving Winik
Alice Winik Bercovitz
Clara Winik Olefsky

Acknowledgments

I am grateful to many people for helping me to research and write this book, but especially to Karen Parker, who graciously shared with me her journals and some of the articles she wrote for *The Daily Tar Heel* during the fall of 1963. I began this book not realizing that the University of North Carolina at Chapel Hill actually did admit its first undergraduate Negro woman that year—and that that woman was Karen. In 1963, Karen wrote in her journal that "It's hard keeping your head up when you know the girls on your hall would like it better if you didn't live there. . . . It hurts hearing people make derogatory comments about you . . . to sense that many people assume you're stupid and can't do anything. . . . All these things . . . make me want more and more to 'show em'."

Thirty years later, when I called her for help, Karen was an editor at the *Los Angeles Times*.

I would also like to thank Westy Fenhagen, Nancy Tilly, Peggy Payne, Kathleen Ford Bonnie, Patricia Ruark, Brooks Preik, Joyce Cooper, Blonnie Wyche, Judy Marshall, Maggi Grace, Jan Dodson, Ruth Gratch, and Beth Perry for their generous help.

1

I hated my mother in the summer of 1963, and as I recall, she hated me back.

The previous fall, just after I began my senior year in high school, my mother's photo appeared in the *Washington Post*, skirt hiked above her knees as police carried her away from a civil rights demonstration near the Washington Monument. I looked at the picture and groaned. My sister Natalie put her hands over her eyes. "I've never been so humiliated," she said.

"Beryl! Natalie!" our father cautioned.

Our grandmother, Miriam, who had moved in with us so our mother could save the world, clunked bowls of oatmeal onto our places at the table. "*Nu?* You're ashamed of her? You should be proud."

I knew enough to keep quiet.

An hour later, as I walked down the hallway of Wilson High School, my history teacher pointed me out to the band instructor. Her dramatic whisper carried above the hubbub of students rushing to class: "That's her. The activist's daughter."

My face grew hot, and I broke out in a sheen of embarrassment. It was a critical moment. I knew two things: I wanted to be anonymous. I wanted revenge.

That night at dinner, Natalie announced her engagement to Barry Gelfand and said she planned to marry in the spring.

"Oh, Natalie," Mother told her dismissively. "You're only a sophomore. You have almost three more years of college."

"I quit school today. I'm going to work full time and save for the wedding."

Mother blanched. Compared to that, what could I do that wouldn't seem feeble? As the months passed and the tension grew, Mother was undaunted by my pointed barbs—even when they had to do with her beloved job.

Mother worked for a civil rights organization with the unappealing acronym FEN, for Freedom and Equality Now. That year, she was busy planning for the great March on Washington, teaching anyone who showed up in her office how to make tactful phone calls asking for housing for the hordes who would descend on the city in August. As the number of marchers increased, so did her hours at the office.

"Come down and help me if you don't have to work," she'd order. "I have two dozen volunteers, and they don't make a dent in it."

I never went. "Your cause, Mother, not mine. If you expect me to feel guilty, don't."

"These are people from all over the country. People who are giving up—who knows what they're giving up to come here?"

"Maybe nothing. Maybe they're coming for a good time."

"They're coming for a great cause. They're coming to see a great leader, Martin Luther King. They're coming because they believe in something." She sighed deeply and uttered the words that became her mantra and exit line: "I'm disappointed in you, Beryl."

2

Dad put a hand on my shoulder. "She's just nervous," he said, pushing his fingers through his springy hair until he found his bald spot, no bigger than a quarter, and massaging it as he always did when he was troubled. "She wants to do it right. You know how she is."

"She's a fanatic."

"That's not fair, Beryl. I don't want you talking like that. It's reprehensible." My father had been losing steam ever since the McCarthy committee had investigated him, but on the matter of Mother he was adamant. "She's very good at what she does. You shouldn't demean it."

"Right. Any excuse not to spend time with her family."

"If you want to see her so much, go down there and make some calls."

"No."

And so it went. My sentiments were unwelcome, but I couldn't help them. Ten years before, the McCarthy hearings had shifted the balance of power in our family, energizing Mother in exact proportion to the amount Dad was diminished. Before he was investigated, he had been a well-known architect; afterwards he was unemployed. She had been a housewife; suddenly she had an excuse to be a breadwinner. He failed at starting his own architectural firm and ended up buying a dry cleaning store near Gallaudet College for the Deaf. She took a job monitoring voting rights for Negroes and thrived. He had been elegant, animated; he'd worn tailored clothes and highly shined shoes. Now buttons popped off his shirts, his trousers were wrinkled, his jackets grew shiny with wear. She had been a tall, drab woman; now she was striking in a frightening, bohemian way. People glanced at her and took notice; people looked at him and never guessed he was a man who could have his clothes pressed any time he wanted.

Miriam moved in with us the same month Mother went to work in the mid-fifties. Natalie and I were eleven and eight, and although we thought Miriam was old, she had plenty of energy for us. She'd immigrated from Russia as a teenager and spent most of her life running a tailor shop with my grandfather while raising my father and his sister and supporting leftist causes. Now Papa was dead, and she needed to fill her time. She cooked us enormous meals, cleaned the house, went to Workmen's Circle meetings, tended our great-aunt Gussie during Gussie's crazy spells, made lunch for her friends Mrs. Frank and Mrs. Silverman once a month on Thursday. She kept us fed and clothed and tended.

By the time Mother's office began sending her on short trips to the South, there was nothing for her to do at home anyway.

"Any job, it has to do with colored people voting, it's dangerous," our great-aunt Gussie informed us. "Especially in the South. *Ach.*"

Natalie and I were horrified. It was bad enough Mother left us; it was worse that we had to fear for her safety.

"Gussie, *g'noog,*" Miriam said sharply, which meant *enough.* Natalie and I had been taught very little Yiddish because our elders enjoyed having a private language we couldn't understand. But we understood *g'noog* and we understood what Aunt Gussie meant about the South.

We had known about the South ever since we could remember, because of a joke Dad used to make about our great-grandmother, Bubby Tsippi. "We're off to see Mississippi, girls," he would bellow as we prepared to go visit her, back in those days before Senator McCarthy robbed him of his sense of humor.

"Leonard!" Mother would admonish, pretending to be angry. "She's an old woman. Treat her with respect!"

"What's disrespectful?" he'd ask. "She's a missus, isn't she? And her name is Tsippi." Then he'd wink at us before putting on a sober expression.

We all knew what the word Mississippi implied. At the bottom of the deepest South, Mississippi was a hot, hellish place where slaves had once picked cotton, where Negroes were forced to wait in separate rooms from whites even in a doctor's office, and endure other terrible insults. Mississippi was as cruel to Negroes as Russia had once been to Jews. The entire South was such a region: steamy and menacing. Leonard Rosinsky would never call his grandmother Mississippi to her face.

So when Mother started traveling to cities like Jackson and Biloxi, we understood the danger. We had seen pictures of slain civil rights leaders; we knew policemen turned hoses on protesters as if they were dogs. Even when Mother came home laughing, brimming with stories she could hardly wait to tell, we knew she was in jeopardy. Aunt Gussie's pronouncements confirmed this, as did Miriam's attempts to silence her. Mother was brave but misguided, we thought.

She believed it was noble to go into the South briefly, for a purpose, on a mission. What was wrong was to stay longer, spend money, support an immoral way of life. She never understood how her friends the Eisners could blow their savings on a vacation to Myrtle Beach. Or how the Gershners, fellow activists from before the McCarthy days, could send their son Stuart to a school in North Carolina just because he'd gotten a scholarship. Some things, she said, were simply beyond comprehension.

In the end, this gave me courage. By the time Mother's picture appeared in the *Washington Post* and embarrassment took up permanent residence on my skin and in my soul, we'd all agreed I would go to George Washington University next year to study medical technology. I would do as Natalie had done: live at home and work part-time to earn tuition.

Instead, I sent applications to three colleges I was sure Mother would hate: The University of North Carolina, the University of Alabama (in the state where that devil incarnate, George Wallace, reigned), and Ole Miss.

"There's no money to send you away to school," Mother fumed. "Especially schools run by bigoted blockheads."

"Don't complain. I paid the application fees out of my own savings."

"Why throw away money on such nonsense?" Her expression froze; her eyes widened. "To insult me!" she gasped.

After that, we avoided each other or spoke only in clipped, acid tones. When she wasn't working, she devoted her attention to Natalie. She tried hard to bully her into going back to school, but Natalie refused. Natalie was getting married *no matter what.* In June. At home. By a rabbi.

"A rabbi!" Mother exclaimed. Except for Bubby Tsippi, no one in our family believed in God. "Our faith is in the possibilities of man, not God. A rabbi would be hypocritical."

"I don't care. Barry's parents will expect it." Natalie crossed her arms and stood firm.

Dad fingered a thread on the front of his shirt and spoke softly. "Leah," he said to Mother. "So she wants a rabbi. Why not?"

By spring, the wedding was planned and I'd been accepted by all four schools I'd applied to. I sent letters to each one saying I was coming. I found a part-time job at Kitty Kelly Shoe Store on F Street.

"You're showing some sense for once," Mother said. "You can keep working in the fall when you go to G.W."

On a balmy Sunday the week before I graduated from high school, a bearded rabbi married Natalie and Barry in our living room, under a not-so-traditional Jewish *chupah* of colorful African shawls borrowed from Mother's office. For the reception, Miriam fashioned her famous sponge cake into three layers, and her friend Mrs. Silverman decorated it. Natalie threw her bouquet to me, and we hugged and cried as she prepared to leave. We agreed that I would come to New York often to visit.

As the heat of summer kicked in, Mother threw herself

back into finding housing for marchers while I tried harder than ever to keep out of her way. She was restless and edgy; she blamed me for not helping her. No matter that she hated being office-bound. No matter that the job was impossible. The way she acted, the entire looming housing shortage might have been *my fault.* The air between us bristled.

"Everyone in this house is trying to do what they can to help others less fortunate," she sniped. "Except you."

"What do you mean? I'm working at Kitty Kelly! You're the one who wants me to earn money for school."

"You're not working full time."

"No, but I'm earning my tuition. Earning it by exploiting Negroes, if you want to know the truth."

"Spare me, Beryl." She narrowed her eyes. "Exploiting them how?"

"Every time they pay for their shoes, I have to give them my spiel about buckles and handbags."

"That doesn't sound exactly criminal." She opened the phone book to dismiss me, flipping through to find a number.

"Nobody needs doodads they can't afford. Think what the markup must be. I get thirty percent commission."

"A shoe store isn't a charity. It has to pay the help. It isn't exploiting."

It was true that nothing in the store cost much, and that my commissions weren't making me rich. The stock ran to cheap, colorful shoes in shades of lime and lavender and fuchsia that no white person had the courage to wear.

"No one needs shoe buckles," I maintained.

"If it bothers you so much, find a spare moment to come to my office. Work off your guilt."

"What's wrong with you, Mother? I don't see you asking Miriam to help. I don't see you asking Dad."

"Miriam has to run the house. And don't you think Dad has enough on his mind? Think what it's like, going from important architect all those years and now dry cleaner to the deaf. He works as many hours as I do."

"Oh, please."

She slammed the phone book shut. "Fine, then. Don't make phone calls. Don't tax yourself. Charity begins at home. You can help Miriam get ready for Bubby Tsippi. She's coming next week. You can get your stuff out of your room."

She lifted the phone book and threw it onto the top of the refrigerator. "And Beryl. This isn't optional."

❊

Bubby Tsippi was ninety then and nearly deaf, a tiny woman whose face looked like a shrunken apple and whose sweet-natured smile revealed a line of pink gums and no teeth at all. Her wardrobe consisted entirely of faded housedresses and the tattered scarves she wore to cover her head. Her real name was Zipporah, which meant "little bird" in Hebrew.

I threw my clothes into boxes and lugged them into the hallway. Ever since Bubby had gotten too frail to run her own house, she had divided her time among her children. She had borne eleven of them, and six were still alive, four in Baltimore, and Miriam and Aunt Gussie in Washington. All of them kept her for a few months except Aunt Gussie, whose crazy spells could come on without warning.

Aunt Gussie complained because she wanted to keep her mother in her own apartment, but Miriam wouldn't hear of it.

"Sure, and what if you have a spell?" Miriam shook a clean sheet from the dryer in her sister's direction.

"So if I have a problem, so Abe will watch her."

"Abe!" Miriam scoffed at the mention of Gussie's husband. "Abe got his own problems!" The little fingers on both of Uncle Abe's hands had been amputated long before I was born—for what reason I didn't know—and the stubs were tight and shiny as the top of a drum. His middle and ring fingers were frozen into claws.

"I might be fine her whole visit," Aunt Gussie said. "Sometimes I'm fine. Like when the Cossacks came."

"What are you mixing, her visit and the Cossacks?" Miriam asked as she folded the sheet into sections.

"I'm not mixing nothing. I was fine when the Cossacks came. When I was living in Kiev."

"You weren't living in Kiev, you were living in Slobotsky." Miriam had left the subject of Bubby Tsippi somewhere in Russia at the turn of the century. "Jews weren't allowed to live in the city proper," she explained to me. "Slobotsky was a suburb."

"So what does Beryl need to know, Slobotsky or Kiev?" Gussie, too, turned to me to clarify. "We lived in a court apartment. The Cossacks didn't come down our block. We were fine the whole time."

"Hhmph," Miriam snorted, and closed the dryer. As often happened between them, they dropped the subject before it was settled.

Being an orthodox Jew, Bubby Tsippi had kept kosher all her life. Being a family that didn't believe in God (only in the possibilities of man), we didn't. Miriam had solved the kosher problem by buying two sets of cheap dishes, one for meat, the other for dairy. She'd also bought special pots for cooking her mother's food, and she went to great lengths to prepare dishes Bubby Tsippi could eat with no teeth. Miriam made cold beet borscht and a spinach borscht called *schav*. She made chicken noodle soup and matzoh balls soft enough for Bubby to gum. She cooked vegetables to a fine pulp, her preparations for one meal often blending into the next.

In the dank, moldy basement the first night of Bubby's visit, I woke up twice with my heart thudding until I remembered where I was. I'd never minded the dungeon-like quality of the basement before, but without Natalie for company, it was creepy. In the morning, I stumbled up the steps into air already so hot and muggy the kitchen floor stuck to my bare feet. I waylaid Mother in the dining room.

"I hardly got any sleep," I complained. "The place is like a jail cell."

"What do you know about jail cells?" Mother asked, not looking up. She was dressed for work, shuffling through the mess of papers she always kept on the table.

"I'm going to be late," she muttered, stuffing papers into her briefcase. She was as tall as most men—but attractive, too, which was the more infuriating. She had large blue eyes which Natalie and I hadn't inherited, and silky black hair which we had—except that hers hung almost to her waist and was always shoved haphazardly into a bun. That morning it was pulled back even more carelessly than usual, with several long strands hanging into her face. This ought to have looked sloppy but instead looked like a fashion statement.

"So you're ten minutes late," I told her. "You stayed at the office till midnight. Are they going to fire you for missing your bus?"

"I'm not going to the office. I'm giving my abortion talk. I can't find my notes."

"Oh, Jesus," I groaned. She was the only woman I knew who carried a briefcase to work, the only one who wore horn-rimmed men's glasses for reading. "If you wouldn't give personal talks, you wouldn't get nervous and lose your papers."

She gave me a stare of blue ice. Her own abortion was the basis for her speeches, not easy for her to talk about. "Just help me find the notes."

The phone rang in the kitchen. I ran in to answer. It was Uncle Abe for Miriam.

"I think she's getting Bubby settled out on the porch," I told him.

"So you'll go find her," Uncle Abe said.

My mother poked her head into the kitchen. "Got it." She held up a sheaf of papers.

"Miriam!" I yelled. Most of my friends called their grandmothers Bubby or Grandma, but Miriam—a woman who addressed her own best friends as Mrs. Frank and Mrs. Silverman—had rebelled against that custom after the McCarthy hearings and ordered us to call her by her first name.

Miriam appeared, fully made up and powdered, wearing her usual dark dress covered by an apron, along with stockings and sensible shoes. She took the phone and listened.

"*Nu?*" she told Abe finally. "So you'll go in and take it away from her." I knew she must be referring to the blueing Aunt Gussie used on her hair. This was serious business.

Aunt Gussie's hair had turned white when she was twenty-five. She had been blueing it ever since. She was proud no one had ever seen her with yellow streaks, even after her appendix operation. During her crazy spells, Gussie applied the blueing every day, and for weeks afterwards amused the neighbors with hair the color of a cloudless sky.

"Take the box from her right now," Miriam ordered fruitlessly. We all knew Gussie wouldn't let Uncle Abe within five feet of her during these times. "You'll tell her I'm coming over," Miriam added, and hung up.

She took off her apron and reached for her purse.

"The woman certainly has interesting timing," my mother said.

Miriam ignored this. "You'll take me by machine," she said. To Miriam, a machine was a sewing machine or an automobile or anything in between.

"Leonard has the car."

"Fine. Then I'll go by myself on the bus." Miriam was the only one Gussie trusted at these times. On the bus, Gussie's apartment was ten minutes away.

"I'll be back when I can." Miriam clutched her purse to

her chest and fled out the kitchen door, nearly bumping into the barrel of brine she'd set out to make the old-fashioned dill pickles Bubby still liked to mouth, even though she couldn't chew. Her sturdy shoes clunked down the steps and along the sidewalk toward Connecticut Avenue.

"I have to go, too," Mother said. "I'll try to be home by noon, but don't count on it. You need to watch Bubby until I get back."

"I have to work," I objected.

"Not till later. It's Thursday." On Thursdays the downtown stores stayed open until nine. I wasn't expected at Kitty Kelly until five.

"You might have to give Bubby lunch," Mother added.

"Give her *what* for lunch?"

"I don't know. Miriam must have left something." Mother, too, marched out the door and was gone.

Still in pajamas and robe, I shuffled out to the front porch where Bubby rocked. Her housedress hung from her as if from a hanger. Her head was covered with a faded brown kerchief that hid her few remaining wisps of hair—the kerchief Natalie and I insisted on calling Tsippi's *schmatte* because the term meant "rag" and annoyed our mother immensely.

"Nu, v'as machst du, Bubby?" I shouted. *How are you?*

Bubby looked up and gave me a toothless smile. *"Goot. Goot."* Though the humidity was eighty percent and the temperature even higher, Bubby never complained. Where her kerchief met her forehead, a line of beaded sweat glistened.

I sat on the porch steps at a level with Bubby's ankles, white above rolled-down stockings, the skin so translucent I imagined I could see gray bone beneath. I'd exhausted my few words of Yiddish, so there was nothing for us to do together but sit. We stared at the bumpy sidewalk, heaved into ripples by the roots of old sycamore trees. The neighborhood was shabby but genteel, safe enough for her to stay out here all day if she wanted to, and she often did. From the distance came the hum of traffic heading up Connecticut Avenue toward Chevy Chase Circle three blocks away, or beginning the long trek downtown. I had always liked the distant sound of cars; I found it comforting. I didn't think Bubby could hear it. She sighed deeply. I did, too.

"What do you like to eat?" I asked in English.

She said nothing. She couldn't hear; she didn't understand. After a minute, she began to snore. I got up and went into the house for the cotton afghan Miriam had crocheted for her. At ninety, she chilled easily even in the middle of summer. I draped the cover over her shoulders. Without opening her eyes, she reached up and took my hand. Her skin wasn't leathery, just soft and warm, like much-laundered cloth.

2

At lunchtime I checked the refrigerator for something Bubby could eat. Miriam usually took a few days to get into her cooking mode, and since Bubby had just arrived, there wasn't much choice. A carton of small-curd cottage cheese, creamed and soft, would have to do. I reached into the cabinet where Miriam kept Bubby's special plates.

I hadn't expected Mother to get back in time to help me, and of course she didn't. She rarely came home when she said she would, and after an abortion lecture she'd be surrounded by women wanting information and advice. I'd seen this first-hand once, after Natalie and I both reached puberty and Mother told us she wanted us to come hear her.

We arrived late and stood at the back of the small auditorium looking for seats. The room was packed with women. Mother was clinging white-knuckled to the lectern.

"My husband had been investigated by McCarthy and was about to lose his job," she confided to the crowd. "I couldn't have afforded another child then, financially or emotionally. I could barely afford the children I already had."

Natalie and I slunk into seats in a far corner, shrank into ourselves, wished ourselves invisible.

Mother smiled bitterly, and her tone grew crisp and sharp. "It was an axiom here in Washington that if McCarthy robbed you of your livelihood, you went into the dry cleaning business. But we didn't know that yet."

A few wisps of nervous laughter rose from the audience. Natalie and I were catatonic.

"Fortunately, I was solvent enough to find a reputable doctor. Fortunately, there were no complications." She raised her voice a notch. "But it cost ten times what it should have. It still does!"

A murmur filled the room, women nodding and agreeing.

"It's also still illegal. Still a dirty secret! And it isn't going to change unless you and I change it. You and I!"

A burst of applause rose and crested, and women leapt from their seats to shake Mother's hand. Natalie and I rose with them—her living, unaborted children—and hustled out of the room. I hadn't been to another abortion lecture since.

I thought about that as I snatched a plate from the cupboard and spooned some cottage cheese onto it. I set out silverware, then went to the porch and guided Bubby inside to the table.

"*Danke,* Beryl," she said, eyeing the cottage cheese but making no move to eat. I picked up her spoon as I'd seen Miriam do in previous years, put some cottage cheese on it, and offered it to Bubby. She opened her mouth. After I fed her a few bites, she took the spoon from me and began to eat on her own. I sat down across from her and nodded encouragement.

A moment later Mother shouldered her way through the back door. She looked spent.

"I'm going to do some paperwork here this afternoon."

She yanked off a high-heeled pump and rubbed her foot. "I'm not going into the office."

Her gaze shifted to Bubby, who was still eating. She watched for long seconds, narrowing her eyes. Her expression hardened. She pointed to the cottage cheese.

"That's a dish for meat," she said to me.

"It is?"

Mother believed the kosher laws were twelve centuries out of date, as impractical as segregated lunch counters. I was surprised she knew which dishes were which, much less cared. I myself thought the plain white ones were for dairy, but couldn't be sure.

Mother mumbled something in Yiddish to Bubby, who looked up, uncomprehending. *"V'as?"*

Mother repeated herself, louder.

Bubby put down her spoon but didn't seem alarmed. She shrugged and replied briefly in Yiddish. Then she pushed herself away from the table, rose slowly, and began shuffling toward my bedroom for her afternoon nap.

"What did she say?" I asked Mother.

"She said, 'So what if I eat *milchig* from a *fleishig* dish? How could it be so important?'"

I was relieved.

"Why did you bother to tell her?" I asked. "You might have upset her. What would be the point?"

"Beryl," Mother said stonily. "After all this time you should know one set of dishes from another."

"Miriam is the one who cooks, not me! Besides, those dishes haven't been handled for a year! You know what this is like? The High Holiday thing. I suppose I should have known about that, too!"

"That was ten years ago. Are you still dredging that up?"

"Seven years!" I shouted.

"Seven, ten, who cares?" She shrugged as if it didn't matter.

17

I felt blood rush to my face. Seven years ago I'd come home from school with flower bulbs to sell for a fundraiser, and I remembered like it was yesterday how Mother had urged me on. It was early autumn, a sunny day. "Why not go sell them right now? Look how warm it is."

So I went. Up and down the block without making a single sale. At the Katzes' on the corner, I hesitated. Not long before, Robert Katz had invited some of us in to listen to his player piano, and five minutes later his mother had appeared in the room. "Enough," she said, pointing us to the door in the middle of a song. "Right now."

As afraid as I was of her, I was more afraid of returning to school without selling any bulbs.

There was a long pause after my knock. Then she flung open the door and frowned down at me. Dressed in a formal brown suit, she was in the process of attaching a gold earring to her ear.

"What?" she demanded.

I began my spiel. She raised a hand to stop me.

"Flower bulbs! Don't you know what day this is?"

"No," I said honestly.

Mrs. Katz's lips turned down in displeasure. Her eyes narrowed to slits above her puffy cheeks.

"It's Yom Kippur Eve," she spat. "How can you be out selling flower bulbs when people are trying to get ready for *shul* on the holiest night of the year?"

I muttered an apology, but Mrs. Katz drew herself up and closed the door. I fled. Bitter tears burned my eyes as I ran. My skin stung as if I'd been slapped.

At home, an ordinary dinner was being prepared. No one was dressing for *shul*. No one had mentioned that it was a holiday. When I blurted out my story, Mother said, "To each his own. But the woman should have more manners."

So how was it that now, when she saw I'd given Bubby

the wrong dish, her expression was an exact mirror of Mrs. Katz's, all distaste and disgust?

※

I decided to shower and leave for work early. Downtown I could window-shop until it was time to clock in at Kitty Kelly.

"Wake up Bubby before you go," Mother called when I came up from the basement. She sat in the dining room, papers all over the table, reading reports, too important to rouse herself. She was twisting a loosened strand of hair.

I went into my bedroom where Bubby slept. She never undressed for naps, just got into bed under a thin layer of covers. Each of the bedrooms had a little window air conditioner. Usually Bubby turned hers off, but not today. She lay on her back with her toothless mouth open, her scarf askew. A few wisps of gray hair curled around her ear.

"Bubby, time to get up." As usual, I stroked her forearm to awaken her. After sleeping, her skin grew silky and cool. But that day it was cold, and the darkened room was also cold, not just from the air conditioner which hummed in the window, but from some aberration in the nature of things, some lack of living spirit, trapped in the unnatural halo of chill. I knew at once she'd died not long after I fed her cottage cheese in a dish meant for meat. Mother was right to be angry. I had fed her unfit food and brought down the wrath of her God.

I went screaming into the dining room, trying to say what had happened but unable to form words. Mother grabbed me, yelled, "Stop! Stop!" then rushed into the bedroom. I kept screaming as she made the appropriate phone calls. I howled and sobbed. By the time Dad burst into the door as if he'd run the entire way from the dry cleaning shop, I'd worked myself into a state of hysteria.

"Breathe deeply," Mother kept urging. "Say something. Then breathe."

But I was too upset to be coherent. Dad guided me to the couch; Mother brought me a glass of brandy.

"Shh, Beryl. It's okay," Dad said, touching the brandy snifter to my lips. "Bubby was an old woman. She was lucky to live so long, not to be sick. These things happen."

I pushed the brandy away.

Mother motioned Dad to move. She sat down beside me.

"Settle down," she commanded. "I mean it."

I kept wailing. I hiccupped. I began to gasp for breath.

"They say you should slap them when they're hysterical," she said to Dad.

"She's not hysterical, she's in shock."

"Then she should lie down. She should prop up her feet."

Dad arranged my head on the couch cushions. Mother put pillows under my feet.

I was not comforted. I was only so exhausted that I fell asleep.

For the next two days, I was unable, or perhaps only unwilling, to speak. I felt quite removed from the activities of my family as they prepared for the funeral. I heard what they said but didn't answer. I registered their concern but didn't care. I lived in a bubble of silence.

"Beryl, what's wrong with you?" Natalie asked when she and Barry arrived for the funeral. She took my hand and stared into my eyes. "Oh, Beryl," she whispered when I didn't reply. Then she burst into tears.

Back at the house after the funeral, people spoke in low tones and pointed to me.

"Poor thing, she was the one who found her."

"Well, of course she's upset. It was a terrible shock."

The sound swirled around me. I stood apart, listening but unresponsive. I had dressed for the funeral entirely in black, borrowing a blouse from Natalie and hose from Miriam to complete my ensemble. I had wept silently at the funeral home; I had leaned on my father's arm at the cemetery and clutched a handkerchief to my nose. Back at the house I had been surprised at the large number of people who came to pay respects, considering that Bubby was ninety years old and all of her friends were dead.

"Is she going to be all right?" A woman gestured in my direction with a slice of cocktail rye slathered with chopped liver.

"She'll be fine," Mother said impatiently. "She just needs another day or two."

I rose from my seat. Leaving the hungry mourners to their whitefish and coffee cake, I drifted out to the front porch and sat on the swing. People greeted me as they came or left. I nodded but didn't speak. Dusk began to gather. The street fell into shadow. A man approached from around the corner, a tall Negro with a jaunty, loose-hipped walk. There was something familiar about him, though I didn't recognize him at first. I hadn't seen him since the day of my grandfather's funeral, nearly ten years before. It was Rayfield, who had been the presser in Miriam and Papa's tailor shop. I had always liked him.

He hadn't changed much. He was still bony, angular, pleasant-looking. One of my first memories was of falling off the high counter in the tailor shop, and of Rayfield plucking me from the floor and saying "Bingo!" in a large, cheerful voice.

He came up the porch steps to offer condolences and smiled a greeting. I leapt off the swing, ran toward him, catapulted myself into his arms. "Oh, Rayfield," I wailed, the first words I had spoken since Bubby's death. "Oh, Rayfield, I killed her!"

Fifteen minutes later I was lying in Miriam's big bed upstairs. Rayfield had handed me over to Dad, who had given me a glass of schnapps and helped Natalie and Mother guide me up the steps. Now they were all staring down at me, open-mouthed and astonished.

"You thought you killed her?" Dad asked. "You really thought that? No wonder you're upset." He patted my right hand over and over again, and Natalie, on the opposite side of the bed, did the same with my left.

"It stands to reason," I said, my voice tremulous after two days of silence. "Why else would she die right after breaking a kosher law? I fed her from the wrong dish."

"Coincidence, Beryl," Dad said. "An irony. But certainly not your fault."

Mother and Miriam stood soberly at the foot of the bed, looking on. Aunt Gussie, who had snapped out of her crazy spell when her mother died, was downstairs with Uncle Abe tending the guests.

"You saw it," I said to Mother. "Because of me, she ate *treif*. So God struck her down. You said yourself I should have known which dishes were which."

Mother waved a hand to show how preposterous I was. "If God exists, why would He strike her down for eating off the wrong dish now? Why not five years ago? Those dishes were never really kosher."

"It's true, *tochter,*" Miriam said. "A kitchen, it can't be kosher if you keep bacon in the ice box. It was always just pretend."

I looked at Mother. "Then why did you make such a big thing of it?"

Mother shrugged but didn't answer.

For the next week, Miriam observed the traditional mourning period for Bubby's death, not by sitting a formal *shivah* but by setting out platters of bagels and sweet rolls for anyone who might stop in. Aunt Gussie came over early in the morning and stayed all day to help. Natalie and Barry had to go home to New York, and my parents, not given to mourning just because tradition called for it, went back to work.

I did not go back to Kitty Kelly. I slept until the sun was high and hot, and I spent my days in the living room, staring out the window. Who said I hadn't killed my great-grandmother? How could they dispute it? She hadn't even been sick.

The instant the week of mourning ended, Miriam and Aunt Gussie attacked Bubby's belongings. They boxed the contents of her suitcases in cartons for the Progressive Women's Club rummage store. They stripped the bed and opened the windows. "All aired out," Aunt Gussie said. "You can move back into your room."

"I could never sleep in there," I told her.

"What will you do then, live like a mole in the basement?" Miriam asked. "When you start college, you'll need your room, your desk."

I tried to picture myself taking the bus to George Washington University every morning and returning at night to study in the cell where my great-grandmother had died.

"I'm not moving back into that room," I announced. "I'm not going to G.W."

"Of course you are," Mother told me when she heard. To the others she said, "She's just in her scrap box, this isn't the first time." She was referring to a box of rags Miriam and Papa had kept in the workroom of their tailor shop, which I would fashion into imaginary garments with such absorption that when they spoke to me I didn't make sense.

"Say what you want," I told her. "You'll see."

Although she wouldn't say so, Mother was miffed that I was taking time out of her schedule. The March on Washington was approaching. She had a lot to do.

"Beryl will be fine," Miriam assured her. "Look at her. Good hair. Almost black."

"Yes, very silky," Aunt Gussie agreed. "Very durable."

Miriam and Aunt Gussie believed dark-haired Jewish children, having inherited their coloring from a thousand years of survival in the desert, were sturdier and more intelligent than blondes. Mother hated this superstition. She pointed to Gussie.

"Your own hair was black once," she snapped, "but you had your share of troubles." It was well known that Gussie's crazy spells had started back in Russia in 1910, when the boy she loved was killed in a pogrom. She'd fallen into a depression and hadn't recovered until four years later, when the boat trip to America had proved such a new and different experience that it cured her. She hadn't had another crazy spell until she married Uncle Abe. Since then they'd averaged three times a year.

If Gussie was insulted, she didn't show it. She only touched her newly-set curls, which were still the cerulean color she'd left them after her recent spell of madness. "Almost blue," she said to me, and winked.

The period of mourning ended, but I wore black every day and moved through the house with deliberate slowness. I picked at my food and imagined myself pale and thin. I was surprised I never actually lost any weight.

"It's no good she should be like this," Miriam said. My father agreed, and my mother would have, too, if she hadn't been so busy working. The midnight sessions grew more frequent. She came home with a distant brightness in her eyes. She paid us no attention.

The day of the March on Washington, she returned late, too buoyed up to stop moving. She paced the kitchen, rubbed her arms as if she were cold, although the living areas of the house had no air conditioning and the fans were only shifting the heat from one place to another. "Such response!" she exclaimed over and over. "Imagine, a quarter of a million people!"

She recited passages from Martin Luther King's "I Have a Dream" speech. She sat down and got up again. She told my father he should have joined the crowd.

"I meant to. But the store— I saw some of it on television." The truth was, he hadn't been to a gathering of activists since McCarthy.

"Well, you should have been there," she gushed on. "It's days like this you feel you're finally getting somewhere. Back in action. Moving." She sat down once more and looked around the table coyly. "In fact," she said, "they asked me to go to Alabama!"

"Oh?" Dad raised his eyebrows and tried to look noncommittal, but his fingers searched the crown of his head for his bald spot.

"The Birmingham schools are being ordered to integrate. They're expecting disruption. They need people to—"

"Leah, I thought after they dragged you off and put you in the paper you wasn't going to get in trouble no more," said Uncle Abe, who had arrived to take Aunt Gussie home.

"No, no, this is purely behind the scenes. Meetings. Training sessions. Nothing dangerous." She looked from one to another, as if asking for permission. "Do you think I'd go South for fun?"

The day she left, a Saturday, Miriam made a sponge cake, cleared the table where Mother's papers had been, and served tea in the dining room, a steaming kettle of it even though the fans were running full force.

"I'm against giving her psychotherapy," my father said, nodding in my direction.

"Why? Because she'll tell some doctor family secrets?" Miriam didn't look at me either.

"Because they'll give her drugs," Dad said. "I'm opposed to giving her drugs."

"Or electric shock," Aunt Gussie added. "God forbid, electric shock." It was well known that Uncle Abe had once put her in the hospital during a crazy spell. After she'd been given electric shock therapy against her will, she'd stopped trusting him. Later, he swore he hadn't consented to such a thing, but ever after, the moment she began to lose touch with reality, she insisted she needed Miriam.

"What are you talking, electric shock?" Miriam said, jerking her head in my direction to remind Gussie I was in the room.

Gussie picked up a piece of cake with her fingers and shredded it into a pile of crumbs. "Me, if I have problems, usually I don't advertise. After electric shock, I had to ask help for everything. I couldn't remember nothing for a week."

"Huh!" Miriam snorted, angry at her for not dropping the subject.

In reply, Gussie dropped her fork onto her plate, spraying crumbs across the table.

"Look what she does with her food," Miriam said to Dad. "She's afraid if she eats it she'll get fat like a balloon. She thinks it's better to drink seventeen cups of tea, then she'll keep her weight down." To Gussie she said, "At our age we're not going to win no beauty contests. Not with mashing up cake and not with blue hair."

"My hair may be blue, but at least I have my mind. Without no electric shocks, neither."

The two sisters glared at each other.

"She don't eat cake, she never got fat, neither," Uncle Abe defended, patting Gussie's hand with the stub of one of his amputated fingers.

Miriam, twenty pounds heavier than Gussie, turned a scathing gaze to Uncle Abe's deformity. Abe put his hands in his lap and said nothing further.

I went out onto the front porch, sat on Bubby's old chair, and stared out at the street as she had. Lulled by the whoosh of sycamore leaves blowing in the air, I fell asleep. I woke up to find Aunt Gussie staring down at me. Her eyes swam behind thick bifocals. I felt she'd been watching me a long time.

"Grief, it's one thing," she said. "Making yourself crazy is another. Craziness is no pleasure, believe me."

I had to agree. Gussie was certainly in a position to know.

Miriam wandered onto the porch behind her sister, untying the apron she always wore over her dress. *"Nu?"* Miriam said.

"I'm telling Beryl she didn't do nothing to make herself crazy," Gussie explained.

"You think Beryl don't know that? Of course she knows."

"I'm not crazy!" I protested. "Bubby didn't even want to eat! I actually had to feed her!"

"So did God make her choke on it?" Gussie asked. "Did he give her a belly ache? She died in pain? No."

"Gussie, *g'noog!*" Miriam shot her sister a withering glance for upsetting me.

"How do you know she didn't die in pain?" I asked. "You don't know!"

I started to get up, but Miriam took my chin in her hand and turned me toward her. *"Tochter,"* she said. "Your Aunt Gussie makes some sense. What she means is, better you shouldn't make from cottage cheese a mountain you can't climb over." I tried to dislodge my chin from her grip, but Miriam held firm. "Old superstitions, they're never good," she told me.

I jerked my head out of her hand and jumped up. "How do you know they're superstitions? How do you know God doesn't expect a person who believes in kosher laws to follow them?"

I stomped into the house and slammed the screen.

✺

That night at dinner, Miriam wore her best black dress and a pair of rhinestone earrings I had given her for her birthday. She waited until the brisket had been handed around the table and then said, "Gussie and me, we got an idea."

"An idea about Beryl," Aunt Gussie added, glancing at me meaningfully.

"Maybe we have too many ideas about Beryl." Dad began to cut his meat.

"She should emigrate," Aunt Gussie said boldly.

"Emigrate?" Dad looked up from the brisket.

"Sure," Gussie said. "Emigrate. Like I done."

He held his knife poised in the air, waiting.

"For a cure," Aunt Gussie added.

"Emigrate where, Aunt Gussie? Back to the old country?" he asked.

"It's funny?" Gussie said, insulted.

"Sometimes when there's a death, it's good to get away," Miriam said. She cocked her head slightly in Gussie's direction. I thought of the boy who'd been killed in the pogrom.

"Natalie invited her to New York," my father said. "She said no."

Miriam shook her head. "Not send her to visit nobody. Send her to live."

"What did you have in mind?" he asked, indulgent now, smiling.

Gussie's eyes shone behind her glasses. "Somewhere

different from Washington like Ellis Island was different from Russia."

"Someplace foreign," Miriam explained, "where she can forget and be well."

"Is this just a general idea?" Dad asked. "Or were you thinking of someplace specific?"

"She goes to college soon," Miriam replied.

"So?"

"She don't want to stay here in Washington," Gussie said. "She said so herself. We got a plan."

"All afternoon they discussed it," Uncle Abe put in proudly.

"Emigration," Miriam nodded. "Foreign countries."

"You mean those places I applied to?" I mumbled, beginning to catch on.

Dad narrowed his eyes at Miriam. "Those were in the South. Leah would never permit it."

"Leah wouldn't help her own child?" Miriam asked. "Of course she would."

"She don't have to go to Alabama or Mississippi," Aunt Gussie assured him. "She could go to the other school she got in."

Dad opened his mouth to speak, but then didn't. The miasma of guilt that had been hovering over me began to lift. In order to make my mother miserable and escape from her at the same time, maybe killing my great-grandmother was the only thing I could have done.

Or maybe I hadn't killed her. Of course I hadn't. What had gotten into me?

"It's settled, then." Miriam lifted her napkin from her lap and put it on the table to show the decision had been made.

Aunt Gussie grinned. "See?" she said to my father. "This is what we're trying to tell you all along." And that was why, in the fall of 1963, I began college not at George Washington University in D.C., but at the University of North Carolina in

Chapel Hill, a foreign country in the warm but evil heart of the segregated South.

3

My father said he would drive me to Chapel Hill himself.

"Five hours by machine," Miriam complained. "I sit that long, my legs get stiff."

"Mom," Dad protested. "You don't have to come."

"Not come!" she fumed. "Of course I come."

Mother couldn't join us because she was still in Birmingham, riding out the troubles created when President Kennedy federalized the National Guard to help integrate the schools. She spent her days in meetings that lasted well into the night, then slept in the homes of sympathizers, moving once or twice a week. She called us from pay phones in noisy corridors, shouting in order to hear herself.

"Feeling better?" she asked me on the night we meant to tell her about my new plans for college. "I knew you would. I hope you're getting ready for school."

Dad rubbed a stain on his shirt and watched me worriedly, trying to judge the tone of the conversation.

"Yes. Next week. I'm going next week."

He actually sighed; he thought I'd told her. I raised my voice so she'd be sure to absorb the shock of what I was about to say, "I'm going—"

"Listen," she said. "They need me back in the meeting. I'll call tomorrow." And she was gone.

The next time she called it was the same thing, and the time after that. She asked the usual questions about the family; she listened for a moment before events or noise overtook her. She loved us, she said. She missed us. But it was clear her mind was on higher causes.

By the time I was ready to go, she still didn't know where I was going. Even Dad realized this and seemed resigned. "Better let things be, for now," he cautioned.

Imagining Mother's eventual reaction, I felt a thrill of anticipation.

Just wait, I thought.

Miriam ransacked my closet and ordered me to try on everything I owned. At the sewing machine she'd kept from her years in the tailor shop, she repaired the rips and straightened the hems. There was no question of a new wardrobe. Sending me away at all was expensive enough.

"I'll mail you fifteen dollars a week," Dad said. "Fifteen should be enough for meals."

"Plenty," Miriam echoed.

"And for starters, here." He pressed a wad of twenties into my palm and closed my fingers around it. "For books and shampoo and all the things you have to buy."

A quick pang of guilt shot through me. They were sending me off because they thought it would restore me—off to a land they believed was evil, even though money was tight. Mother would hit the roof.

The night before I left, one of the clerks in the dry cleaning store was rushed to the hospital with pneumonia—the only one who could hear and speak. The others were all profoundly deaf and communicated entirely by sign language. My father couldn't leave after all. I'd have to go to Chapel Hill on a Trailways bus.

It was a cloudy September morning. I hadn't slept much the night before; I was too excited. "You'll call every Saturday," Miriam instructed when they dropped me at the bus station. Dad gave me a quick hug and turned away. Miriam took my chin in her hand. "Good luck, *tochter*," she said, and for a moment I had to brush back tears because until then *tochter*—daughter—was all I'd ever been.

Below Richmond we veered west, and below South Hill, Virginia, we crossed into North Carolina. When the miles of countryside finally gave way to the outskirts of Chapel Hill, the sun came out and a hot breeze began to blow. We drove into town beneath an arch of stately maples, their leaves rustling softly as if to mark my arrival.

At the bus terminal I claimed my mounds of luggage and called a cab. Five minutes later the driver deposited me in front of a quad of three identical red brick dorms: Alderman, Kenan and McIver. Each one was a massive three-story building with a front porch supported by white pillars. Each one could have been an antebellum plantation house. Each might have been Tara. I stood in the clinging heat and caught my breath.

Alderman Dormitory was the one on my left. The quad buzzed with girls and their families bringing in their belongings. I lugged my suitcases and boxes inside, into a high-ceilinged parlor furnished with several groupings of sofas and chairs in stiffly formal arrangements.

I nodded to some of the other girls and they to me, but nobody paid me much attention. I seemed to be the only one moving in without a cluster of friends and family. The massive front door was flung open, and so were a series of French doors leading into secondary parlors from the columned porch, but still the heat was oppressive. In Washington, where the summers were steamy, mid-September was already cool.

A bank of mailboxes stood at the back of the parlor. In front of them a gray-haired woman signed people in at a desk. I piled my things where I could keep an eye on them and stood in line. If only Miriam were here to scout for a water fountain! But I couldn't picture her in her dark, blocky dresses and oxfords among these stylish fair-haired mothers. My father I could see, his chin stubbled with whiskers as he studied the columns and crown moldings with his deposed-architect's eye. "Neo-Colonial," he would say, and grow thoughtful. My mother, surveying the scene, would snort, "All *white* girls, you'll notice," and fix me with a meaningful stare.

But she'd be wrong. As if on cue, a pretty black girl emerged from a hallway and passed through the parlor and out the front door. The crowd hushed and gathered into itself as she went by, then resumed its hum. This might be a foreign country, but some of its customs were familiar.

At last the woman at the desk took my name and handed over my key. "I'm Mrs. West. The housemother." She looked around. "Who brought you?"

"A bus," I said.

She frowned and pointed to the wing across from where the black girl had emerged. "One-oh-five," she said.

Wrestling with my largest suitcase and a couple of boxes, I was about to shoulder my way through the heavy swinging door to my hallway when a tall, ungainly girl rushed across the lobby, waving her hands at a soft-spoken family just in front of me.

"If your father's going to bring your things in, yell 'Man on the hall' first," the girl ordered. "Always yell first."

Startled, the daughter blocked her father's way and in a strained, shrill voice called out, "Man on the hall!" As if the poor man were vicious and deranged.

I wondered if treating men like wild beasts was another Southern tradition.

My room turned out to be the first on the right. Not wanting to disturb anyone, I unlocked the door and peeked in tentatively, but no-one was there. I was greeted by green walls, a soaring ceiling, a jumble of desks, wardrobes and unpacked boxes that filled almost every inch of floor space. At the back, a huge window looked out onto a shrubby bank. There were three beds, one neatly made up with a white chenille spread and dotted with dozens of decorative pillows like something out of *Good Housekeeping;* the second unmade and piled high with mattress pads, boxes of records, a jumble of sheets, a pink quilt. Pinned to the quilt was a note in large, sloppy letters: *Went to my old buddy Lenoir. Back soon. Susan.*

The third bed was mine, pushed against the left-hand wall, stripped and uninviting. I dropped my suitcase on top of the mattress, trudged back to the lobby and brought in the rest of my boxes.

Despite the enormous open window, the room was stifling. My hair clung to my neck, my blouse to my skin. Spotting a tiny sink by the wall, I turned on the spigot and splashed cold water on my face and into my hair. I cupped my hands and took a long drink.

Behind me, the door flew open. I jumped back and splashed water everywhere. Into the room rushed the blondest girl I'd ever seen—blonde hair, blonde eyebrows, eyelashes so blonde they were lighter than her skin. She didn't see me. She slammed the door behind her, leaned her back against it, and sighed. When she turned in my direction, she opened her pretty pink lips and put her hand to her white throat as if to protect it.

"Lord, I bet I scared you to death," she said, looking like she'd been scared to death herself. "Honey, I'm sorry as I can be. I'm Ashley Vance, one of your roommates. I'm—"

And then she burst into tears.

She hates the idea of rooming with me, I thought. Then I came to my senses. "Are you okay?" I asked.

"I'm sorry. This is no way to—It's just that I thought—" She leaned back against the door and sobbed until her shoulders shook. I decided this had nothing to do with me.

I grabbed a box of Kleenex from the rumpled pink bed and thrust it at her.

Ashley sniffed. She plucked out a tissue and tried to stop crying. After a time she blew her nose.

"I thought Mama would never leave," she hiccuped.

"It's okay," I said. "I know about mothers."

"These are tears of relief, really." She wiped an eye, breathed deeply. Her voice was even, her drawl lilting and smooth. "Mama and Daddy hate Paco so much I reckoned they'd lock me in my room till he graduated and went back to South America. I thought they'd—" She stopped herself. "You poor thing. You don't have the first idea what I'm talking about. I didn't even ask your name."

"Beryl," I said.

"Well, Beryl. Mama and Daddy sent me to Chapel Hill to meet nice Southern boys, but Paco turned out to be from a little farther south than they expected." She looked at me, sly now, and both of us laughed. I felt a moment of kinship with Ashley for having come to Chapel Hill as I had, for other than academic considerations.

She blew her nose again. "There," she said, and moved toward the bed with all the pillows. "Beryl what?"

"Pardon?"

"What's your last name?"

"Rosinsky."

"Rosinsky." She let it play on her tongue. She looked at me earnestly; she didn't drop her gaze. "That's a *Jewish* name, isn't it?" Her eyes were such a pale blue they seemed translucent.

Oh no, I thought. Here it comes. I didn't know how to

react. When you were in a foreign country, you didn't. "If that bothers you, my being Jewish—"

"Lord, no. Paco's Catholic. I don't care a whit. I don't know where my manners are."

"It's okay," I said quickly. "I don't mind you asking."

She began rearranging the little pillows on her *Good Housekeeping* bed, all in shades of pink and lavender and blue, pastel presences like her own. "Did you just get here?" she asked. "Did you meet Susan yet?"

I nodded toward the note pinned to the pink quilt. "She went to Lenoir's." I handed her the note.

"Lenoir's not a person,"Ashley said. "Lenoir's the dining hall."

I made a comic face. "Newcomer," I said. And both of us laughed.

※

I had no time to settle in. I had just enough time to change clothes, pull my wet hair back into a pony tail, and venture out onto the campus, before attending the orientation meeting for freshmen.

The campus was lovely. Grassy and shaded, with ancient trees arching over the brick walkways. Some of the red brick buildings sported columns; others stood in unadorned splendor. In the classroom where the meeting was held, a bearded professor instructed us about the university's Honor System. Everyone had to sign an agreement not to give or receive help on tests. The boys signed a sheet promising to act like gentlemen, the girls vowed to act like ladies. In the classroom where we sat, there were perhaps twenty "gentlemen" and only three of us ladies, probably because girls could come to Chapel Hill as freshmen only in certain majors and otherwise had to wait until junior year. I felt I should be wearing a hoop skirt. I thought our vows sounded quaint and charming.

On the way back, doors opened magically before me, responding before I touched a handle. The gentlemen from the classroom held them. Other gentlemen, scores of gentlemen, traveled the brick walkways outside, nodding to me and smiling. The ratio must have been four or five boys to every girl. If this was typical of life in a foreign country, it boded well.

Back in the dorm, my other roommate had arrived—a short, sweet-faced girl with glossy brown hair teased into a perfect circle. A sprinkling of freckles across her pug nose bespoke some redheaded ancestor who had almost, but not quite, passed the trait on to her. Wearing lime-green pedal pushers and a white blouse, she was a compact, carefree-looking girl except for her fingernails, which were sore-looking and bitten down to the quick.

"Susan Tillery," Ashley said by way of introducing us when I came in. "All you need to know about Susan is that she's from Winston-Salem and her father's the town's most famous internist. So, if you get an ulcer or the flu during your stay here—"

"All you need to know about Ashley," Susan shot back, "is her parents didn't really make a mistake and name her after that fella in *Gone With the Wind*. Her daddy's from Charleston and they named her for the river."

"Oh, Susan."

"You also need to know if we weren't kin her daddy would never have let her come back to Chapel Hill. He's too scared Paco might scoop her up and take her away."

I stared from one to the other. Ashley, tall and elegant, smoothed a piece of shelf paper into one of her drawers and set a pile of neatly-folded sweaters inside. Susan, petite and bouncy, dumped her clothes onto her disheveled pink covers and abandoned them to arrange boxes of records next to a thick-spindled record player for 45s. Ashley's face was narrow and too sharp to make her a great beauty, but she stopped me cold with her absolute blondness. Susan's face, round and pert, was the kind people would call "cute" even when she was fifty. The two of them looked and acted as different as relatives could.

"I know we don't favor," Ashley explained, "but her mama and my mama are cousins. Not close, but they grew up together down on the coast."

"But there's bad blood between the daddies," Susan confided, grinning at Ashley and setting a stack of records on the spindle. "For years we only saw each other at family reunions."

"Bad blood?" I asked.

Susan smiled wider. "Her daddy called mine a Whiskey-palian."

"A what?"

"Susan, don't," Ashley said, but she was grinning, too. "Beryl doesn't know about all that. She doesn't even go to church!" Then she caught herself. "I mean, she goes to—"

"It's all right," I said. "A whiskey—?"

"Whiskeypalian," Susan said. A record dropped and "Sugar Shack" began to play, about a little coffee house along the tracks. "See, Ashley's Baptist and we're Episcopalians, and Baptists don't drink. So one time my daddy was having a Scotch and he and Uncle Toby were disagreeing about politics, and Uncle Toby called him a Whiskeypalian. Normally nobody would have thought a thing about it—people call Episcopalians that all the time—but they were in this big argument that made it worse. After that Mama and Aunt Sally Ann had to meet on the sly."

Both of them laughed.

"When Mama heard Susan was coming to Chapel Hill," Ashley added, "she called up Aunt Peggy and they decided the least they could do was get their daughters to room together. In spite of Paco being so unsuitable."

Susan flipped a switch and another record dropped.

Ashley listened to the first few bars and said, "Not 'Ahab the Arab'! Take that off this minute, Susan."

Susan grinned, obviously having chosen the song on purpose. "Bad enough, having a boyfriend from South America. But if he has a roommate from—" She widened her eyes. "Saudi Arabia—" She let another record drop, Ruby and the Romantics, "Our Day Will Come."

"In honor of you and Paco," she said to Ashley.

I guessed I was lucky to have two roommates who were such good friends and so nice to me in spite of it.

Susan picked up a framed picture lying face-down on the floor beside her bed. I expected it to be a poster of the Beach Boys or Bobby Vinton, but it was a Keane print of a big-eyed girl holding a kitten. Susan shrugged as if she recognized the picture was too young for her but didn't care, then stepped barefoot on her bed, atop the wrinkled bedding and clothes, and tentatively held it against the wall for placement. "What about you, Beryl?" she asked. "Are you a junior or a senior?"

"A freshman."

"A freshman!" She dropped the picture on the bed and studied me.

"I just assumed you were a junior transfer student," Ashley said as she cut shelf paper for yet another bureau drawer. "What's your major?"

"Medical technology."

Ashley smoothed the shelf paper, registered satisfaction. "Susan just transferred from Woman's College in Greensboro. I transferred last year myself."

Susan plucked a hammer from the tangle of covers and drove a nail into the wall, which I knew must be forbidden. She hung the print, and the kitten-hugging girl stared down at us with enormous liquid eyes. Susan dropped onto the bed and chewed a mangled nail. "I wouldn't have taken you for a freshman," she told me. "You look older."

"I know." My mother said the advantage of our dark hair

and olive skin was that people treated us like adults when we were still young and later held off labeling us senile because our oily skin kept us from wrinkling. Somehow, I didn't feel this was a family tidbit I should share.

But they were both looking at me expectantly, as if I owed them something in exchange for all they'd just revealed. I debated what to tell them. If all it took to cause a breach in their own families was calling somebody a Whiskeypalian, my father's checkered past was out of the question. And what could I say about my mother? That after the Hearings she had ranted and raved and finally said, "If I'm going to be labeled a subversive, I'm damned well going to *be* one"? That she believed I was going to G.W. because we'd never told her I was coming South? I thought not.

"I'm from D.C.," was all I finally managed. "I was going to go to school up there, but at the last minute I changed my mind."

"Really?" Susan's eyes lit up. Then someone knocked on the door.

It was the first of what turned out to be a parade of Susan's and Ashley's friends dropping in to say hello. I didn't know what had unleashed the stream just then, but I was grateful. There was a Ginny from Ashley's French class last year and a Mary Beth from her church back in Winston-Salem. There were Susan's classmates from her two years in Greensboro and a girl who'd taken piano from the same teacher back home. Each might have been a long-lost sister.

"Hey, Jolene! How was your summer? I was hoping you'd come by." A touch of faces, right cheek to right cheek, the smack of lips kissing the air.

"Look how tan you are! You're about to cross the color line."

"Let me see that darling pin."

"Oh, how dear."

They wore fraternity pins over their hearts and gold circle

pins on the collars of freshly-ironed blouses. Their hair was neatly combed and they smelled of soap and lotion. Some of them draped sweaters carefully over their shoulders even though the temperature was in the eighties.

Everyone said *hey* instead of *hi*. Ashley said *right much* when she meant *a lot* and *I reckon* when she meant *I think*. Everyone said *Durm* instead of *Durham*, referring to the town where Duke University was, eight miles away. They chattered and giggled, and each newcomer greeted me civilly and then studied me coolly, sidelong, appraising. One girl, Penny Blankenship, who lived upstairs on the third floor and said her father was in practice with Susan's, stared with what I thought was outright hostility. I felt I ought to check myself in the mirror for pimples or bits of food caught in my teeth.

But Susan and Ashley remained gracious. They included me in the conversation; they tried to make up for the restraint of their friends. For whatever reason, they seemed to have accepted me—maybe because Ashley had broken down in front of me earlier. Maybe because they felt they had to. Or else—though I had no way of knowing this yet—I was in the grip of Southern hospitality.

The parade of friends had just stopped when a girl knocked on the door and told Ashley her date was waiting in the lobby.

"Come on out, I want to introduce you to Paco," Ashley said.

"And then I'll introduce you to Lenoir," Susan added with a wink.

In the parlor, one look at Paco made me realize why, to Ashley, my Jewishness was only a trifle. His hair was blacker than mine and slicked back in a style that suggested Mafia or Puerto Rican gangs. His shirt looked as if it had just been pressed; the seam in his chinos was knife-edged. He stood so straight he might have been a soldier. He was tall and slender, his cheekbones high and sculptured, his skin whiter than

Ashley's. He was exactly what Natalie and I had once had in mind when we uttered the phrase, *Latin lover.*

"Very nice to meet you." He bowed to me. His enunciation was clipped and exotic. When he put his arm around Ashley's waist and ushered her out of the dorm, his dark head hovered over her blonde one in what could only be a scene from a modern-day *Romeo and Juliet.* This was impossibly romantic. They were star-crossed. It was magnificent.

After they had gone, Susan and I headed over to Lenoir—a cavernous gray place with twenty-foot-high ceilings, similar to the prison dining hall my mother had described after touring a state facility. The student special—meat and two vegetables—cost forty cents. The food had the same gray cast as the walls; some of it was unrecognizable; the meat swam in grease. This must be how Miriam and Aunt Gussie had felt, eating American fare after a lifetime of herring and potatoes.

Back in the dorm, Susan put on another stack of records and made up her bed. She pulled the sheets taut, then lost patience and threw the quilt haphazardly on top. The pink spread no more suited her than the treacly girl-with-kitten picture, but she didn't seem to care. We listened to Martha and the Vandellas, to Frankie Lyman and the Teenagers, to the Singing Nuns, even to the old Bill Haley and the Comets hit, "Rock Around the Clock." Here was another feature of my new country I wouldn't have trouble getting used to. At home we listened only to classical music. Rock was silly, insipid. Classical was worthy. Susan turned up the volume.

Ashley scooted in half an hour before curfew. "Lord knows, I wanted to stay with Paco, but if I don't get this stuff organized before the dorm meeting, I won't be able to sleep." She pointed to her section of room that looked perfectly organized already. With one energetic motion, she swept all the shoes out of her wardrobe and began lining them up in neat rows. She was working fast. "It's just so amazing, being able to see him again without some—well, you know."

I didn't, but she was eager to tell. She was proud of Paco. So what if he was a foreigner? He was hardly some low-class immigrant. His father was a diplomat. His mama—well, she was an ice queen, but no matter. Of course his family was upset! Hers was, too. Her daddy had arrived on campus the instant finals ended last spring and spirited her home to Wilmington, and Paco's father had taken him off to Manhattan. Spending the summer eight hundred miles apart had been pure misery. "If Mama hadn't wanted me to get to know Susan better, I never would have been able to come back."

In the fifteen minutes before the dorm meeting, she rearranged all her shoes, shined a pair of loafers with a neatly folded rag, and set her hair on pink foam rollers. With all that energy, it was clear she was truly in love.

Everyone gathered in the parlor, into one of the perfectly rectangular furniture groupings that broke up the huge room. Girls sat on the carpet, packed themselves four across on flowered sofas, perched on arms of chairs and couches. Some had changed into nightgowns and robes, others were still wearing skirts and blouses. We were more than a hundred, shoulder to shoulder to shoulder.

The only one with an inch of space was the Negro girl. She was very pretty, and so light-skinned she was fairer than I was with a tan. Her eyes were hazel flecked with yellow, framed by thick black lashes. She had a chair all to herself. No one draped over the arm or squeezed in beside her. The carpet at her feet was vacant for a yard in every direction.

"This is Emily Moses." The housemother, Mrs. West, rose to introduce her. "I don't think Emily will mind if I tell you she's the first undergraduate colored girl we've had here at Chapel Hill." Mrs. West's voice was stiff and proper. "I hope you'll all help make her welcome."

Emily nodded shyly, and a few girls applauded. Some looked at their fingernails. Some drew their lips into tight smiles.

"Now, to the election of officers," Mrs. West said, and beckoned to the same girl who'd directed the newcomer to yell "Man on the hall" earlier.

The girl introduced herself as Anna Mae Price, candidate for president. She told us if we voted for her she would oversee the dorm "with honor and fairness." Her hair was on wire rollers and her face was greasy with cold cream. No one seemed to find this odd for a political campaign. Anna Mae was elected unanimously.

In the center of the room, she stood before us in thin pajamas that hung from her lank frame. "Mrs. West asked me to brief you about our rules," she began. At this cue, Mrs. West passed out a list of the women's dorm regulations. "Sign them at the bottom, girls," she ordered. "To show you understand."

We were to be in at eleven on weeknights, one on weekends, midnight on Sunday. "And no overnights except weekends away from Chapel Hill," Anna Mae warned. If we disobeyed, we'd be tried by the women's Honor Council, which could mete out reprimands, social probation, or *strict* social probation. "Or even expulsion, girls." Anna Mae explained each item in a tight voice that said she knew very well the black deeds we were contemplating in the lusty depths of our hearts.

Several girls frowned. One raised her hand. "What's this about the two-couple rule?"

Anna Mae's face flushed with purpose. She reminded me of my mother when she spoke of her causes. "I'm so glad you asked, Alison. The two-couple rule means you can't be in a boy's apartment unless there's another couple present. A very important rule, girls." She breathed deeply.

"That means men can be in the apartment with *you*

alone," Susan whispered, "but if you're in the apartment alone with *them,* you get kicked out of school."

Penny Blankenship maneuvered herself into a space just the other side of Susan and butted Susan's arm playfully with her elbow.

Anna Mae looked in our direction accusingly. "I hope you'll remember, girls, that you signed a pledge to act like ladies."

Only a few hours before, the "ladies and gentlemen" vow had seemed Southern and quaint. Now I wasn't so sure.

"Do boys have curfews?" I whispered.

"Of course not, honey," Ashley said. "They can sleep anyplace they want, drink liquor, and party till dawn, as long as they don't debauch in public."

I saw that being a lady was more complicated than being a gentleman. This must be a Southern tradition. Ladies weren't just mannerly; ladies were *good.*

"Now, read the rules carefully, girls," Anna Mae said, "because you aren't officially signed in until we have your signature."

"What about the Honor System and all that stuff I signed earlier?" I whispered.

Ashley shook her head to warn me. Susan said nothing. They were taking this seriously. You had to be a male to be trusted. Outnumbered five to one, ladies had to be kept pure by fear of punishment.

My gaze swept my dormmates in the parlor, most of them bent to the long list of rules, their faces knotted in concentration. Even Penny Blankenship had lost interest in me. I began to study them for the first time: their gravity about these silly regulations, their clothes, their hair, the way their hands moved as they pored over the papers. I saw at once why Ashley and Susan's friends had raked me with their sidelong glances all afternoon, curious and cool. I wasn't like them.

Most of them wore their hair in short teased bubbles like Susan's, or flips like Ashley's, no longer than chin length. My hair came to my shoulders. The skirt I wore was pleated; theirs were straight. My blouse was plain, theirs were paisley or madras. The girls in pajamas wore bedroom slippers or went barefoot, but the ones who were still dressed wore stockings with brown or burgundy-colored loafers called Weejuns. In the whole room, I was the only one in bobby socks and oxfords that tied. Even Emily Moses, in her straight black skirt and a blouse with a Peter Pan collar, was more in style than I was. Her eyes were downcast to the printed rules, but she looked up and caught my eye as if she felt my gaze.

My agnostic mother often quoted a line from a Hebrew prayerbook: "Remember, you, too, were once a slave in Egypt." She would expect me to introduce myself to Emily, befriend her. After all, both of us were different. But why should I? Why make us both more conspicuous than we already were? I pretended to examine the rules and didn't raise my eyes until I knew Emily had looked away. I was in a foreign country, in disguise, and my parents would never know.

Back in our room, Ashley removed each pastel pillow from her bed and piled it on the floor. "I'm glad she's here," she said suddenly, decisively, obviously referring to Emily.

"Are you?" Susan asked.

"Oh, yes." She clutched a lavender pillow to her chest. "Once, when I was five or six I was in a department store with Mama, and the worst thing happened. Mama was looking at linens, and it was so hot that I went off to get a drink from the water fountain. All of a sudden this saleslady came rushing up and grabbed me by the arm." She yanked the pillow away from her body and shook it as she spoke. "The woman yelled, 'No, no, you mustn't do that. That's for niggers.'

"I was so embarrassed, you can't imagine. After that, I was

always afraid I'd use the wrong drinking fountain or go through the wrong door."

She looked at the pillow in her hand as if just realizing she was holding it, then flung it on the pile with the others. "I think this will be a lot less complicated," she said. "This . . . integration."

"Maybe you want to go live over there with *her* then," Susan teased. Everybody knew Emily Moses lived on the other side of the parlor alone.

"Susan, don't be ugly." Ashley was prim now. "You know what I mean."

We all fell silent. My mother liked to point out the difference between desegregation and *integration,* and I supposed she'd expect me to do that now. I didn't. At dinner Susan had told me our room was supposed to be a double, but a lot of doubles were triples now because so many girls had shown up. Emily's wing, the smallest in the dorm, contained the housemother's quarters, a kitchen, and only two student rooms. Because no one would want to live near Emily, the second room had been left empty. A sign on its door read, "Study Lounge," although the real study lounge was in the basement.

I had listened to her tell me this, and I hadn't said a word.

My roommates had accepted me, and I was grateful. With my unstylish clothes, I was as ridiculous as Aunt Gussie after a crazy spell, shopping in the Safeway with a babushka over her shocking blue hair. If Emily was lonely, I was sorry . . . but what could I do?

Besides, that wasn't what I was here for. I conjured up a vision of Aunt Gussie and Miriam just off the boat, standing on the dusty streets of New York, peering up at the strangeness of the tall buildings. Having left Russia, did they ever look back? Of course not! They learned American ways, gave up the customs of their little village outside of Kiev. They'd sent me here to follow their example, to forget the way we did things in Washington, all passion and politics, and accept this new country with all its strange ways. They knew I was no crusader. They didn't want me to be! They wanted me to adapt.

4

The first thing I needed to do was update my wardrobe. With only one day before classes began, I would have to hurry. Aside from the hundred dollars my father had given me and my money for the week, I had some savings from Kitty Kelly Shoe Store. I'd planned to reveal it after Mother found out where I was and started railing about the expense of sending me away to school. Instead, I stuffed the bills into my bra and walked into town.

Franklin Street was Chapel Hill's main thoroughfare. Running along the edge of the campus, it was lined with restaurants and shops—clothing and shoe stores, a drug store and a bakery, the post office and two movie theatres—where you could buy everything you needed. The sidewalks were bustling. I wanted to transform myself before I made myself even more conspicuous. Thankfully, in their haste to finish their errands, everyone was too preoccupied to point in my direction and snicker.

As I window-shopped and decided what to buy, I saw to my dismay that a sandwich shop called Packard's, smack in the middle of the block, was flanked by picketers carrying signs reading, "Integration Now" and "We Have the Right to Be Served." Here was a scene I needed to avoid. In the basement of our house, similar placards from dozens of old marches languished up against the unfinished walls. I crossed the street, walked hastily past that part of the block, and made my way toward the women's shops.

At a place called The Fireside, I bought two straight skirts and a madras blouse. At the Sally Lynn Shoppe, I bought a second blouse and a silky full slip, which seemed to be the attire for going up and down the dormitory halls to the bathroom. At Lacock's Shoe Shop, I discovered that Weejuns, eleven ninety-five per pair, came in cordovan, red, green and black. I chose cordovan. Everything seemed expensive. At home we usually shopped in cheap stores like Lerner's. But I kept buying.

By the end of the day I had just enough cash left for a trip to Aesthetic Hair Stylists. I watched in the mirror as my hair was lopped off above my chin. I watched as it was teased into a perfect bubble like Susan's. Afterwards, I went into the ladies' room and put on one of my new outfits. Thus disguised, thus unrecognizable, I felt almost Southern.

Out on Franklin Street, the temperature must have dropped twenty degrees since I'd started shopping. The evening breeze was brisk and autumnal. For the first time in years, I felt the air rush across the back of my neck. It seemed the very sensation of freedom. I would walk back to the dorm and begin the task of blending in. Not twenty seconds later, I ran into Stuart Gershner, my one link to home.

Although Stuart had been my inspiration for applying to UNC in the first place, we were not exactly friends. Our connection was that since early childhood we'd sat together in enforced camaraderie along with the other reluctant children at every Workmen's Circle social function. Stuart was two years older than I was, a year younger than Natalie. Even though classes wouldn't start until morning, he was wearing a button-down dress shirt with rolled-up sleeves and had a slide rule protruding from a back pocket of his trousers.

"Beryl?" he asked doubtfully.

"Hey, Stuart." I was pleased with the way I'd learned to say *hey*.

"Jesus Christ, what are you doing here? Is your mother at a rally or something?"

"She's in Alabama," I said.

"So—?"

"I'm here to go to school."

"You?"

"I'm living in Alderman. It was a last-minute decision."

Stuart plucked a cigarette from a pack sticking out of a shirt pocket. "Jesus Christ," he said again. "I can't believe it. You don't even look like yourself. What did you do to your hair? You look like a TCC."

"A what?"

"A Typical Carolina Coed."

"Do I?"

"Christ. Yes." He shook his head and lit a match.

"Thanks," I said, flattered.

"Thanks?" He exhaled smoke into the cooling air and raised his eyebrows. "Never mind, I'll take you to dinner and you can tell me everything."

I almost said no. Stuart was opinionated and judgmental; I'd never liked him. My mother had always thought he was nice. The chances of my telling him "everything" were nil. But I'd spent most of my money and I was hungry. We walked down Franklin Street almost to the post office before he guided me into a restaurant called Harry's Grill.

If I'd known he'd take me to exactly the kind of place our families would have gone, I would have been more cautious.

But after dinner and breakfast in Lenoir Hall, under soaring ceilings where the odor of greasy food mingled with the gray gloom, I was ready for a change. By contrast, Harry's was dim but cozy, with booths along the walls and friendly-looking wooden tables in the middle. Happily, the menu featured, instead of pork chops and greens, common hamburgers and sandwiches.

We'd just settled into one of the booths when Stuart leaned across the table and asked, in his unembarrassed way, "So tell me. Why are you here? I thought you were going to G.W."

I prepared my answer as we studied the menus. "They thought since Natalie got to go to New York, I should have a chance to get away, too," I lied.

"But Natalie got married."

I lowered my voice. "Also," I whispered, vamplike, "I came because of you."

"Me?"

Clearly skeptical, he fished another cigarette from his pocket. I smiled seductively. When I was twelve, Stuart had decided to be the first boy to touch my new breasts. I'd yet to forgive him.

We'd been at a Workmen's Circle Chanuka party—an ethnic event, nothing religious—where we ate potato latkes and sang songs. Natalie and I had known everyone there since toddlerhood. Nothing could have been more boring. After dinner, the adults socialized over coffee while the teenagers went upstairs to a bedroom that served as an office, empty except for a desk and file cabinets. We sat on the wooden floor talking, with the bright overhead light on in case someone came up to check. When I went to the bathroom, Stuart followed and pulled me into another bedroom, held me captive, and circled my breasts with his palms before I thought to squirm away. I felt at once embarrassed and thrilled. Even with a seducer like Stuart, it wasn't entirely unflattering, at twelve, to think that boys couldn't keep their hands off me. Breasts were power.

At home that night, while I stood brushing my teeth, Natalie came into the bathroom and said, "I bet he pulled you into the bedroom and felt you up. He did the same thing to me two years ago. At the same Chanuka party."

In the mirror, I saw myself as I was: an open-mouthed adolescent, drooling a thick foam of white toothpaste. When I recovered, Natalie and I both agreed Stuart was disgusting.

Looking at him across the table in Harry's, I lowered my voice another notch. "I'd never heard of Chapel Hill before you came here," I said. "Really."

He looked pleased. He lit his cigarette and narrowed his eyes against the smoke. "So how come they sent you here? I can't imagine your mother letting you come so far south."

I thought: *she doesn't know.* I thought: *Miriam wanted me to emigrate.* Stuart flicked an ash and set his elbows on the table, waiting for an explanation.

"She thought it would be good for me to get a taste of this part of the country," I lied. "I mean, since it didn't seem to do you any harm."

He settled back, satisfied, and stubbed out the cigarette. Then he grinned. "Wait'll your folks see your getup." He pointed to my madras blouse, tapped one of my Weejuns with his foot under the table. "Are you going to learn the accent, too?"

The more I scowled, the wider he grinned. "I hear it takes at least 'til Thanksgiving to perfect the grit accent."

"Grit?" I asked.

"Carolina-bred. Usually rural. Usually sunburnt on the back of the neck."

"Oh, Stuart."

"Usually not tolerant of anyone different than they are."

"Grits are grain, not people," I told him, irritated at how much he sounded like my mother. Besides, I'd tasted actual grits that morning, after Susan mixed a spoonful of them into the yolk of a sunny-side-up egg. She'd seen me blanch at the sight and suggested I taste them plain to get the right idea. I did, and I could have told Stuart they were no worse than grainy Cream of Wheat.

A waitress appeared, reminding me I was ravenous. I remembered Stuart was paying and cheered up.

We stayed at Harry's longer than I expected. Stuart drank beer and I slugged down Cokes, and we split a slice of cheesecake after we ate our sandwiches. Despite his status as a longtime family friend who felt entitled to ask anything he wanted or make any personal comment, and despite my care never to tell him much, he was easier to talk to than I remembered. When he meant *I think,* he said *I think,* and not *I reckon.* He said *you might be able to* and not *you might could.* He didn't slur his words. He didn't go to some mysterious church where people insulted their relatives by calling them Whiskeypalians. It seemed to me I understood him exceptionally well. One day away from home and I was beginning to fathom what Miriam meant when she lovingly referred to a *landsman* from the old country.

Harry's grew more crowded as evening faded into night. The dinner crowd left and the drinking crowd came in. Because of the sharp change in the weather, the newcomers shed a tang of chilly air along with their jackets and sweaters, which they hung on pegs on the sides of the booths.

Stuart drank three or four beers. I thought he did this partly to remind me I was underage, but I matched him Coke for beer and listened to him talk. Though he'd come to UNC to study math, he sounded as if he cared only about psychology. He was going to take a course with a brilliant professor named Dr. McCurdy, he said. The most sought-out teacher on campus. He went on and on.

After my fourth Coke I was pumped too high with caffeine to care about pyschology teachers, so I watched the other customers. Some of them looked tight and preppy, but most were boys with T-shirts covered by flannel against the chill, or girls in slacks with stringy hair. Bohemians. Conspicuous. One boy actually had a ponytail. The girls in the dorm, I'd noticed, wore skirts even when they were lounging. Slacks were forbidden on campus during classes, and it was easier not to change. In Harry's the girls wore jeans or baggy trousers they must have borrowed from their grandfathers. I told myself that in an hour I'd be back in the dorm and would never have to set foot in Harry's again.

Then I noticed a boy—more a man, really—staring at me intently from a booth a few feet from our table. He was looking openly, not furtively, assessing rather than flirting. Other than his gaze and his good looks, the thing I registered about him was his size. He sat on one side of the booth alone and filled up most of the space. Few college boys lifted weights, but obviously this one did; he had a football player's chest and yet clearly somehow was *not* a football player, not an athlete in that sense.

Across from him were a boy with glasses and a girl with fuzzy reddish hair that cascaded down her back. He was talking to them, but he kept his eyes on me. The three of them were finishing a half-empty pitcher of beer. They must have been there for a while. Why hadn't I seen them come in? I wouldn't have missed this large dark athlete in the midst of these spindly boys. I must have been in the ladies' room.

The boy—the man?—never averted his eyes. Heady with caffeine, disguised in my foreign haircut, I raised my glass of Coke toward him. A toast. He raised his beer and nodded.

Noticing my attention had slipped, Stuart sought the source of distraction. "You're flirting with David Lazar?" He sounded incredulous.

"Huh?"

"David Lazar. Don't you even know him?"

"Should I?"

"You shouldn't flirt with guys you haven't met."

"Why not?"

"First you should meet him." Before I could react Stuart slid out of the booth and pulled me up with him. "Hey, Dave!" he shouted. "Somebody wants to meet you."

Everyone in the restaurant swiveled their heads to look at us. I shot Stuart an evil glance, but he clutched my hand and dragged me toward the other booth. "Beryl Rosinsky, David Lazar," he said gallantly.

David Lazar smiled. Cow eyes. Deep brown. Thick lashes.

Up close, David Lazar was the most beautiful man I'd ever seen.

David introduced the couple across the table, Gloria and Tripp, all the while looking me up and down. He took in my hairdo. My new madras blouse and Weejuns. He scanned me head to toe and seemed to be adding me up. I was afraid he'd laugh.

"Slide in," he said to me finally, moving toward the wall and patting a place beside him. "Bring over your drinks."

Stuart went to retrieve our glasses. As I sat down, my hand brushed David's arm and registered the hardness of it, the breadth. I imagined him in the gym, covered with sweat. Stuart set my Coke in front of me and pulled up a chair. David asked how we knew each other. Old family friends, we said. Enforced visits since childhood. An approving catch of breath escaped from between David's perfect white teeth. In the low golden light with the promise of cold outside after the warm day, everything seemed vibrant, autumnal, vivid.

"We were talking about CURED," said Gloria from across the booth. Like David, she looked old to be a student, more woman than girl, buxom and curvy. Tripp put his hand on hers. He must have been her same age, but he looked unfinished, like a minister just out of seminary—slender, aristocratic nose, delicate features. Both Tripp and Gloria wore wedding rings.

"Cured?" I asked.

"Citizens United for Racial Equality and Dignity."

Oh Christ, I thought. Activists. Why was I surprised?

But David Lazar didn't look like an activist. Not at all! His clothes were adult, formal, chinos and an open shirt. He might have just pulled off a tie, might have just come from work. His clothes were a little like Paco's.

"We used to have COB," Gloria went on, "the Coalition for Open Business. But it fell apart last month." Her big bosom shifted as she warmed to the topic. She was so white-skinned that the stretch of her arm beneath her floppy shirt looked nude instead of just bare.

"There was a huge march," Tripp added. "Quite a few people were arrested."

"*Tripp* was arrested." Gloria grinned at him.

A hush fell on the table. Everyone looked at me. I was being tested. I looked like a TCC; Stuart had said so himself. They were waiting for me to say something disapproving about Tripp's arrest. If only they knew.

"She knows all about it," Stuart interjected, defending me. "Her mother works for FEN."

"Freedom and Equality Now," I felt compelled to explain. "A small civil rights organization in Washington."

"In Washington?" Gloria's brown eyes flashed. I could feel an inquisition coming. The hair on my arms bristled. What right had this floppy big-busted woman to question me? Did they think my mother had sent me here to dispense her propaganda? Quite the opposite! *My mother doesn't even know where I am!* I wanted to shout. Now that I was in disguise in a foreign country, what right had Stuart to mention my past? If I waited long enough, he'd blurt out all the details of her arrests, her travels, her picture in the *Washington Post*.

"Listen," I said, checking my watch. "I've got to go."

"Me, too," David agreed. It was later than I thought: after

ten-thirty, and curfew was at eleven. I slid out of the booth as Stuart picked up our bill.

David pushed himself up, one big hand on the table, the other reaching back for something in the tangle of clothes that hung from the peg at the top of the booth. I expected him to retrieve a jacket or a sweater. He came away instead with something long, solid, glinting silver. It took me a moment to recognize a pair of metal crutches, the kind with a circular brace that went around the arm just below the elbow. He swung out of the booth and fit his fingers around the padded hand grip. My breath caught in my throat. These were not crutches for a broken leg. These were the expensive, custom-made kind, fashioned for a permanent disability.

"Polio," David said without inflection. "When I was twelve."

Stuart, eyebrow raised almost imperceptibly, caught my eye: I told you so. I felt rooted to the spot. Stuart set his hand on my spine at waist level and pushed me forward.

David was a step in front of us, next to Gloria and Tripp. His legs looked solid. They didn't hang slack. It took me a moment to figure out that he put no weight on the left one. I watched him maneuver. Sitting down, he had been perfect.

David balanced himself by the register, a massive arm on one crutch as he pulled out his billfold. I tried not to stare, but it was too late. His jacket was suede, his hair the color of night. We walked out into the cold air. My new clothes were too summery. I tried not to shiver.

"I'll walk you to the dorm," Stuart offered.

"You don't have to."

"She doesn't have a coat," David pointed out. "Where do you live?"

"Alderman," I told him.

"I'll drive you," David offered.

Stuart pointed to a cluster of men's dorms across the street. "I live right there in Pettigrew." He waved and crossed the road. The married couple, Tripp and Gloria, were halfway down the block.

David jiggled his crutches, shrugged off his jacket and dropped it around my shoulders. "Car's down there," he said.

We walked down Franklin Street, or rather I walked and David half-walked, half-glided, borne along by the muscles of those arms, that massive chest. We stopped beside an old Chevy. David opened the door for me; he got in the driver's side and swung the crutches into the back. He was graceful as a dancer and yet lumbering, too. As if, no matter how fine the natural gait, the crutches turned it ugly.

Inside, the car was perfectly ordinary. None of the customized controls I'd heard of on the steering wheel so cripples could control the car with their hands.

David's jaw tightened as he noticed me studying the dash. "Don't worry, only the left leg's affected," he said. "You work the gas and brake with the right foot, if you recall." There was ice in his voice, and his face had frozen into a scowl. He started the motor and drove me to the dorm without another word.

If he was going to be so sensitive, why had he bothered?

He parked on Raleigh Street and walked me to the door, swinging himself up each step to the porch. A dozen or more girls stood outside, talking to their dates or kissing them good-night. I gave David his jacket. He leaned a crutch against one of the pillars while he put it on. He watched me watching him. His thick lashes made a shadow on his cheekbone as he adjusted the coat. The golden wash of appreciation he'd bathed me in at Harry's was gone. Now he was—what? Disdainful? No. Angry.

What terrible thing had I done?

"My legs don't work very well," he said. "But let me tell you so you won't wonder. My legs are the only thing that doesn't work. The *only* thing."

He swung himself down the stairs. At the bottom, he turned back. "I'll call you," he said.

Which puzzled me even more.

I fled into the parlor to sign in. My hands were shaking so badly I could hardly write. If David was angry at me for noticing his infirmity, why hadn't he stayed seated at Harry's when he had the chance? Why had he let me see?

Just an irony, my father would say. Not your fault. But it was. After cutting my hair and thinking I was going to fit in, why had I gone into a place like Harry's—with Stuart Gershner, of all people!—and fallen for David Lazar while he was still sitting down?

5

School started in a blaze of sunshine, with light so sharp and metallic that I was reminded from moment to moment of the exotic landscape I'd been sent to, where nothing was normal. I was taking English, chemistry, history, zoology—all the required freshman courses for medical technology. I darted under the overhanging shade trees, finding my way from one classroom building to another. My list of books to buy was lengthy. I'd have science labs three days a week, leaving me no free time until evening. "My reading assignments are endless," I complained to my roommates.

"You'll be all right if you go to the library between classes," Ashley advised. "That's what I always did. The dorm's noisy, even in the lounge."

Ashley spoke with assurance, but as the days went on, she didn't crack a book. Maybe seniors didn't have to. While I worked feverishly, she spent most of her time primping to see Paco. After classes, she rolled the ends of her hair in foam rollers and went down the hall to shower. She returned with her face scrubbed and applied a sheer film of makeup. She put on a new outfit for the evening, then removed the rollers and brushed her hair into its perfect silvery flip. When she was dressed and ready, she sprayed Golden Autumn cologne into the air and walked into the mist. "Mama says you never want to smell like the red-light district," she said. Leaving her untouched books where she'd set them after classes, she rushed to the parlor to meet Paco, and she never returned until seconds before the doors were locked at eleven.

Moments later, mourning as if he'd been amputated from her, Paco appeared at our window from a hiding place in the bushes. Ashley kneeled on her bed and whispered to him through the screen. His dark head bent to her blonde one; their hands pressed against the wire mesh and touched, palm to palm, Romeo and Juliet. I'd turn away and realize I'd been holding my breath.

Tactfully, Susan and I retreated to the study lounge with our books and later went into the bathroom to change. Our return to the room in pristine gowns and full-length robes finally cued the lovers to say goodnight. Were the meetings at the window illegal? Probably so. One night, just as Susan and I left the lovers to their privacy, the dorm president, Anna Mae, made her way down our hall, hair pulled into rollers, nightshirt flapping at her knees.

"Hey, Anna *Mae!*" Susan and I both shouted, trying to distract her. Susan slammed the door shut behind us. My heart beat doubletime. Had we been found out? But Anna waved and sped by on her way to other business. We rushed back into the room to tell Ashley it was all right. Paco was sprawled flat behind the bushes outside.

She whispered out to him. He reappeared at the window, unmussed, unfluttered, distant, and mysterious. Shrouded in formal manners and formal good looks, he made Susan and me feel somehow—excluded. And yet honored, too, to be involved in the romance even as roommates.

The room felt so empty afternoons when Susan and I came in just as Ashley was hurrying out, so close and hot and filled with Ashley's Golden Autumn and the scent of love that it was often impossible to stay there until it cooled off and aired out.

Penny Blankenship was rushing sororities, as were most of the junior transfer students, and wished Susan were rushing, too. She took pleasure in coming down from the third floor every afternoon to report on the doings at the first set of parties.

"Ashley off with the Latin lover?" She'd flop onto Susan's bed with a Coke in her hand and make herself comfortable. Then she'd list the various houses she'd been to, speaking in Susan's direction while turning her back to me as best she could. There was at least one Jewish fraternity on campus, but if there were Jewish sororities, I hadn't heard.

"I'm not wild for the ADPi's," Penny would say with great casualness, taking tiny sips of her Coke. "But maybe the Kappas. Or the Chi O's."

"The snobs, the richies, the beauties," Susan responded, turning up the volume on her favorite record, "Sugar Shack."

"Honestly, Susan. I don't know what's got into you." Penny shot a malicious glance at me, as if to suggest I was responsible for Susan's defection. Then she apparently dismissed that idea as too repulsive because she said, "You decided not to rush because of Ashley, didn't you? Don't say you didn't."

"Don't be ridiculous." Susan raised the volume once again, letting the words about the little sugar shack along the tracks blare into the room and out the open window. Undaunted, Penny reached over and turned the record player down to a whisper.

"Ashley could have pledged Chi O in a minute last year if

she hadn't met Paco and decided there were better things to do," she argued. To me she added haughtily, "Her mother was a Chi O, so she was a legacy. That's half the reason her parents are so upset. That and he's foreign."

Susan's pert face congealed into formal pleasantness. "They're mainly upset because he's Catholic," she said. "Her Daddy's a deacon, you know how he feels."

"Don't you wish," Penny sniffed. "Don't tell me he'd say everything was plum peachy if Paco decided to turn Baptist."

"He might. You don't know he wouldn't. Listen, I have to read this history."

But Penny leaned back against the wall beneath the print of the girl-holding-kitten, took another sip of Coke, and rolled the liquid around in her mouth as if she were going to stay there forever. Finally she swallowed and said, "He wouldn't like Paco any better if he decided to become a Baptist preacher." She pointed to Susan. "And you know it."

The nostrils of Susan's pug nose flared as she took a deep breath, but she said nothing. I felt compelled to defend her.

"Susan's right," I said. "Ashley and Paco aren't that different. It's not as if one of them were Jewish. After all, Christian is Christian."

Penny spewed Coke and hooted.

"Well, isn't it?" I demanded.

A key turned in the lock and Ashley reappeared. "I forgot my bracelet." She took in my stony expression and Penny's mirthful one. "What's going on?"

"She thinks Christian is Christian." Penny nodded in my direction.

"Leave her be, Penny," Ashley said. "Beryl probably knows about it better than we do. Going to that—what do you call it? Temple?"

"Yes. Or synagogue. We don't go, though."

"You mean not every week." Ashley plucked a silver bracelet from a tangle of jewelry on her dresser.

"Not ever."

"*Never?*"

"Except for a wedding or Bar Mitzvah or something. It's mostly in Hebrew. You can't understand a word."

Ashley held the bracelet poised above her wrist. A hush fell on the room. "Paco's church is in Latin. *He* goes."

I wondered how I'd gotten into this discussion. Penny was taking in my every word, probably storing it for ammunition. "My parents don't really believe in it," I said weakly.

For an instant Ashley stopped moving entirely, then regained herself. "Then they're denying you your heritage." She lowered the bracelet decisively to her wrist and latched it in place.

"They're not really denying me," I said. "Not going to temple *is* my heritage."

※

Ashley left a moment later, with Penny close on her heels, clutching her half-empty Coke. Susan giggled. "Ready to eat?" she asked. I nodded, pleased she still wanted to break bread with me, someone as foreign as coolie hats and saris.

We left the room so hurriedly that Ashley and Paco were only a few steps in front of us when we got outside onto the sidewalk. They strolled along, unaware of us, holding hands, touching arms from wrist to elbow. We were so close that Ashley's cologne carried into our faces, along with her languorous drawl and the clipped edge of Paco's accent. Surely they heard our footsteps? But they seemed not to. They laughed and gazed at each other rapturously, and finally disappeared into Paco's car.

"She's so pretty she could have anybody," Susan remarked when they drove off. "Sometimes I don't understand it. Why she wants a foreigner."

A quick stab of adrenaline shot through me. She might as well have called Paco a Jew. A psychopath. A murderer.

I took a deep breath and waited until I thought I could make my voice sound neutral. "Are you being judgmental?" I asked. "Or only sad?"

"Neither. Just realistic."

"But he's so handsome. So polite."

"I guess so," Susan agreed halfheartedly. "But elegance isn't everything."

It was not turning out to be a good afternoon. The word *elegance* conjured up a picture of David Lazar, who'd looked so elegant till he stood up. I knew well enough what he'd meant when he said his legs were the only thing that didn't work.

So why hadn't he called?

A hundred times, I had told myself that maybe he'd tried. There was only one phone on our hall, and getting through was a major undertaking. The moment someone hung up, it rang again, some boy urgently looking for some girl. Considering the ratio of men to women on campus, we all had our admirers. I'd been invited to Saturday's football game by three different boys, two who also wanted to study with me in the library, another who offered to buy me dinner at the Zoom Zoom Room on Franklin Street, which wasn't cheap. We could all have as many dates as we wanted.

Susan and I walked on in dreary silence, Susan probably despondent because her friends kept razzing her about not rushing sorority, me because I feared I was being ignored by a boy—a man—on crutches.

In Lenoir Hall, the usual collards and turnip greens languished on the steam table before us, vegetables I'd finally learned to distinguish because the turnips were dotted with little cut-up pieces of white turnip root. I never ate either one. I motioned the server to put some sweet potatoes on my plate. It didn't occur to me until I tasted them, coated with a sweet brownish syrup, that what I'd had in mind was not this sticky mess at all but Miriam's *tsimmes*—a holiday dish of sweet potatoes and carrots and prunes she might be serving even now. It was probably Rosh Hashonah. Of course it was! Notices from Hillel had been appearing in my mailbox for days, inviting me to New Year's services. I'd thrown them all away.

At home, the family was probably dipping bites of gefilte fish into horseradish or spooning up Miriam's chicken noodle soup. Swept by a wave of homesickness, I pushed the foreign-looking sweet potatoes to the side of my plate. We didn't go to temple on Rosh Hashonah—certainly not!—but we always marked the holiday with Miriam's festive dinner. "To cele-brate the New Year," my mother would explain annually. "Fall really *is* the new year—not the first of January, for heaven's sake. It's not a religious thing."

Even with my mother in Alabama and me in North Caro-lina and Natalie in New York, I counted four at the table. My father, Miriam, Aunt Gussie, and Uncle Abe. Last year, there had also been Bubby Tsippi. I tried to remember—but couldn't—what my great-grandmother ate at those ritual nonkosher family dinners.

"What's the matter?" Susan asked.

"I just remembered I'm supposed to call home." I waited for Susan to finish, and then dashed off to Graham Memorial, the student union, to use the pay phone on the second floor.

So far I hadn't been a sterling correspondent. During the summer, the post office had added a five-number zip code to all addresses. Five numbers! Addressing a letter suddenly seemed exhausting. I didn't write to friends; I didn't write to Natalie; I didn't even call home every Saturday as I'd been instructed. Instead, I waited for Miriam to get through to the dorm, as she eventually did, and then was annoyed because our conversation was tense and unsatisfactory, with other girls lingering in the hallway to use the phone.

That night in Graham Memorial, I was relieved to find the phone free and the hallway deserted. My father accepted the charges and sounded delighted to hear from me. For long moments he interrograted me about my classes, my room-mates. I warmed to his attention; the wave of sadness and homesickness disappeared. In the background, Miriam picked up the extension.

"You'll write letters to your mother," she commanded, wasting no time on small talk. "You'll send them here, since she keeps moving from house to house. Your father always has the latest address. You'll send the first letter tomorrow."

"When will she be home?" I asked.

"A week, maybe," my father said. "Maybe two."

"Who knows, soon enough," Miriam interrupted. "In the meantime it's not necessary you should be specific where you are. You'll tell her you're fine. You'll tell her how your classes are going. You'll tell her what she needs to know."

So she still didn't know where I was. And nobody was going to tell her until she returned. It seemed fitting. If she left us, we had every right to carry on without making her privy to our decisions. My father and grandmother would protect me from her wrath. They would hide my location from her until the last possible moment. I might be in a foreign country, but I had powerful allies. When I hung up, I caught sight of myself in the glass of a trophy case. Staring back at me was a Typical Carolina Coed, smiling wide, showing teeth.

6

A pack of dogs roamed the campus. They belonged to students who lived in town, and they came to school every morning. While their owners went to class, the dogs sniffed about on the grass, chased squirrels, greeted whoever came by. There were eight or ten dogs altogether, daunting from a distance but not at all wild close up. At the end of each hour, the pack split, most of its members trotting to wait loyally outside the various classroom buildings for their owners. They'd walk the students in question to the next class and then rejoin the pack to sniff and paw for another hour.

As I came out of Bingham Hall from English, a few dogs stood by the door, tongues hanging out, panting, expectant. I noticed them absently as I started to hurry away toward chemistry class on the other side of campus. Then I heard a voice I recognized instantly.

"Ivan, over here, boy! Ivan!" David Lazar called. A black-

and-white hound—little more than a puppy, certainly not Russian—perked up its ears.

"Ivan!"

The dog ran and leaped, planting big clumsy feet on David's thighs as he leaned against the building, one crutch propped against the bricks, one hand free.

"Hey, fella. Hey, fella," David said, rubbing the dog's ears. Unaware that I was watching, he looked fresh and open and loving.

Sun dappled his hair, which after all was not Spanish-black like Paco's, but a deep rich brown with mahogany highlights. Even leaning against the building near his crutch, anyone would notice him more for his strong broad chest and the wide fingers stroking the puppy, than for his weakened legs. The sight of him made my mouth go so dry that I had to swallow a few times before I could speak. I walked over to confront him.

"I didn't know you were a student," I said, forgetting chemistry class. "I thought you were—older."

He looked down at me with so much light in his eyes that I knew he hadn't forgotten to call. He grinned. "I am—older," he mimicked. "And you, I understand, are—younger."

So. He hadn't called because someone—it had to be Stuart—told him I was seventeen. Maybe he thought he'd get arrested.

"How old is older?" I blurted, afraid he'd say thirty, something outrageous.

"Twenty-three."

"That's not so old," I said.

"I work part time in the psychology department. I'm taking a couple of courses so I can go to law school."

"I see." A positive sign. I had placed him as a clerk in an insurance office, in a dim corner hidden away from the general public.

"That's what most people do here," he said, his voice

taking on the same hard edge as it had the other night. "Most people go to school." He kept petting the dog, watching me.

"Well—sure."

The dog closed its eyes, let him knead its ears.

"I was a couple of courses short for law school. It's not so unusual."

"No, I didn't say—"

"That suits you, does it? Law school?" Sudden heavy sarcasm. I set my face into neutral.

"Yeah. Sure. Why not? Law school or whatever. Doesn't make any difference to me." The dog came over and sniffed my hand.

David retrieved the crutch from against the building and positioned it under his elbow. When he began to walk, Ivan stayed at his heels. Helpless, I matched him stride for lumbering stride, bathed in David's grim silence. Halfway across the quad I remembered: chemistry!

"Oh, no, I'm late!" I said. Then I set my two good legs into graceful, grateful motion and bounded off.

Instead of spending time with David as I had hoped, I did what every other Carolina coed did: went out with whoever looked interesting, whoever asked me first.

I went to my first football game with a boy named Reese Chambers. He was late because he had two other couples to pick up, and by the time I went up to the ironing room on the second floor to press my skirt, there was no one left in the warm, sundrenched rooms of Alderman Women's Dormitory except me and the housemother, Mrs. West. Ashley had gone off with Paco, Susan was with a boy named Colby Lee. Every other girl had either been asked to the game or fixed up with someone, a boy whose first name was likely to be two words, like Colby Lee, or else whatever his mother's maiden name had been, Carter or Morgan or Steadman. He would have excellent manners; he would open doors for his date and guide her up curbs and steps; he would pay her way wherever they went.

Reese and two friends arrived dressed in blazers and ties, carrying flasks of whiskey in their pockets, which they (but not their dates) began drinking as we walked to the stadium. The afternoon was hot. While the boys got drunk, we girls cheered and perspired and got sunburned. Afterwards, we walked to Reese's fraternity house for more bourbon, and then we drove to the Saddle and Fox restaurant in Durham, where they ordered 7-Up and poured liquor into it under the table.

Back at the Deke house, Reese and I danced to exactly two records before the color drained from his face and he lurched out onto the lawn to throw up. Then he passed out on the grass.

One of his fraternity brothers tapped me on the shoulder. "I'll take care of you," he said. "I'll take you home later."

"How about right now?"

He said, "Aw, baby, the night is young."

The fraternity house was on the opposite side of town from Alderman Dorm. In the end, I walked. I went under the sweeping streetlights of Franklin Street, past the post office onto the tree-lined residential stretch, and finally onto dimly lit Raleigh Street. I took off my shoes the last half mile, intending to jab any attacker with a wicked spiked heel. My mother would have been proud.

When I signed in, an hour before the one o'clock curfew, Mrs. West noted my disheveled state and said, "Are you all right, dear? You haven't been drinking, have you?"

It seemed to me anyone could see I was flustered but not drunk. "I haven't been drinking, but my date was. He got sick and I walked back alone."

"Oh, dear." She came close enough to smell my breath

and eyed me suspiciously a few seconds more. "In the future you really need to be more careful." As if I, not he, were guilty of the breach of manners.

On Sunday, I went to Graham Memorial to read chemistry. I'd taken to studying in the student union because the buzzing fluorescent lights and unnatural quiet in the library put me to sleep. In Graham Memorial, the reading room had dark paneling and wooden floors covered with thick Oriental rugs, and overstuffed leather couches and chairs. Lamps on the end tables shed soft, homey light instead of institutional brightness, and classical music was piped in from an office outside. There was no enforced quiet, but rather a murmur of voices from people playing chess or cards at the tables scattered throughout the room. In Graham Memorial, I could study for hours.

But that day, I was too restless. Shafts of sunlight streamed through the tall windows and were blotted up by dark wood, making me feel caged. I wanted to be outdoors—on the shaded square of grass bordered by Alderman and Kenan and McIver, or in the arboretum across from the dorm, or *somewhere*—outside, in the light. I gathered my books and left.

On the quad in front of Graham Memorial, I stopped to read the inscription on the statue of a Confederate soldier everyone called Silent Sam—silent because he was supposed to shoot his gun every time a virgin walked by. Ironically, the deeply Southern message at his feet was about the utmost importance of duty, a sentiment my mother would have cheered. A few hundred yards away, down on Franklin Street, a protest march was just ending in front of the post office. Casually dressed students mingled with formally-dressed men and women, equal numbers of colored and white, the men in suits and ladies in printed shirtwaists, neat purses hanging from their arms as if they'd just come from church. The participants had been carrying signs, but they'd lowered them now. I couldn't see the writing.

On the campus where I stood, some boys who'd been throwing a football back and forth stopped to joke and gesture toward the marchers. I remembered being the butt of such jokes. I averted my eyes.

But before I turned completely, I noticed a black-and-white dog sniffing its way through the dispersing crowd. Ivan. Subversive Russian name and floppy, cheerful walk. When I looked up, David Lazar had spotted me and was waving.

I had no choice but to cross the street. He stood with the couple I'd met the other night, Gloria and Tripp; a beautiful black-haired girl I didn't know; and the Negro girl from the dorm, Emily Moses. None of them carried signs, so it was unclear whether they'd been in the parade or just watching.

"You know Beryl Rosinsky?" David asked Emily. "She lives in your dorm."

Emily smiled politely. She had glorious eyes, the color of dark-flecked mustard, but the smile didn't reach them. She had no idea who I was.

"On the other side of the parlor," I offered.

"Oh. Sure," she said. Then the pretty dark-haired girl pulled Emily away and David latched onto my arm and said, "Come on, I'll show you where I live."

After our previous frosty encounters, this sent blood trumpeting through me in such a rush that I felt dizzy. I neglected to say I had to study chemistry. I forgot I'd wanted to be outdoors. We went to his car on Rosemary Street around the corner, Ivan loping between us.

David lived not far from Franklin Street. Anyone with better legs could have walked. He had a tiny duplex with no front yard and a side yard dominated by an oil tank. Inside, most of the living room was taken up by a huge built-in space heater hooked into the wall, with piping out to the oil tank. I had never seen such an arrangement. But though the furniture was sparse and tattered and the wooden floors dark with age, the rooms were surprisingly neat. Inside a thumbnail kitchen, the counters and table were clean and all the floors were swept. How he'd managed this while balancing on crutches I didn't know. I only knew the cottage was charming. A sugar shack. A real-life version of Susan's favorite song.

I caught a glimpse of a bedroom to the left—a double bed, a white bedspread—before David made his way over and pulled the door shut. It occurred to me then that being in a man's house alone put me in violation of the university's two-couple rule. I felt a little shiver of excitement.

Ivan bounded up onto a threadbare sofa and thumped his tail in invitation. David motioned me to sit. Above the sofa, a large poster of President Kennedy smiled down on us, giving me pause. An identical poster graced one of the walls in my mother's office. These weren't sold in stores; you had to be politically connected to get them. I sat on David's sofa anyway. He set his crutches against the wall and dropped down next to me. Ivan thumped his tail harder and set his face in my lap.

"So what's with you and Emily?" David asked.

"Me and Emily?"

"She didn't even know you."

"Why should she?"

"She lives in your dorm."

"So do a hundred other girls."

"She's colored," he said.

"You sound like my mother," I said. "There are some people, if they were white, she wouldn't care if I had anything to do with them. But because they aren't, we're supposed to be good friends."

David grinned. "And is Emily the kind that, if she were white, you wouldn't have anything to do with?" He scooted closer and inched his arm around my shoulder, and I was so glad he was only teasing that I didn't move away.

"She wouldn't care that we have nothing in common," I continued. "Or that we probably wouldn't have two words to say to each other—"

"You have in common that you're both students here." His voice was low and seductive. It was so warm inside the circle of his arm that I forgot what I'd been saying.

"Ummnn," I muttered.

He pulled me close against a clean cotton shirt that smelled of detergent.

Ivan bounded off the couch as if on cue. David brought his face closer. I noticed the fineness of his olive skin, the thickness of his dark lashes. I closed my eyes. We progressed quite rapidly from the first tentative kiss to tongues in mouths and his hands on my breasts. I wasn't prepared. I grew dizzy and faint, and amazed that I could breathe and kiss at the same time.

Soon we were lying down, David sprawled on top of me, rubbing his hand up my thigh. I forgot about his questionable bohemian friends, his crippled legs, the possibility that he might be an activist. Something momentous drew me toward him, canceled out all that. *It's only sex,* my mother would have said. But it didn't feel like only sex; no. It felt far more important, a magnet drawing me to the heart of the world. I never even opened my eyes until he started tugging at my underpants.

Ivan lay curled on a throw rug before us, one black-and-white ear flopping against half-closed eyes. He was watching intently.

"No, David," I said, wriggling out from under.

David paid no attention. I removed his hand from my leg. "No," I whispered urgently.

This time he didn't argue. I bolted into a sitting position. I began to understand the need for the two-couple rule. I rearranged my clothes.

"Were you in that march today? Or just watching?" I asked, seeking safety in conversation.

David stroked my arm, his fingers close to my breast.

"Answer me," I said.

He whispered so that his breath tickled my ear. "Does it really make any difference?"

Well, yes, it did. But the way his lips were caressing my earlobe, the way his hand moved against my arm, I couldn't keep focused. We resumed kissing and slid down on the couch. He unbuttoned my blouse.

"Come into the bedroom," he said.

"No." I caught sight once more of Ivan, almost asleep, so comfortable about this, so—*accustomed* to seeing David do this. I sat up again.

David sat up, too. He slid to the opposite end of the couch. His warm manner vanished. "I know what you're thinking," he said. "Let me give you a little education. Polio's a virus, that's all. Just a virus."

"I wasn't thinking about that at all," I protested.

"It feels like a bad flu. It races through your body in a couple of days and wipes out some of the connections between muscles and nerves. It can be very specific. It can leave you so you can move your little toe but not your big toe. Or it can wipe out whole systems. In my case, it wiped out most of my left leg. I can feel the leg, but I can't move most of the muscles. That's all. Just that. Nothing else."

I felt childish, scolded. "I don't care about that," I said. "I wouldn't be here if I did."

Ivan got up, stretched, came over to lick my hand.

"Come into the bedroom," David said, smiling.

"No," I said.

We spent the rest of the afternoon and most of the

evening on the living room couch, breaking only to cook hamburgers for supper. David sprinkled the meat with Worcestershire sauce and balanced himself against the stove as he maneuvered the skillet. As soon as we washed the dishes, we returned to the couch. John Kennedy smiled down on us from the wall as music wafted from the record player. David's collection was not rock 'n' roll 45s like Susan's, but folk music albums, long-playing. Pete Seeger. Joan Baez. Bob Dylan. By the time we left for the dorm, my lips felt bruised.

It was almost midnight, Sunday's curfew. A dozen couples were saying goodnight on the porch. Ashley and Paco were among them, but the two of them weren't embracing, just staring at each other as if already sorrowful about the long hours they'd spend apart until tomorrow. David leaned against a pillar and pulled me to him with a free arm. As we kissed, I thought about the ethereal quality of Ashley's romance, compared to the solid earthiness of—this.

David let me go. A few people were watching us. One girl smiled at me sweetly. I knew what she was thinking: *Dating a cripple, poor dear, how sad.* I said goodnight and darted quickly into the dorm. I wanted David to touch me—oh, yes—beneath my bra, in private places, but not on the lips in public. I knew from my mother's picture in the *Washington Post* that drawing the spotlight was never, ever a good thing.

Also, I suddenly remembered why I was here. I was here to stand up to Mother. David was exactly the kind of boy she would approve of, downtrodden and victimized. I should avoid him entirely.

This resolution lasted less than forty-eight hours, when David found me after class and asked me to meet him at Harry's for dinner. We ate and then spent several hours tangling on his couch. I refused to go to his bedroom or let him take off my underpants. I made him bring me back half an hour before curfew. I bolted out of his car at the curb and ran to the dorm alone.

On the way to check my mailbox, I almost bumped into Emily Moses. I said hello but didn't start a conversation. In my mailbox was a check from Dad and a notice from Hillel, inviting me to services for Yom Kippur, the Day of Atonement. I wouldn't go to services; I never had. But after avoiding Emily and being ashamed of David, I decided the least I could do on Yom Kippur, for the first time in my life, was fast.

I didn't, of course.

7

On September 15, 1963, a bomb went off in a church in Birmingham, Alabama, killing four little Negro girls in their Sunday School class, which is why my mother didn't show up in Chapel Hill until October. She was sitting on Ashley's bed when I came back from class, legs tucked under the full skirt of her shirtwaist, possibly meditating. I didn't know who'd let her in. Nobody ever sat on Ashley's bed except Ashley. The pastel pillows were scattered everywhere. Ashley was due back in an hour.

The first thing my mother said to me was, "Nobody told me they sent you here until I got back to Washington. I thought you were at G.W."

A cold shiver skittered across the back of my neck. I'd prepared exactly what I'd say when I finally saw her: What kind of mother doesn't know what school her child has gone to? What kind of mother is so negligent? But the words didn't come.

"They wanted me to emigrate," I whispered.

"So I heard." She untangled her legs and slid off the bed, studying me with piercing intensity. "I was worried."

"You couldn't have been too worried. I've been here for a month." I let my books drop onto the desk. Mother didn't seem aware of my anger. She strode over and engulfed me in a bear-like hug. Then she held me at arm's length as if to check for signs of illness. As her grip loosened, I made myself step back out of her reach.

"They should have told me where you were," she said.

"They tried to. I tried to myself. You were too busy."

"I'm never too busy for family." She moved toward the window, cutting me off from Ashley's bed and the disarranged pillows. "It's true I get caught up in things. Maybe I shouldn't. But I'm never too busy for family." She looked wistful and apologetic, but I didn't reply. She turned to stare out at the golden afternoon light.

"If you live in a certain section of Birmingham, they call it Dynamite Hill," she said. "They expect a certain amount of trouble. But when you start blowing up children—"

Her voice trembled and her right hand balled into a fist as if to assert she wasn't showing weakness. I wasn't surprised the bombing evoked so much emotion. In the paper there'd been a photo of a critically wounded girl, the sister of one who was killed. She lay in a hospital bed, her small dark face swollen and her eyes covered with huge gauze pads. I wasn't sure whether or not she'd been blinded.

My mother turned from the window. "You cut your hair," she observed.

"Do you like it?"

She picked up one of the pillows, a pale yellow with the silhouette of a cat appliquéd in white. "It's expensive—a new hair style, a new wardrobe." She gestured toward my Ship 'n Shore blouse. It was borrowed from Susan, but I didn't say so.

"Well?" I patted my hair, bracing myself. I willed her to

move away from Ashley's bed so I could straighten the covers.

"I liked it long," my mother said.

The light hung thick between us, coming from the top of the Palladian arch over the window, above the venetian blind. My mother ran her fingers over the cat appliqué on Ashley's pillow without looking down at it.

"Why didn't you tell me you were coming, Mother?" I asked.

"The better question is, why didn't you tell me where you were?"

"I told you, you were busy. I didn't even have your address."

"You sent those letters."

"I sent them to Miriam. She sent them on."

My mother unhanded Ashley's pillow and stood straighter. "If they were going to play this—this game, you didn't have to."

We stared at each other, neither wanting to give ground. "Once I found out you were here, I tried to call you at least a dozen times," she said. "The line was always busy." A few strands of her hair had dislodged themselves from her French twist; her maroon lipstick had faded so that her lips looked brown.

"Miriam calls," I said. "Miriam always gets through."

My mother took a deep breath. "You never intended to come to school here. You were angry because I was arrested. Because of that picture in the paper. Because it didn't look dignified."

"Mother, don't."

"Don't tell me 'don't.' Doing what's right isn't always pretty. Appearances aren't everything."

"No? Well, looking ridiculous doesn't help anything, either! Being dragged off like that. As if singlehandedly you could change anything."

"There's no point rehashing—"

"No, really, Mother. Do you honestly love those colored people so much? I don't see you bringing them home in droves. They're not your friends, your close companions."

"You don't have to be best friends to fight with someone for a cause."

"Oh, that's it?" I addressed the fourteen-foot ceiling. "She believes in war. In armed confrontation. No—pardon me. Passive resistance."

Mother sank onto Ashley's bed. "I didn't used to," she said slowly. "Not until after the Hearings." She balled her hands into fists again, then unballed them and shook her fingers as if they'd gone numb. "But I'll tell you what. It wasn't until I started believing in war that I ever got anything I wanted."

"Oh, sure. Look what you got. Notoriety and ridicule."

She gave me a sharp exclamation point of a look. "And also a sense of purpose," she said. "In the end, you're always fighting for yourself."

She stood up and crossed her arms. "I think what brought you here was an unnecessary, and if you'll pardon my saying so, self-indulgent guilt trip because Bubby Tsippi died after she ate something that disagreed with her."

"Well, I no longer feel guilty," I said.

"You wouldn't be here if you didn't."

"Just tell me what this visit is all about," I demanded. "To make me come home? You might as well know right now that I'm staying here. I'm not going to G.W. I'm not living in a house where we have to bail you out—"

"For godsake, Beryl!"

"Well, I'm not!"

"I didn't come here to drag you off!"

"Then why did you?"

As if reading my mind, she set Ashley's pillows in place and tugged at the spread. A long silence ensued. "I came," she said finally, "to take you to dinner."

My mother offered to drive us to a restaurant, but it was too early to eat. Since it was sunny and unseasonably warm, I decided to show her the arboretum, then lead her on the path past the planetarium to Franklin Street, and take her to the only place I thought she'd fit in—Harry's Grill.

Her skirt was wrinkled, but otherwise she looked respectable. Serious civil rights activists in those days dressed modestly, in ordinary dresses with stockings and heels. I could hardly remember my mother ever wearing anything else. She had on a burgundy-colored shirtwaist and black pumps, the sort of clothes she'd worn even before my father was accused of being un-American.

But I did remember—or thought I did—that it wasn't until after the McCarthy hearings that my mother began adopting slightly outrageous gestures and accessories to go with her modest clothes. She'd tie her long hair in a knot smack on top of her head, carry a conspicuous shopping bag to the market, wear enormous red earrings and matching beads. No matter how often people told us she was beautiful, Natalie and I found her ridiculous. She didn't look or act the way a mother should. She was too big, too strong, with such a striding, masculine walk that even her large eyes and straight, aristocratic nose didn't make her look ordinary. It didn't matter to us that, in those months after the Hearings when my father began to fold into himself and my grandfather had the heart attack that killed him, the women fared better because they vowed not to care what anyone thought. Let people criticize! Bring them on! Miriam made us call her by her first name and Mother transformed herself into an activist, a rebel. And she survived.

But we didn't forgive her. We held her accountable for embarrassing us; we wanted a family like everyone else's. We hated her for drawing attention. She was noticeable even when she was trying not to be.

That day in Chapel Hill was no exception. As we strolled down the path that led toward the planetarium, she slipped off her shoes and carried them in her hand, and drew the eye of every student who passed.

Oh, I understood why she did it! I did—and that made it worse. Except for its brief cold snaps, autumn in Chapel Hill was warmer and sweeter than in Washington. The honeyed light slanted from the west, dappling the leaf-strewn pathways with sun and shadow. We walked beneath the grape arbor, then cut across a lawn dotted with yellow-leaved maples so luminous that they might have been lit from within. After the long day, my mother's feet must have hurt. It was only natural for her to take her shoes off. But the moment she did, the moment she began walking barefoot on the grass, she ceased to look like anyone's mother. At that moment she became an aging vagabond, a woman who rode freedom buses with students half her age, a woman whose unflattering picture of her arrest landed on the pages of the *Washington Post*. She looked like a woman who, if she'd lived in the Garden of Eden, would have organized a strike against the Creator.

"Put your shoes on, Mother, it's too cold," I said.

"Soon." Students wandering through the arboretum back to their dorms smiled at each other conspiratorially, as if to say: look, a weirdo. Mother paid no attention. She dangled her shoes from her hand. She commented on the size of a wisteria vine as we strolled past the trellis where it was trained. "Just look at the width of that stem!" She might have been a tourist on vacation.

"Aunt Gussie had another one of her spells while I was away," she informed me, idly running her hand along the back of a concrete bench to test the texture of the masonry. "Did Miriam tell you?"

"No."

"It didn't last long, thank goodness. Of course it would be

easier if Gussie let Uncle Abe take care of her when she gets like that. But she insists on Miriam."

"I know."

"She doesn't trust Abe at those times. Even now."

"I know, Mother." We rehashed this every time Gussie acted up.

"I'm not saying she doesn't care for him. I'm talking about trust."

"Mother, they've been married almost forty years. If she didn't trust him, she could have—"

"Gussie was pretty once, the prettiest of all the sisters," she interrupted. "She could have had a lot of men."

"I thought she didn't have boyfriends because it took her so long to get over that boy who was killed in the pogrom. I thought the trip to America cured her."

"Not entirely."

"But she got better. You said so a million times." Wasn't her miraculous recovery the reason Gussie and Miriam had insisted that I, too, emigrate?

"She did get better for a while," Mother said. "But she didn't get married. And now look at her." She dropped her shoes onto the grass and slipped into them, one by one. "When she was thirty—in those days thirty was an old maid. That's when Bubby Tsippi called the matchmaker. And what did the matchmaker do? Found a man with claws for fingers."

"Obviously she's adjusted," I maintained.

"After forty years," Mother said quickly. "But imagine her at thirty, having to marry a man with claws."

We came out of the arboretum, from dappled shade into the sunlight in front of Morehead Planetarium. Mother took a sudden deep interest in the roses around the sundial in the center of the parking lot.

"Uncle Abe had been a chemist, but his fingers had been burned," she said. "In those days they thought they could treat him with X-ray, but it made him worse. The little fingers had to be amputated, and the middle and index fingers froze into claws."

Why hadn't I heard this before? It occurred to me that Natalie and I had never asked. As children, we'd been too afraid of his hands to want to know more. His nails had a yellowish cast to them. And they were long and neatly filed like a woman's. Only as the years went by and Uncle Abe never pointed toward us or tried to touch us did our fear melt into curiosity. Who filed his nails? we whispered to each other. Could he do it himself? Or did Aunt Gussie have to help him? It seemed a terrible, intimate task.

When I was eight, we were at a funeral for a distant cousin, waiting for the casket to be lowered into the grave, when someone pointed to another area of the cemetery and said, "That's where Abe's fingers are buried." Natalie and I weren't meant to overhear. We were appalled.

The rest of Uncle Abe's remains, our father told us, would someday go into the coffin with the fingers. In Jewish law, you were supposed to bury the whole body, he said. This was a common practice. For days Natalie and I huddled together and discussed this. Imagine! That someone would buy a coffin to bury *fingers!* We pictured them, greenish and rank, rotting in the empty coffin in the dark.

"Think of it," my mother said. "Aunt Gussie was a virgin. Imagine being touched by those hands."

I shuddered. Then I wondered how Mother knew Aunt Gussie was a virgin. How did she know Gussie hadn't slept with the boy in Russia? After all, the breakdown began after he was killed. And now, all these years later, what difference did it make?

We stepped from the planetarium parking lot onto Franklin Street. "I'm sure she learned to love Abe after a while," Mother said. "They seem content enough. But at first it must have been terrible. She got well when she came to America, and as soon as she married him, she began having the spells again."

As if to echo the terror of this, at that moment the light receded from behind the buildings on the other side of the street and cast the block into shadow.

"And of course she couldn't trust him. Imagine being given shock therapy against your will. She was terrified. Who wouldn't be? It's barbaric."

"I thought Uncle Abe didn't know they were giving it to her."

"I'm sure he didn't. At least not the first time. He tried to take care of her, I'm not denying that. But finally he put her in the hospital. Not once, several times. Miriam never did that, never. No matter how bad she got. You can't blame Gussie for asking for Miriam."

"Oh, Mother."

"Not that Abe hasn't been good to Gussie in other ways. Of course he has. All these years. But still." My mother sighed.

"The point being?"

"The point being, if she's unstable, maybe it's because she ended up in a marriage she never wanted. A marriage her own mother forced on her. Bubby Tsippi called the matchmaker because Gussie was thirty years old. She wanted Gussie off her hands. Whoever the matchmaker brought, that was who Gussie got."

"I thought you said that's what they *did* in those days," I said, exasperated.

"It was. The point is, number one, Bubby wasn't some saint. Number two, it's ridiculous to think you killed her, especially since nobody told you about the dishes. She was a ninety-year-old woman who sold her daughter into marriage. And that daughter has been unstable ever since."

She sounded so earnest that I didn't have the heart to say I hadn't felt guilty since the day I'd been told I could go away to school. Since that day I'd been set free of the burden of living with a mother whose picture could end up in the *Washington Post.*

"Let's cross," I said, pointing to the other side of Franklin Street. If Mother had wanted to make speeches about Bubby Tsippi's unworthiness, she should have made them last summer before she ran off to Alabama.

But she persisted. "You know, Gussie isn't really her name," she said as we dodged traffic. "Her real name is Shamona."

"I know." I'd always thought Shamona a more romantic name than Gussie, but nobody called her that, and I didn't think it mattered. Lots of people had nicknames.

"You know what Shamona means, don't you?"

"No." Some curse that would discredit Bubby further? We reached the curb on the other side of the street and slowed down.

"It's the Hebrew word for eight."

"Eight?" How disappointing.

"Gussie was the eighth child. Bubby didn't even bother with a name for her. She saddled her with a number. What kind of a person gives her child a number?"

"Maybe one who has eleven children. Maybe one who likes the sound of the word. She thought of a name for Miriam."

"That was because Miriam was younger. Bubby had two boys in between. She had plenty of time to think of a girl's name." In the colorless dusk, my mother's face was flushed, triumphant. "What if I'd named you Two?"

"Oh, Mother," I said, and sighed.

"I'll tell you another thing," she said. "You know how Bubby always wore that scarf?"

"Sure. I thought orthodox women had to cover their hair."

"When Bubby was young, she started wearing a wig like all the other women. Then someone told her wigs could get bugs in them. And that was that. She never wore a wig from that day. She covered her head with the kerchief. If she'd been such a saint, she would have tolerated the bugs."

"That's ridiculous," I said.

"She was human, that's all. It's not so terrible to be human." She raised her hand quickly so I wouldn't interrupt. "I know you cared for her. Of course you did. But to think you were responsible for her dying, when she was in her nineties anyway—"

"Mom, I never thought—" The street lights blinked on and the evening air cleared my head. Why should I tell her the truth? Let her feel guilty for neglecting me in my time of need. Let her suffer.

But as we went into Harry's, I couldn't help being touched that, in spite of everything, she'd driven five hours to Chapel Hill just to comfort me.

8

In the weeks I'd been meeting David for dinner, I'd never told Susan or Ashley anything about him—and particularly I hadn't told them we ate at Harry's a couple times a week. Harry's was a beatnik hangout, a place for weirdos. No point branding myself as one of them. If it hadn't been for David, I would never have set foot in the place.

Besides, I didn't go there for politics. I went for sex—or more accurately, the prelude to sex. Not something I'd confess to my roommates anyway. As soon as David and I finished our sandwiches, as soon as Tripp or Gloria launched into a discussion of the segregationists who ran the grocery out on the highway, or whatever the evening's topic proved to be, David and I excused ourselves and escaped to his house. My stays at Harry's usually lasted less than an hour.

Then why, that evening in the company of my mother, did Harry's wife wave to me as if I were a regular? Even Harry himself nodded in our direction. I was so rattled I introduced

Mother to both of them. I acted as if I spent most of my time with leftists and campus radicals. Who was I trying to impress?

It was still early. I judged that we could eat and leave with an hour to spare before David and his cronies showed up. After we ordered drinks, I asked Mother as casually as I could how long she was staying, and where.

"I'm not staying at all. I have a meeting in Greensboro first thing in the morning. I'll drive there tonight."

"Greensboro?"

"Nonviolent resistance," she said. "I'm teaching a class."

My stomach tightened into a knot. So. Mother hadn't made the trip to offer me comfort. She'd come for business. I was merely on her way. I attempted a smile. At least she wouldn't have time to chat with my roommates and perhaps regale them with stories of her arrests. This could be for the best. By the time the waitress brought my roast beef on rye, I had managed to relax.

"Leah!" Stuart Gershner bellowed to my mother. My back was to the door and I hadn't seen him come in. "I didn't know you were in town!"

"Stuart!" Normally Mother thought it disrespectful for my friends to call her by her first name instead of Mrs. Rosinsky. That evening she made no mention of it. She smiled and beckoned Stuart to our table. "Sit down," she gushed, patting a chair. "How've you been? Have you eaten?"

Stuart hadn't eaten. He sat next to her and let her buy him dinner. He gobbled two hamburgers and poured half a bottle of ketchup on his French fries as she quizzed him about his courses. No one would have imagined she thought it "unconscionable" for the Gershners to have sent Stuart to school in North Carolina. She listened to his spiel about his psychology teacher, Dr. McCurdy, as if spellbound. She gurgled pleasantly at his tales of campus civil rights activities. She seemed flattered when he asked her about her work.

"I guess you heard about Birmingham," she said. "I should have been finished by the day of the bombing, but there was so much anger, so much hate—" She shook her head.

"Christ," Stuart commiserated.

I looked at my watch. "Mother, if you want to get on the road—"

"So Leah," Stuart interrupted. "I guess you came here because you wanted to meet David." Puzzlement registered on my mother's face. Stuart shot me a *gotcha* look.

"David?" my mother asked.

"Beryl's boyfriend. He just walked in." He pushed his plate away, pointed to the door.

"The one with the crutches," he said.

I turned. David, Tripp, and Gloria stood in the entryway, along with Laura, the beautiful black-haired girl who'd been around ever since the day when David first invited me to his house.

"David's not my boyfriend," I whispered. "Just a guy I've been out with a couple of times." They were scanning the place for a table but hadn't seen us yet.

Stuart lit a cigarette and blew smoke in my direction. "I guess Beryl told you," he said to Mother. "David had polio when he was a kid."

"I see." For a long moment Mother froze, her Coke raised halfway to her mouth.

David, Tripp, Gloria, and Laura all spotted us at the same time.

"Beryl?" David asked. I brought them over to the table.

"This is my mother," I said.

"Oh, the civil rights organizer!" Gloria exclaimed.

"It's an honor to meet you," Laura told her.

David leaned on a crutch and stuck out his right arm. "David Lazar."

Mother shook his hand. "I've heard so many nice things about you."

She shot me a wicked glance.

"I'm Gloria, and this is Tripp," Gloria said. "It must be exciting, your work. I mean, especially now, with President Kennedy and Martin Luther King—"

"It is exciting," Mother said, but she didn't take her eyes off David. She'd always championed the rights of the poor and the dark-skinned, never the rights of people with physical disabilities, but I knew she'd approve. Any handicap was better than none. I wanted her to know as little as possible about my new life—the life she'd come to spy on because it happened to be on her way to Greensboro. I didn't want her approval.

"We were just going," I said. "Mother has to drive to Greensboro."

She looked at me skeptically, but she stood.

The moment we got outside, Mother said, "I hope you won't take up smoking just because your friends smoke. Or because you're in a tobacco state. It's a nasty habit."

"I don't smoke, if that's what you're asking," I said. "You could have said something if Stuart's cigarettes bothered you. Why were you so nice to him if his habits are so nasty?"

She stopped walking. "You know what I'd like? Some ice cream. Where can we get some ice cream?"

I was bewildered. Mother rarely ate sweets, not even Miriam's sponge cake. I took her across the street to the Carolina Coffee Shop. She ordered vanilla and asked for two spoons.

"One of Dad's clerks quit—the one who hears." She'd grown suddenly warm and chatty. "He'd like to hire another hearing person so he could get away from the store sometimes. But he feels guilty. After all, who really needs the jobs? The deaf do."

The ice cream arrived in a tall parfait glass. She pointed to my spoon, but I left it on the table and shook my head. She picked up her own spoon and ate slowly. Her voice grew languid, dreamy, its tones apparently softened by the rapture of sweetened cream. "Do you know if someone asked your father to speak on this campus about architecture, he wouldn't be allowed?" she asked.

"He wouldn't?"

She took another spoonful of ice cream and held it in her mouth. "Imagine," she said when she'd swallowed. "He used to be a famous architect. Even now, it's possible someone would ask him to speak at a college." Her eyes were half closed as if she were dreaming of it.

"Sure. Of course," I said doubtfully. He'd stopped giving lectures years ago. I was touched that she was still hoping he'd be asked. "Did someone invite him to speak?"

"No. But if they had, he wouldn't be able to. Not here, anyway."

"Why not?"

"Beryl, look at me. Do you have any idea what I'm talking about?" She pointed at me with her spoon.

I didn't.

"He wouldn't be able to speak because there's a speaker ban in this state. Did you know that?"

"I think so," I lied. Actually, I knew that Tripp and Gloria were upset about an English scientist who'd been scheduled to give a lecture on campus and was forced to cancel. Beyond that, I hadn't paid attention. Tripp and Gloria were upset about ten or twelve issues at any given time.

"The speaker-ban law was passed last June," Mother said, schoolteacherish. "No one suspected of being a Communist is allowed to speak on a state campus. Not about politics. Not about anything."

"Oh." A strangled, sinking feeling tugged at the back of my throat.

"It's a terrible thing, taking away an individual's freedom to speak. A lot of people think it's unconstitutional."

"It probably is," I agreed.

"You never gave it a thought until now," Mother said sharply. "You never do. But I'm sure Dad did. I'm sure he thought about it the whole time he was debating whether to drive you here."

"He wanted to drive me. The only reason he didn't was because his clerk was sick."

"Nonsense. He wouldn't be welcome here. This is a place he not only wouldn't be allowed to forget his past, he'd be ostracized for it."

"All he would have done was help me with my things!"

"That's not the point." She jabbed the air with her spoon and dripped ice cream onto the table. "He sent you to a school like this because he thought it was for your own good. Did you ever consider that? The sacrifice." Her voice rose a notch, the way it did when she gave her speeches. I knew people must be watching us. I looked down at the table and blinked back tears.

"I didn't know," I said when I could talk without my voice wavering. "About the speaker ban, I mean."

"No? Why didn't you? If you're old enough to go away to school, you're old enough to investigate the kind of place you're going." She dropped the spoon into the half-empty parfait glass. "The point is, you could have known. You should have known."

I said nothing. In front of us, the ice cream had melted and black specks of vanilla bean clung to the glass. Mother probably hadn't tasted anything after the first bite. The languid voice and dreamy expression were all for show.

I couldn't stand it anymore. "I have a quiz to study for," I said. "I have to get back."

"Fine." She raised her hand and motioned for the check.

We walked toward her car in silence. If she expected me to confess the error of my ways and abandon Chapel Hill because the university had offended our family honor, she was mistaken. I was here and I meant to stay.

100

Then she started talking again. She told me about Miriam's swollen ankles and the way the washing machine had broken down. I found myself telling her about my chemistry class and the awful goggles we had to wear. When she asked about Susan and Ashley, I told the truth: Susan was smart, Ashley was pretty, both of them were nice. I didn't mean to reveal this much, didn't mean to reveal anything. But the night was mild and we walked slowly, and it happened before I could think. When we reached the car, she unlocked the trunk and lifted out a box.

"Some things I thought you could use," she said.

I took the box.

"I'd like to meet your roommates, and then I have to get going. You know how I hate to drive at night."

She sounded anxious to be on her way. I remembered I didn't want her to meet Ashley and Susan. "Ashley never comes in until curfew. Susan's probably at the library. If you're in such a hurry to get to Greensboro, maybe you should go now."

I thought she'd argue, but she didn't. She looked a bit defeated.

"Well," she said finally. And two minutes later, she was gone.

9

One day in the middle of October, Ashley woke up with what seemed like food poisoning. This was no shock, considering that she and Paco often ate in Lenoir Hall. Just as the first light seeped through the window, she bolted from her bed and rushed out the door for the bathroom. Susan and I wrenched ourselves awake long enough to register that she'd left without putting on her bathrobe and returned looking drained, hugging herself against the chill. She collapsed onto her bed and pulled the covers up to her chin.

"You okay?" I mumbled.

"I will be."

She was up again five minutes later, stumbling across the room to the sink, vomiting until she was empty and heaving.

I was cold and wanted to sleep, but I got up, turned on the spigot and wet a washcloth, and held it cool and damp against her forehead—Miriam's formula for nausea. Ashley braced herself, arms outstretched, hands clutching the side of the basin, and caught her breath. In the morning light, her skin looked parched and gray.

"I'll be all right," she said, and hobbled back to bed.

Susan put on her robe and dragged the trash can over to Ashley. "Just in case."

"Oh no—not in a trash can." Ashley turned to the window. With the covers bunched in her fists, she curled into a fetal position and closed her eyes.

She was still in bed at noon, when both Susan and I came back from classes to check. "I'm some better," she said. Although still deathly pale, she wore a cream-colored slip instead of her nightgown as she crouched under the covers. I noticed that she'd laid a skirt and blouse over a chair. She must have showered and was trying to dress, step by step. "At least I want to go to Spanish," she said.

"I wouldn't. You probably have one of those twenty-four-hour viruses," Susan told her. "Or else you ate something. Tomorrow you'll be okay."

"I think I'm okay now." Ashley rose and pulled on the rest of her clothes. She gathered her books. Susan and I walked her to class. When we got back around four, she was sound asleep in her bed.

The next day, she was still sick, and we went through a similar routine. She slept the morning away, then made herself get up and go to art history. She returned to throw up again and take a three-hour nap. "You ought to be in the infirmary, not in class," I said.

"It was probably something I ate, like Susan says."

"After two days? Even Lenoir Hall doesn't put out anything that malevolent."

"Sometimes food poisoning doesn't show up for twenty-four hours, and then it can stay with you for a while," Susan told us. Having worked three summers in her father's office, she spoke with authority. "You really should check it out." But Ashley did nothing.

For the rest of the week, all she could hold down were Cokes from the soda machine. She dropped weight suddenly and alarmingly, more than eight pounds. Despite the foam rollers she used every night, her hair hung straight and oily.

Sick as she was, she managed to revive each evening and go out for several hours with Paco.

On Sunday morning, Ashley made her usual early-morning trek down the hall to the bathroom. To my surprise, Susan also slung her feet over the side of the bed, stood up, and pulled on a white sweater and her favorite green pedal pushers.

"Where are you going?"

"I'll be right back."

She closed the door softly behind her and reappeared half an hour later holding a small paper bag, which she thrust at Ashley. "Eat this," she commanded.

"I couldn't," Ashley mumbled.

Susan pulled a rectangle of wax-paper-wrapped saltines from the bag and held them out. "Try," she said. "You think it's easy finding somebody who has food in her room and who's up at this hour on Sunday morning?"

Ashley looked as if a long day's nap would serve her better than breakfast, but she sat up in the bed she'd just settled into. Dark rims edged her eyes; a crust of dry vomit clung to a strand of her rolled-up hair. She opened the box and nibbled the crackers slowly. Usually Susan put on a record or her radio as soon as we were all awake, but that morning we watched in silence as Ashley ate. Susan gnawed a fingernail. I put on a pair of slacks. Ashley chewed. Two crackers. Three. Gradually, a trace of color seeped into her face.

"I bet it stays down," Susan said. "Crackers do."

Ashley leaned back and relaxed her shoulders against the window sill. Susan pulled a chair from Ashley's desk and sat down directly in front of her. "This is no stomach virus," she said. "This is no food poisoning."

Ashley closed her eyes. Susan grasped Ashley's chin between her thumb and index finger the way Miriam sometimes did mine. "Look at me, Ashley."

Ashley opened her eyes. Susan locked her jaw and stared her down. I was confused.

"He came to the beach last summer," Ashley said finally. "He and a couple of friends. No one knew. They drove down from New York." Wrightsville Beach, I'd learned, was a fifteen-minute drive from Ashley's house in Wilmington. "They were only there a couple of days."

"When?" Susan demanded.

"Middle of August."

"Why didn't you tell me?"

"I didn't want Mama and Daddy to find out he was there. Not that you would tell, but—I mean—nobody has ever questioned—I always go to the beach." She paused and wiped away a tear that had formed in the corner of her eye. "I'm sorry."

Susan handed her a Kleenex. "When was the last time you had your period?"

"Beginning of August," Ashley whispered, and then she started to cry.

✺

Maybe it shouldn't have, but the possibility of Ashley's pregnancy shocked me. Given the diaphanous quality of her romance with Paco, it was the last thing I expected. To me, they were still Romeo and Juliet, star-crossed, but ethereal. If the lovers couldn't live happily in this world, it was only natural that they'd hold out for the next. I'd never minded that Juliet died. I would have been horrified if she'd gotten pregnant.

As I struggled to revise my notion of a relationship between a tow-headed Southern belle and a black-haired

Latino, Susan sat on the chair by Ashley's desk and began to question her. Until then, Ashley had seemed older and more remote than the rest of us, but illness and fear had broken her down. She sat before Susan silent and questioning, like a repentant child.

"Have you been to the doctor?" Susan demanded in the take-charge manner she must have learned in her father's office.

Ashley shook her head no.

"Does Paco know?"

"Not yet." Ashley stared at the floor, at the mounded pillows at the foot of her bed, at anything but Susan. "I wasn't sure. I mean, that there was anything to tell him."

"Oh, Ashley," I blurted. "How awful!" She'd been lying there night after night, fearing the worst, while Susan and I slept. She'd been in the grip of a desperate torment while we—I felt as if a hand had closed my throat, then suddenly let go. "Oh, Ashley, what are you going to do?"

"She can't decide what to do until she finds out what she's dealing with." Susan's tone was sharp. "The first thing she has to do is go to the infirmary."

I nodded, feeling foolish and stupid and foreign.

Ashley rubbed her eyes as if she wasn't sure she was awake. "The infirmary? On Sunday?"

"Sure," Susan said. "Why not?"

❄

It was after lunch before Susan convinced Ashley the two of them should walk over for the pregnancy test before consulting Paco. "Getting out will do you good," she insisted. "It's such a nice day."

It wasn't a nice day. It was chilly and overcast. I summoned up enough Southern manners to refuse when Ashley asked me if I wanted to come along, aware from the

McCarthy days that some issues had to be settled by family only. But as soon as they closed the door behind them, I felt left out and resentful. I picked up a book and put it down. I changed my sheets. I sorted through my laundry. It was proper to stay away from the infirmary while Ashley's blood was being tested. It would also be polite to be out of the room when she came back. I'd better think of somewhere to go.

I put on a jacket and went for an aimless walk through the arboretum, past the planetarium, past the shuttered stores on Franklin Street. It didn't occur to me until I was nearly there that I'd been carefully making my way to David's house.

Two mahogany-skinned girls whizzed past me on roller skates as I reached David's corner. I hadn't realized before that David lived on the very edge of colored-town. One block north, there wasn't a single white residence; on David's street, not a single colored one. But though David sometimes waved to his colored neighbors as they passed and headed toward the next block, I'd never heard him speak a name. Maybe he didn't know any. I meant to bring this up the next time he criticized me for not being friends with Emily Moses.

Then Ivan bounded up from the front stoop to greet me, wagging not just his tail but the whole hind half of his body, and David saw me and opened the door.

For a while, I felt like a traitor. David invited me to his bedroom, as always, and when I refused we spent an hour making out on his couch, as always, while John F. Kennedy smiled down on us from the wall and folk music drifted from the record player. Even as I writhed beneath David's seductive touch, I noticed that his version of "Blowin' in the Wind" was by Bob Dylan while Susan's was by Peter, Paul, and Mary. Since nobody in the dorm listened to Bob Dylan, I wondered if this signaled some unbreachable social chasm between him and my roommates. Of course it did! That was why I never mentioned him. They thought I came in late most nights because I had study groups for all my hard science classes.

They'd be horrified to think I was testing the two-couple rule with someone who hung out with radicals and walked on crutches. Right now I didn't even want to be with him. I wanted to be at the infirmary, privy to Ashley's secrets.

Then David's kissing escalated into rubbing and tangling with clothing. I stopped thinking and gave myself over to pure sensation.

I didn't go back to the dorm until late afternoon. Susan was at her desk, studying. Her radio played softly. No records. Susan and Ashley had both switched on their desk lamps, which cast a cozy glow against the murky sky outside the window. Ashley sat on the floor, polishing her toenails. I'd never seen her do this before. The whole picture seemed falsely idyllic.

"Well?" I asked.

"I had my blood drawn," Ashley said. "They say the blood test is the most accurate."

"And?"

"And she finds out in a couple of days." Susan told me.

"A couple of *days?*"

"Days. Yes."

Ashley brushed pink polish onto a toenail and also onto the flesh all around it. She dabbed at the mess with a cotton ball, which clung to her sticky skin. As she groped around the floor for the polish remover, I saw that her eyes were glossy with tears.

❋

Until Mother's visit, I hadn't realized that once relatives began dropping in on their college-student children, there would be a steady stream of parents in Chapel Hill until the end of the semester. The next to appear was Ashley's father, who arrived the day before Ashley was to get her test results.

"He could have picked a better time," I said.

"Parents give you a month to get settled. Then they descend," Susan replied. "They don't give you a choice."

Like my mother, Mr. Vance was going through town on business. Unlike my mother, he called first to invite his daughter to dinner.

"He won't stay long," Susan reassured us.

Ashley sat ramrod straight on the bed, hands clenched into fists, almost catatonic.

"We have to clean the room," Susan told her. "He'll want to see what it looks like."

"I thought you can't have a man on the hall," I said.

"You can show your father your room," Susan snapped. Her tone said she was trying to distract Ashley and I shouldn't interfere.

"Daddy saw the room when they brought me up to school," Ashley mumbled.

"I mean he'll want to see how it's decorated." Susan waved at the walls and bedspreads and Ashley's decorative pillows.

Ashley blinked herself awake. I watched her hands as she slowly unclenched her fists. Straightening the room was her forte. She loved to refold sweaters, untangle the jewelry on her dresser, arrange her pillows. She stood up and swung into action. We picked up clothes, stacked our books into neat piles, dusted the desks. For the first time in weeks, Susan retrieved her pink quilt from where it sat rumpled on the floor and smoothed it across her bed.

"Take Uncle Toby to Lenoir," Susan suggested while we worked. "Tell him you want to show him where you eat every night. There'll be too much commotion to talk about anything serious."

"I think I took him there once."

"Then take him to the Pine Room." This was the casual part of Lenoir Hall downstairs, where hamburgers and barbecue were served instead of full meals. "Talk to anyone who passes by. You'll know plenty of people."

"I don't think . . ."

"Beryl and I will happen to come by. We'll introduce him to Beryl. Maybe he'll invite us to sit with you."

Ashley lowered a shirt she'd been in the process of hanging up and stood bland and listless. "There's no way I can eat a whole dinner in front of him. I'll be running for the john halfway through."

"Of course you won't," I said.

"Ashley," Susan said urgently. "You don't have any choice."

❀

To her credit, Ashley pulled herself together and followed Susan's plan. It must have worked better than we'd expected, because when we saw him sitting with Ashley across the crowded Pine Room, her father was laughing, and Ashley was laughing, too. They were clearly having—fun. Puzzled, we set our trays on a table out of their line of sight and waited for their expressions to grow more solemn, ten full minutes. Then we went over for introductions.

Ashley's father was tall and as fair as she was, with luminous blue eyes and hair that must have grayed early, making him look distinguished. I'd been told he owned a car dealership, but he wasn't paunchy or overbearing; he looked more like a golf pro. He stood up and hugged Susan, then held out his hand to me. "Tobias Vance," he said. "You must be Beryl. Sit down."

He was charming—oh, very. Sometimes the people who ought to be the most malignant, whose appearance or evil vibrations ought to sound an alert, are perfectly presentable at first, even pleasant. Someone once told me McCarthy had been that way. Susan's father focused his attention on me as if he'd been waiting years to meet me. He said Ashley was glad to be rooming with me, and he hoped I was enjoying the South—although, in its way, Washington was the South, too.

"My parents don't think so."

"Oh, yes. It's below the Mason-Dixon line, it's more a Southern city than people think." I didn't have the presence of mind to disagree.

Watching him talk was like watching Ashley, the same fluid motion of the hands, the small graceful turns of the head, all of it identical except that Tobias Vance's mood seemed more open than his daughter's had ever been, even before the crisis.

Mr. Vance finished eating and Ashley finished pushing her food around on the plate. She looked surprisingly rosy.

"Come see our dorm room, Daddy," she suggested.

"Yes, come on over, Uncle Toby," Susan urged.

Earlier, we'd decided that if we showed him the room after dinner instead of before, he'd have to cut short his visit. There wasn't much tolerance for a man on the hall, even a father, for more than a few minutes.

The four of us walked together to the dorm, where Mr. Vance complimented our decorating efforts. "That high ceiling's a blessing, isn't it? You don't feel crowded even with the three beds."

He plucked a toothpick from his pocket and brandished it in front of us before setting it between his teeth. "I know toothpicks are rude, but you know what they say—if you know the rule, then you can break it." He gave an exaggerated wink, then continued walking around the room to check out the floor space.

Even with the door open to the hallway as required and girls gawking in, he seemed perfectly comfortable. He teased Susan that she hadn't grown since tenth grade. "But it becomes you—being a petite young lady." No one would have suspected the friction between the families. He flicked the toothpick from one side of his mouth to the other with his tongue and seemed entirely at home.

He was almost ready to go, actually edging toward the door when he cocked his head as if something had occurred to him only that moment. "You still seeing that boy from South America?"

"Well, sure," Susan said. "We see him all the time."

He wasn't distracted. "I mean Ashley."

Ashley put her hand on the edge of her desk to keep from falling. "Yes," she said. "I am."

Family matters, I thought, and began to collect some books.

"I hate to run off," I said, "but I have to get to the library. I'm meeting someone. It was nice to meet you, Mr.—"

He took the toothpick from his mouth and pointed with it to my chair. "Please stay." Never had such an affable voice dealt such a weighty order. I clutched the books to my chest, helpless, and sank into the chair.

At the center of the room he perched on my bed, leaning forward a little, arms on his knees, rolling the toothpick between his fingers. He had a view of all three of us, but it was me he addressed. "Her mother and I—we don't think Paco's a bad boy. I don't want you to think that." He glanced at Ashley. "It's just that he's so different from her," he said to me. "You in particular should understand."

Ashley continued to clutch the desk, and with her free hand, fingered a tiny pearl earring. Her discomfort gave me courage.

"You mean I should understand because I'm Jewish? Or because I'm from D.C.?"

"What concerns us," he said, "isn't so much his being South American. It's that you young women are at the age when you're beginning to get serious about the young men you meet." He looked in turn at each of us. "Of course that's normal. That's what God intended you to do. Her mother and

I, and I'm sure your parents, too, want you to associate with boys with backgrounds similar to yours. Not because we're cruel, but because we know from experience that the more different you are from the young men you choose, the more difficult it's going to be for you later."

He waited, as if he expected each of us to nod and agree, which none of us did. "You, Beryl, I'm sure you date boys of your own religion, don't you?"

His voice was friendly, confiding, as if the two of us were compatriots in a matter too complex for the others to fathom. I said nothing.

"Our family is a church-going family, too," he said. "Church is a very important part of our lives."

Between his thumb and forefinger, he broke the toothpick in two.

"Ashley's mother has sung in the choir for years. Back in high school, Ashley was in the youth choir." He turned to her. "You enjoyed that, didn't you, princess?"

Ashley managed a frozen nod.

"Every year the youth group had a spring retreat. I believe most all of your friends went on that, didn't they?"

"Yes, sir," Ashley said.

"Church was never just a duty for us, is my point. It's been a pleasurable part of our lives, wouldn't you say?"

"Yes, sir."

He sat straighter on the bed. "So you can imagine how difficult it would be for Ashley to give that up, if it came to it." He drew his eyebrows together. "Have you ever gone out with a boy from another country?" he asked me.

"No," I said, and then added, "sir," which I'd never done before in my life.

"See?" He chuckled dryly and stood up. He flicked the pieces of the toothpick into the wastebasket. He put his arm around Ashley's shoulder and squeezed, as if something between them had been settled.

"See? Even Jewish girls from the big city don't date foreign boys. Their families wouldn't allow it, either."

Actually, I was sure my family *would* allow it, probably encourage it.

Ashley stiffened under her father's touch, but he was jovial now, triumphant. "Why, I hear that down there in South America the women have to walk three steps in back of the men," he said. Another chuckle. Ashley didn't move.

"I thought that was in the Orient or somewhere," I muttered.

"It *must* be the Orient," Ashley said. "Not South America. Not if your family are diplomats." Her father took his hand off her shoulder.

I summoned the energy to stand. I was still clutching my books to my chest. "I really have to go."

This time no one protested. I stayed in the library until curfew. The next morning, Ashley's pregnancy test came back positive, as we'd known all along it would.

☀

I thought she'd cut classes that day, but she went to every one. When Susan and I walked into the dorm in late afternoon, she was standing at the mirror, removing rollers from her hair as she always did at that hour. "Now what?" I asked.

"I'll talk to Paco. There's no point in not telling him now." She looked at Susan. "Is there?" When she pulled a brush through her hair, the right side flipped up as usual, but the left hung strangely limp.

"No point," Susan said.

Ashley wet her brush at the sink, dampened her hair, and rolled the whole left side again. She pulled on the bouffant cap of her dryer and turned it on. It hummed agreeably. Suddenly she switched off the motor. "I don't want to lie to you." She looked from Susan to me and back again. "I called him this morning."

"And?"

"We'll probably get married. Well—of course we will. We just have to work out the details." She switched the dryer back on, lay down on her stomach, hands under her chin so as not to disturb the rollers, and turned toward the window.

Even from across the room, it was impossible not to register her lack of conviction.

"You wouldn't necessarily have to get married," I said. "There are lots of things you could do." I thought of the Florence Crittenden Home for Unwed Mothers in Washington. I thought of my mother's abortion speeches.

"Like what?" Ashley looked at me dully.

"You could go away and have the baby and come back to school later."

"Oh, I couldn't. I'd be kicked out."

"No one would have to know."

"Everyone would know," Ashley said.

"The Women's Council would expel her on morals charges," Susan explained. "She has to get married if she even wants to finish the semester."

"The semester? What about the year? You're a senior!"

"After we get married, I'll get some kind of a job. Paco has to finish school. The baby's due in May."

There seemed to be no question of her finishing school. The complete flatness in her tone left me tongue-tied. Even last summer when I believed I'd killed Bubby Tsippi, it had never occurred to me that, even in a desperate situation, there would be only one thing a person could do.

"Did you ever think—" I turned to Ashley. "Maybe you don't want to have this baby at all? Maybe you want to get rid of it?"

"That's illegal," Ashley said.

"Your father's a doctor," I told Susan. "Doesn't he know someone who could help her?"

"He wouldn't," Susan said.

Ashley reached under her dryer to feel if the curls were dry. Even before she unrolled them, I sensed that the left side would be as lank and limp as before.

"There are other people who could help you," I said. "Not necessarily people in North Carolina." I would give her my mother's abortion speech. I would confide that my mother still knew people in the business. I would offer up everything.

But both Susan and Ashley looked at me like I was mad.

10

I wasn't quite seven when Mother had her abortion. It came at the end of the time we always referred to quietly as the Hearings, just as one day Ashley would probably speak in hushed tones about her Senior Year.

No one mentioned babies or pregnancy until after it was over. Natalie and I were completely in the dark. All we knew was that we had to go to Miriam's every day after school instead of walking home, and wait in her house above the tailor shop until our parents returned from meetings they attended to prepare for the Hearings.

Natalie was livid. She wanted to go home and play with Stephanie Gittleson as she'd always done. She wanted to be normal! Secretly, she was afraid Stephanie would find another best friend, which in the end was precisely what happened.

"I appreciate the bonds between ten-year-old girls," Mother said early on, "but I just can't have you in the house by yourselves right now, or with some sitter who isn't family."

"What about Aunt Selma?" Natalie demanded.

"Selma has her hands full with the baby." Selma was Dad's younger sister. Our cousin Eddie had arrived at Halloween, red and screaming. At family gatherings, Natalie was allowed to hold him, but I wasn't.

So we went to Miriam's. Every day while Miriam and Papa worked downstairs, Natalie lay on the living-room floor, on a maroon-colored rug with a pattern of ferns, sulking. It was winter, but on sunny days I opened the French doors to the front porch overlooking Georgia Avenue and beckoned Natalie to come out.

"You're freezing me here!" she'd scream, leaping up, slamming the doors shut, trapping us inside. "If you want something to do, go get me a drink!"

At home I would have hit her and made her chase me through the house until Mother yelled to stop. Above the tailor shop, this was forbidden because the customers below might hear. Natalie fixed me with a look of disgust. Her hatred for me shivered through the air. She flopped down on the rug and directed her vile and angry gaze at the ceiling. It was then that I conceived the idea of a poisoned potion.

I retreated to the kitchen, where every morning Miriam put meat, potatoes, onions, celery and carrots in a heavy iron pot to cook while she worked. The smell was heavy and pungent; the idea of the poisoned potion was sweet.

I took a clean glass from the cabinet and filled it with orange juice. I added a few teaspoons of salt and a handful of Babo cleanser from under the sink. The mixture frothed prettily as I stirred it. For an added flourish, I took a few cookies from Miriam's Aunt Jemima cookie jar and set them on a plate.

When I returned to the living room, Natalie was watching a test pattern on TV. She looked away disdainfully as I set the glass and cookies beside her. After a moment, she slid her hand toward the plate and took a cookie. She bit into it. She chewed and swallowed. Then she took a swig of the juice.

Long seconds ticked by. Her nostrils flared. The muscles in her face twitched. All this seemed to be happening in slow motion.

"You're dead, Beryl," she gasped.

I bolted through the dining room, down the kitchen stairs into the back of the store. Natalie was older, but I'd always been faster. In the workroom, my grandparents sat at their sewing machines, bathed in soft artificial light. Papa's bald spot was covered by gauzy specks of lint, and his chair was pushed back from the machine. He was pinning a piece of cloth with straight pins that he spit out of his mouth. He looked at me curiously as I slowed down. Running in the tailor shop was forbidden.

"Papa, don't you ever swallow those pins?" I asked.

"No. I been doing this fifty years." He spit another pin and held it in his hand. "I don't advise you should try it yourself."

Miriam looked up from her machine. She didn't meet my eye but deliberately stared at the skirt she'd just finished sewing. "Hungry?" she asked. She couldn't see me shake my head no.

Except for Rayfield the presser, no one looked me in the eye that winter. Everyone made a point of staring just beyond me. Rayfield stood in front of the pressing machine, about to step on the foot lever and release a hiss of steam onto a pair of trousers. Getting close to the pressing machine was also forbidden for me and Natalie because the steam inside was under pressure and could cook us. I would have been terrified if Rayfield hadn't always winked and made faces to reassure me. He did this now.

The pressing machine hissed and grew silent again. Since no sound came from upstairs in the kitchen, I knew Natalie would probably wait to ambush me later. Or else by the time

Miriam served dinner, she'd forget. We ate at Miriam's every night because Mother was too pale and listless after the meetings to cook. We thought this was because of nerves. By the time we went home, Natalie would have more important things on her mind than poisoned potions. I was already thinking of something more important, myself. I was remembering the mystery of the Fifth.

The night before, our parents and their friends had had one of their meetings in our dining room. Usually these were cheerful, raucous affairs, but this particular get-together was odd because no one laughed or even argued. Natalie and I were supposed to stay out of the way, but I couldn't help hearing Sam Gershner say in his deepest, lowest voice: "What are you going to do, Leonard?"

"Of course I'll take the Fifth," Dad said. "As a matter of principle. What'd you think I was going to do?"

I was confused. The fifth what? Or just *the* Fifth? And why did my father sound so upset?

The door of the tailor shop jangled. Papa pulled his vest down and disappeared into the front, fingering the tape measure draped around his neck. Rayfield hung up the trousers he'd just pressed. Miriam stood.

"Maybe you'll help Mr. Rosinsky close up," Miriam said to Rayfield. "I have to go give everyone eat."

"Yes, ma'am."

Miriam's thick figure retreated up the stairs. In the front of the store Papa was talking to someone in Yiddish. This meant it might be a long conversation.

"Rayfield, can I ask you something?"

"Shoot, baby," Rayfield said. I felt I could count on Rayfield to tell the truth. In this respect, he was unlike other adults. Even after his wife, Jasmine, became visibly pregnant, Rayfield was forthright. He hummed a little as he pressed a shirt: collar first, then sleeves and back. When he was finished, he arranged the folds with swift, long fingers the color of coffee. But his palms were pink. I waited for him to turn his hands so I could see the pink. It was like waiting for someone to tell a secret.

"What's the Fifth?" I asked.

Rayfield turned from the pressing machine and looked down at me through friendly black eyes. He laughed. "A fifth is a bottle of whiskey, sugar—nothing you need to know about right now."

"You sure?"

"'Course I'm sure." He took the shirt off the machine and hung it on a hanger. "Don't be asking your grandma or grandpa about no fifth. Hear?"

He winked again, which cheered me. But only momentarily. My understanding of whiskey was this: pale golden liquid Papa referred to as *schnapps,* which he and my father (but not the women) drank out of shot glasses on Rosh Hashonah. They drank to herald the new season, I had been told, to celebrate happy times. I didn't think my father would take whiskey to the Hearings.

A few days after that an article about our father appeared in the *Washington Star.* Arriving at Miriam's, Natalie leafed frantically through the paper until she found it. The headline said: "Prominent Washington Architect Called Before McCarthy Panel." Dad's picture smiled out from beneath the words.

"Can't read it, can you?" Natalie taunted.

"Yes, I can! I'm in the top reading group. Give it here!"

I knew *architect;* that was what our father did. I knew *Washington,* of course, and *McCarthy* ran the Hearings.

"What's p-r-o-m-i-n-e-n-t?" I asked.

"Prominent. Important. Well-known. God, you're dumb."

This was untrue. I wasn't dumb. I knew from Dad that a

man named McCarthy could summon anyone to the Hearings, and they had to come. It wasn't fair, Dad said, but in the end it wouldn't matter. "Let me tell you something about witch-hunts, sweetie. Most people know that when you go on a witch-hunt, you're bound to come up empty-handed. Most people don't hold the victims liable." A shiver skittered down my back at the mention of witches, but he smiled and made it go away. On the day of the article, I said to Natalie, "I don't see why people can't refuse to go. Why can't they just stay home?"

"Because they can put them in jail for not showing up!" she shouted, hands on her hips, hating me. "They have to go, but they don't have to answer."

"Then they shouldn't," I asserted.

"You jerk! If they don't answer, McCarthy thinks they're Communists. He thinks they want to share everything. He thinks Daddy's one. And you're not allowed to be a Communist—or didn't you know that?—baby."

Natalie's voice pierced my skin with its small, sharp points. I blinked back the stinging in my eyes and went down to the store.

Papa wasn't at his sewing machine but in the front, sorting dry cleaning from laundry on the wide counter. Strong light came into the window and reflected off the three-way mirror where Papa measured customers for suits.

"Here, you'll help me do this," he said. It was unheard-of for him to let me help. "You'll put the laundry in one pile, the dry cleaning in the other." His bald spot shone in the light, and the brightness picked out tiny white whiskers on his face. Less than a year later, he'd be dead from a heart attack, but no-one knew that yet. In the light from the storefront window, he looked wrinkled and wise.

"Natalie says they think Daddy's a columnist," I told him.

Papa froze for a minute, a blue suit jacket in his hand. "A columnist," he said finally. He looked down at the jacket.

"Leonard Rosinsky is an architect," he said. "A columnist is somebody who writes for a newspaper."

This was a lie. Dad *was* a columnist. A newspaper story he'd written once was a source of family pride. It was about a house he had designed, where two or three families could live at once, sharing kitchen chores and babysitting. In that way, some of the mothers could work and some stay at home; everything would be easier. Mother had hung the article on the bulletin board in our kitchen.

Nobody would tell me the truth! Tears stung my eyes, and I couldn't see to separate the laundry from the dry cleaning. I knew Papa's lying had something to do with the Hearings, but I didn't know what. I was about to begin sobbing in earnest when Rayfield came out of the workroom carrying a bunch of hangers. He winked and set the hangers on the counter. The wink was a secret between us which gave me courage. I tried to wink back. As usual, both eyes closed instead of just one. But when I opened them, the tears had disappeared.

The day my father went to the Hearings, Rayfield's wife, Jasmine, called to say she was about to have her baby. Rayfield left the store half running and half dancing. I saw him go because Natalie would not let me stay upstairs with her in the living room.

"Get out of here, Beryl," she'd snarled when we got in from school. Our parents had said they might be late getting home, and Natalie was furious. There was no dealing with her. I spent the whole afternoon down in the store.

After Rayfield left, Papa's workroom felt unnaturally quiet. I didn't feel like playing in the scrap box or rummaging through the tin of spare buttons. I picked up Papa's statue from the counter—a white stone carving of a man's head down to the shoulders. On the bottom was inscribed: Eugene Debs (1855–1926).

"He was a great leader who helped the working people," Papa said as he ironed a cuff with the hand iron. "He ran for president five times."

"Did he ever win?" I asked.

"No."

"How could he be such a great leader and never win?"

"It happens more than you think," Miriam said. She was basting the hem of a skirt. She bit off the thread with her teeth.

I rubbed the statue against my face, the cool, white stone. I missed Rayfield. I remembered Jasmine coming into the store one day in a red dress with her hair hanging straight to her shoulders like a stiff black sheet. Now that she'd be busy with a baby's bottles, she'd probably tuck her hair under a scarf like Bubby Tsippi's or braid it like Miriam's. She wouldn't let it hang free. She and Rayfield would hold the baby the way my Uncle Nate and Aunt Selma held my cousin Eddie, stiffly and awkwardly in their arms.

Papa took the jacket off the ironing board. "Some people, when they work for somebody else, they have to work even if it's bad conditions." He was talking about Eugene Debs, but I didn't understand at first. "Somebody like Rayfield needs the money to buy what to eat. Let's say his wife is having a baby, he wants to go home. But the owner says no, he needs some suits pressed. What can Rayfield do? He can go home and lose his job. Or he can stay."

"You wouldn't make him stay."

"No, but some people would. So let's say he works in a big tailor shop, ten pressers work there. All the pressers can get together and say, either you let Rayfield go home, or none of us will work here anymore. That's called organizing. That's what Eugene Debs taught the workers to do."

"Oh." I put the statue back on the counter. I didn't care about organizing. I cared that, after today, Rayfield would have a baby. After today the Hearings would be over and Dad

126

would have to stop being a columnist. I liked his story about the house where several families could live. After today, nothing would be the same.

※

I was right. After the Hearings, Mother was sick in the mornings and Dad had to fix breakfast and get us off to school. He lost his job and began looking for another. No one would hire him. Mother's skin grew very white.

One afternoon the house was empty when we came in from school. No Aunt Selma, no sitter, no-one. We found the key in its hiding place. Our parents didn't come home until dinnertime. Mother was leaning on Dad's arm. Her face was the color of ash. Dad put her to bed.

The next day she claimed she was better, but she didn't cook any meals. She made Natalie and me sit quietly in the living room while she explained what an abortion was and how she'd had one. It was illegal, but it shouldn't be. Many women had abortions. There were times when they had to. She was going to be honest with us.

She recovered slowly. She'd start each day rushing around and then suddenly have to rest. In time she grew well enough to come with us to Miriam's for Sunday brunch. "Later maybe we'll ride over to see Rayfield's new baby," she said brightly. Her voice was airy and false.

We ate bagels and cream cheese and lox in Miriam's dining room. The adults spoke in Yiddish so we wouldn't understand. Aunt Selma jiggled Eddie up and down on her lap.

"Oh, let me have the baby," Natalie cooed.

"Good, you can feed him," Aunt Selma said.

"I'd love to," Natalie said in her superior way.

Aunt Selma warmed Eddie's bottle and Natalie gave it to him while my parents drank tea and Papa sipped milk and *vasser* out of a glass. The way he held a sugar cube between his teeth and let the hot liquid pass over it, he could talk just as easily as with a mouthful of pins.

The adults grew careless, speaking partly in Yiddish and partly in English. I caught the word *blacklist* and guessed it didn't refer to a list made with a black pen. I now knew Communists wanted a different kind of government and columnists wrote for newspapers. But I didn't know *blacklist* and wasn't going to ask.

"Zuh den?" Uncle Nate said. "It happened in California, it could happen in Washington."

My father said he didn't think so; he wasn't worried about a blacklist. Steam fogged the kitchen windows. Aunt Selma smiled at me and said, "It's Sunday, isn't it? Isn't something nice on television on Sunday? Run in the living room and see."

Outside, it was cold after the hot house, even in the sun. Mother, Miriam, Natalie and I got into Papa's car. Dad left for a meeting. Aunt Selma and Uncle Nate took Eddie home. Mother gave me a wrapped package to give to Jasmine. It was a sweater for the baby.

I wasn't looking forward to this. Jasmine would be fat like Aunt Selma. She and Rayfield would hover around the baby like everyone did around Eddie, protective and closed.

When Rayfield opened the door to their apartment, Jasmine stood behind him holding a tiny brown infant with fine, fuzzy bristles of hair. Jasmine's middle was still round, but her arms and legs were thin. She said the baby's name was Luther.

"He doesn't look big enough for that name," I said.

Everyone laughed. Rayfield and Jasmine didn't turn away from me, they looked directly at my eyes. Rayfield said, "Well, I guess he ain't big enough, not yet." I gave Jasmine the wrapped package. She said, "Just for that, you get to be the first one to hold him." She put the baby into my arms. He was small and light. He didn't cry until after my mother gave him to Natalie.

"That's the dinner bell," Jasmine said when the baby kept crying. Her hair hung down like always, straight and black against her neck and shoulders. "Rayfield, stay in here with Mr. Rosinsky while I feed him," she said. "You ladies can come with me."

Mother's face grew pale. She looked like she might throw up. "I'll just wait here," she said. She clutched Natalie's arm to hold her back. Miriam didn't get up either, but I was out of their reach. I followed Jasmine into the kitchen.

The two of us sat down at a wooden table. I waited for Jasmine to put on a bottle to warm. That was what all mothers did as far as I knew—warmed a bottle and tested the milk on their wrists, then fed it to the baby.

But Jasmine did the most astonishing thing. She lifted up her blouse and revealed a naked breast the same brown as the kitchen table. The breast was not nearly as private-looking as Mother's white ones. She arranged the baby so he was close to it. Maybe I was rude to stare, but I didn't turn away.

The baby stopped crying and rooted around until his mouth took hold of Jasmine's nipple. He made his hands into tiny fists and sucked as if it were hard work. A line of milk appeared on his mouth, but he didn't choke or turn purple the way Eddie did when he got too much milk from his bottle.

"You like your teacher this year?" Jasmine asked.

"She's okay."

We talked as if everything were perfectly normal. Soon the baby's eyes closed and his little fists opened. Rayfield came in to pour Cokes for everyone. Standing behind Jasmine's chair, he put his hands on her shoulders and asked me, "Well, whatcha think?" He sounded as if he were talking just about the baby, but I knew he meant the secret, too.

Colored babies could get milk directly from their mothers. There were no bottles or pots or pans. Jasmine shared her milk. It was like the tasks families could share in the house my father had designed, where everything would be easier.

"Nice," I said, as if we were talking only about the baby. I would never tell Natalie. Rayfield winked. Everything was gray and cramped around me, but the secret of the milk had light in it, like the hidden pink of Rayfield's palms.

❄

We left as soon as I came out of the kitchen. In the car on the way home, Mother began to cry. This was something she never did, something she would never do again.

"What's the matter?" I asked, but she kept weeping.

"She's tired is all," Miriam explained.

My mother sniffed.

"What I want you to remember," she told me, "is that some things are hard to do. But even if they're hard, you do them because otherwise the situation would be worse."

I didn't know what she was talking about, but I reached over and patted her hand.

"Some things are just not possible," she said, and blew her nose into a hanky.

Some things were just not possible.

I wished I could tell that to Ashley.

11

For the next few weeks, Ashley and Paco negotiated the terms of their marriage—if indeed there was to be a marriage at all.

"Of course there will be," Ashley said. "It's just—not so simple."

Paco planned to go to graduate school in political science, then return to South America and follow in his diplomat father's footsteps.

South America! It was one thing to *be* from there, another to go back. To live among anacondas and poisonous frogs! Among people who spoke in rapid, tongue-twisting cadences. Worse, while most everyone in North Carolina (except me) was Protestant, everyone in South America was Catholic. Paco refused to marry outside the Catholic Church. Ashley would have to convert.

"Impossible!" she said. "Daddy and Mama always thought

I'd get married in our church at home. I'm an only child. I couldn't do that to them."

"And I," Paco replied. "I cannot disappoint, either."

"If I converted, it would kill Daddy," Ashley murmured, her voice reduced to a whiny thread.

"Of course it will not kill him," Paco crooned, stroking her hair. Sympathetic but unyielding, he drew her head onto his shoulder.

Was killing Daddy such a bad idea? I wondered. Tears brimmed at the edge of Ashley's eyes. I dismissed this thought as disloyal.

Ashley returned day after day with nothing resolved. She loved Paco, she said. She loved Mama and Daddy, too. Unaccountably, I thought. But still.

The only time a trace of color returned to her face was when she thought of some new argument to bolster her case. "Why, if Paco marries a U.S. citizen," she declared, "he'll be eligible to live here all his life." They could wed in the Baptist Church and simply stay in North Carolina.

But no. To be a South American diplomat, Paco had to spend the early part of his career in his native country. Living in North Carolina was not an option.

The after-hours discussions at our window grew longer and more turbulent. At curfew, Susan and I retreated to the dim study lounge in the basement for longer periods of time. We returned to find Ashley's face streaked with tears, the room frosty with the night air.

"Even if I convert, his parents may not go along. Maybe back in his country, they could have the marriage annulled."

"Did he tell you that?"

"No."

"Then don't be silly. They don't annul a marriage when a baby is involved."

Or did they? After all, Paco's parents had whisked him up to New York over the summer. They were powerful people.

132

But unknown quantities. Every day I meant to broach the subject of my mother's abortion, to give Ashley at least *that*. Every day I didn't.

Susan, too, looked frustrated. Ashley's troubles were part of a complicated adult world we hadn't dealt with before and didn't quite grasp. To compensate, we protected her from the dangers we could understand.

Each morning, when Ashley rushed to the bathroom, Susan and I took turns standing guard so no one would suspect her trouble. Throwing up in the toilet would have been a public act; everyone would have heard. We made it possible for her to vomit in the running shower instead, privately and secretly while other girls used the johns. We stood at the sink, washing our faces, reminding our hallmates about their manners: "There's someone in the shower, don't forget to yell 'flush!'" The commodes drew off all the cold water. A person caught in the shower without being warned would be scalded. Sometimes Ashley vomited so long that people forgot she was in there. I washed my face until my skin grew cracked and dry. Scrubbing, primping, I kept watch for impromptu flushers. Then I waited for the bathroom to empty so I could signal Ashley it was safe to turn off the water. I told her she could come out. I was on a mission.

She emerged wet and white-faced. She dried herself, put on her bathrobe, brushed her teeth. Some days the toothpaste made her feel better; other days the taste sent her lunging once more for the shower stall. I manned the door, scanned the hall, waylaid intruders. Sometimes Ashley was so weak afterwards that we had to walk shoulder to shoulder back to the room, her leaning on me without seeming to.

Between Paco's nocturnal visits and Ashley's grief and nausea, we averaged only a few hours of sleep each night.

For comfort, I met David at Harry's. Ashley's predicament should have made me question his intentions, but I was too reckless to care. So what if other boys wanted to buy me meals, take me to films and sports events to earn my favors; so what if David didn't? For an hour we'd listen to Tripp and Gloria talk about civil rights, then we'd make our excuses and sneak away to his house. We were always rushing off.

Despite our hurry, I became Gloria's grudging admirer. She would gurgle on unself-consciously about anything that came into her head—Alabama's blustery school desegregation, the maniacal ranting of Alabama's governor George Wallace, the liberal reputation Chapel Hill enjoyed when really it was reactionary, evil, vile! Gloria's white face would flush; she'd wave her arms and gesture without a thought to how ridiculous she looked—when I, by contrast, never forgot for a moment about the impression I was making. I didn't approve of her, but I thought it must be luscious, to feel so free.

"All we want is a public-accommodations ordinance," she said one night to a newcomer who had strayed over.

"What's a public-accommodations ordinance?"

"A law to keep businesses from discriminating because of race."

"You'd rely on good will to pass a public-accommodations law?" David asked rhetorically. "In the few places in Chapel Hill that aren't already integrated, there *is* no good will."

"The few places? The few!" Gloria cried. Her big bosom heaved. She pulled her sweater down and rearranged the loose, flowing dress beneath it, that looked more like a costume than street clothes. "Over twenty businesses discriminate against Negroes. Five restaurants. One grocery store. All the barber shops. What dirtbags!" She'd count the offenders on her big square fingers. "The barbers say they'd have to provide extra training to serve the Negroes. Extra training! What a bunch of shooblakadoo. What schnipps!"

I admired her way of sounding as if she were forever cursing, though no standard cuss word ever passed her lips, only inventions she made up on the spot.

I admired David more—the way he regarded her with his assessing, level gaze, like an indulgent but disapproving parent, though they'd grown up together in Charlotte. "My money says the elected officials won't force a public-accommodations law," he said. "Not yet. Not now."

I admired the lack of fire in his pronouncements—so different from Gloria's emotional outbursts—so different, I reflected, from my mother's. Even when Emily Moses sat at our table and the others grew frenzied with purpose because of her presence and darkness, David would look at me sidelong and sly. He knew what was going on. He sympathized with the activists, but he wasn't one of them. He wouldn't be drawn into foolhardy public displays that wouldn't do any good. I was proud of him.

I was also so wild to touch him that it was difficult to focus on the fact that our meetings at Harry's weren't true dates, that he paid for my food sometimes but usually didn't, that the objective was always to go back to his house. It didn't bother me that after he invited me into his bedroom and I refused, we always tangled for an hour on the couch while Ivan looked on from the floor, and then he took me back to the dorm, and that was all we ever did together. We were having what my mother would call "a good old roll in the hay," a phrase she used with the utmost contempt. Except that our union was never fully consummated, David's behavior fit exactly into my mother's description of what all young men wanted from girls they didn't respect.

No matter, I couldn't stop, even when Ashley and Paco were deepest into their debate. I wanted to go back to David's little sugar shack even on the nights when he was being touchy about his legs not working well, or getting ornery because someone treated him like a cripple.

Once, as we were leaving Harry's, a student I hadn't seen before tried to open the door for us—a fraternity type, dressed in chinos and a crewneck sweater (dressed, I noted, a lot like

David). He'd been sitting with a couple of friends at the front of the restaurant when he spotted us at the cash register and sprang from his seat to push open the front door for us.

"I can do it, man," David said. He pushed the boy aside and moved to open the door himself. He glared at the Good Samaritan and motioned me to go out. The do-gooder and his friends all looked away.

On the way to the car, David lumbered along faster than usual, grimly silent, face twisted into what I supposed was fury. Ivan, waiting outside the restaurant for him, bounded up but then grew subdued and loped along in front of us, not taking his accustomed side-trips to pee on trees and doorways. He turned frequently to wag his tail and sniff at David's feet.

When we got to his house, David didn't bother with his usual prelude to love—which generally consisted of Joan Baez on the record player and some tentative stroking of my shoulder. He began kissing me at once, seriously. He didn't even invite me to his bedroom so I could refuse. In a minute I was pinned on my back on the couch, a position we usually didn't reach for half an hour. Then we'd have a long tug-of-war over my underpants, which I never let him take off. That night he wasn't interested in underwear. He circled his big arms around me less in a lover's embrace than a wrestling hold. I couldn't move. I could hardly breathe.

"David, stop."

He held me tighter.

"What are you trying to do—smother me?" I gasped.

"I'm trying to show you something about having polio. What it feels like to have your chest paralyzed."

"David, what's wrong with—"

He went slack, bore down on me with all his weight. My heart thudded inside its bony prison. My chest felt small and inadequate for the air I wanted but couldn't get.

"Maybe this is what it's like to be in an iron lung," he said.

136

"Stop it, David! I can't breathe."

He let up a little, just until I could draw breath the whole width of my rib cage. "Precisely," he said.

I wriggled but couldn't change position. "You never said you were in an iron lung," I muttered.

"I wasn't."

I waited for him to shift his weight. He hovered above me, face two inches from mine, breath musky from beer.

"*I* wasn't in an iron lung," he whispered. "But a lot of other people were." His eyes grew slick and untrustworthy, dark puddles of oil. Probably he could hear my heart pounding inside the common chest we seemed to share. The sound rose into my ears. A series of loud thumps. Ka-thunk . . . thunk . . . thunk. A rush of adrenaline. Maybe I was having a heart attack.

But no—What I heard was no arrhythmic heart, it was Ivan's tail, beating against the edge of the couch. He nosed his face between us. David sat up. I smoothed my blouse and tried not to show fear. I shifted to the far end of the couch and clutched the arm. David sneered.

"That guy in Harry's who wanted to open the door for us—" he said. "Very noble, didn't you think?"

"He was trying—"

He held up his index finger to stop me. "If you walk on crutches, people like that see your life as tainted."

He inched close again, breathing hard, part school-teacher, part maniac. "They think you live in little closed rooms with stale air. That you can't do anything for yourself."

Goosebumps marched from my wrists to my shoulders. Was this the explanation for his neat kitchen, the tidily made-up bed in the bedroom we avoided? Was neatness his way of showing competence, of proving he could do what everybody else did?

"They're so glad they don't have to *be* you that they open doors for you. Lend you notes from class. God knows what all. I could give you a list—"

"I think he was just trying to be nice," I managed.

He dropped his jaw, incredulous. "You don't have the faintest idea," he said.

I swallowed hard, intending to digest my pride along with his nastiness. I would endure him. Take whatever he dished out. I'd show him I didn't care about his legs, only about his soul.

But the truth was, it wasn't his soul I wanted. His presence robbed me of sense, made me focus on the bulk of his arms, the roughness of his beard, the sly cast of his glance. *Mere sex,* my mother would have sneered, annoyed at my submission to baser instincts. When David slid across the couch to me again, I didn't push him away.

Perhaps to apologize and show he appreciated my mind even if I didn't appreciate his, David decided we should try going out on ordinary dates. We saw *Black Orpheus* at the free flicks at Duke, ate in restaurants I'd never been to before, attended a performance of *The Sandbox* by the Carolina Play-makers—serious art my parents would have approved. We even went to an activist get-together where everyone listened to Pete Seeger and passed around marijuana cigarettes David refused for both of us, which made me feel protected and relieved.

Despite all this, I continued to bound from David's car when he stopped at the dorm, ostensibly so he wouldn't have to walk me to the porch but really so I could keep him a secret. *You're ashamed of his crutches in front of your fancy new friends,* my mother would have griped. And it was true.

At the end of our second week of "dating," we went to a party at Tripp and Gloria's, in the attic they rented on Airport Road. As we approached the steep outdoor stairway, a cacophony of voices drifted out the open door. Inside, someone was playing a guitar. I reached for the six-pack of beer David was carrying. "I'll take it," I offered as we approached the steps.

"No. I got it." From above us came the rasp of laughter. "Go on," he commanded.

The stairs were old, splintery wood, each step two slats deep. I held the banister and sprinted up. When I looked down, David was struggling with the crutches, hugging the six-pack between his arm and body, inching up one painful step at a time. "Go on in!" he shouted when he saw me.

People packed the apartment. I recognized faces from Harry's. Stuart Gershner. Laura and her friend, Fran. Emily Moses with a Negro boy who went to the law school. Two other Negro boys without dates. Across the room, someone was throwing up in the kitchen sink. Stuart came over and handed me a beer.

"Commode-hugging drunk already?" I asked, nodding toward the boy who was vomiting. "I didn't think we were that late."

"He just ate peyote," Stuart said.

"I didn't know you could get it around here."

"You can get it anywhere. Just not necessarily in Fowler's Meat Market."

Then David appeared in the doorway, face flushed, triumphant. He handed me the six-pack.

"You have to throw up before peyote takes effect," Stuart continued.

"You know that from experience?"

"Be serious."

The guitar player stopped and the voices around us filled the void. Shoving me in front of him, David moved into the room and settled onto the floor. All the chairs were taken. I sat down beside him. The boy on peyote began walking around the room, examining each discarded beer can. "Wow," he muttered, before moving on to check another. "Wow." He pronounced each of the letters—B-u-d-w-e-i-s-e-r and M-i-l-l-e-r—as if they contained a revelation.

I sipped a beer and studied our dingy surroundings. The

attic was one large room with a curtain on a long rod that could be pulled across to separate sleeping and living areas. The kitchen was just a wall lined with stove, refrigerator, and the sink the boy had thrown up in. Even the bathroom wasn't closed off by a real door, just a soft bifold that kept sliding open to reveal a cheap shower stall and a toilet with a nicked seat. This place made David's look like a palace.

Across the room, Gloria scrubbed the vomit-soiled sink, then stepped back to examine her work. Her big curvy chest, wet from working, was draped with what might have been a ragtag blouse purchased at Goodwill or a series of veils tied together to look like one. I was moved by the sight. I'd never before known anyone whose clothes and housing spoke of genuine squalor.

"Need a hand?" I called across the room, and got up to help her.

"You could get me those Fritos." She dried her hands and pushed back her hair, fuzzy from the dampness, a reddish halo around her head. I felt a stab of pity for her, soft and draped in veils and cleaning up vomit, trapped in a shape more suitable for a fertility goddess than a real person who'd have to haul it around twenty-four hours a day. Apparently unaware of her plight, she ripped open the Fritos and poured them into a bowl. I opened another beer and went back to David.

The peyote boy lay on his back in the middle of the floor and looked toward a darkened window. He began to moan, whether in torment or ecstasy I couldn't tell. I put my hand on David's for comfort. He pulled away.

"What's wrong?" I asked.

He snagged a crutch and hefted himself up, pretended he hadn't heard. He headed toward the Fritos.

He ignored me the rest of the evening. I drank too much and laughed a lot. When we left, I went down the stairs first, a little unsteady from too much beer. I was careful not to look back at David behind me, not to embarrass him by noticing his infirmity. I was more obedient than Orpheus, promised that Eurydice would follow. Or conditioned like a well-trained dog.

After that, our public dates stopped and we went back to eating at Harry's and tangling in the privacy of David's house. I wasn't sure why, but I wondered if it was to punish me—for witnessing him on the steep, rickety staircase that led to Tripp and Gloria's attic, and seeing the awkward way he had to propel himself up on crutches while anyone who wanted could watch.

All this might have bothered me more if it hadn't been for Ashley's deepening predicament. Girls in the dorm were getting suspicious, and Susan and I had our hands full trying to defend her.

"What's wrong with Ashley, is she sick?" Penny Blankenship asked one day, the first time anyone had broached this subject openly. By then Penny and Susan had reached an agreement. As long as Penny didn't taunt Susan about not pledging Chi O with the rest of their friends, Penny could listen to Susan's records any time she wanted. Penny had even stopped sneering at me, although she hadn't given up her habit of calling endless attention to her pledge pin, secured to one of her expensive blouses or sweaters, by polishing it gently with her fingers.

"Who says Ashley's sick?" Susan asked.

"Lee Anne Morris says she spends a lot of time in the shower in the morning, and either you or Beryl are always with her." She cut her eyes toward me and raised her eyebrows.

Susan didn't let me speak. "Here, listen to this," she said, and plopped "Surfer Girl" onto the record player, Penny's favorite song.

The following Saturday, Ashley's mother called early, before the phone in the hall was tied up, and also before Ashley felt well enough to talk. We found her in the hallway with the receiver to her ear, looking so peaked that Susan and I immediately headed down to the machines in the basement to get her a carton of chocolate milk and a Coke, the odd combination that would usually settle her stomach.

Susan had some coins poised to drop into the soda machine and I was lifting the milk out of the ice when Anna Mae, our dorm president, clicked down the steps in her high heels, fully dressed for the football game later on. Her hair wasn't in rollers for once, but combed into short curls framing her face.

"I thought I'd find you girls here," she said. "I would have talked to Ashley first, but she's on the phone."

She paused, an evil gleam of mistrust in her eye. "What's up with Ashley, girls?"

"Did she do something?" I thought I sounded all innocence, but my hands were shaking and I had to set the milk carton down on the machine. Maybe the jig was up, our subterfuge in the bathroom wasn't working, a pregnancy was not a condition you could hide forever. I regretted once again not having the courage to tell Ashley all I knew about abortions.

"Ashley's sick," Susan said smoothly, shoving her quarter into the slot. I looked for an escape route, but the machines were in a dim alcove flanked by the steps on one side and the study lounge on the other. We were trapped.

"Sick with what?" Anna Mae asked.

"A kind of hepatitis," Susan answered without hesitation. She extracted the Coke and opened it, and paused while the top fell into the bowels of the machine with a little clink. "She's been feeling bad a couple of weeks, but she just got the diagnosis."

142

Anna Mae stood silent as her lips downturned in what I thought meant disappointment. Then a quick surge of new energy flowed through her face like the jolt of an electric current.

"Isn't hepatitis contagious?" She narrowed her eyes. "You can't stay in the dorm with a contagious disease, you know."

"Ashley isn't contagious. Not at this stage."

"I see," Anna Mae said, meaning she didn't.

"If it doesn't clear up, she might have to drop out next semester to rest. We hope it won't come to that." Susan raised Ashley's Coke to her lips and took a long swallow, a liberty she never would have taken if she weren't more nervous than she was letting on.

"Well. Poor thing." Anna Mae's voice was clipped and dutiful. She took a step toward us and hesitated. Then she patted both Susan and me on the shoulder. "I'm glad you told me this, girls. Some of the others on your hall were getting worried. It's always good to confide something like this so I'll know how to help you if I can. If there's anything else, don't hesitate to come up to my room any time."

She turned and clicked her way back up the stairs.

When we got to the room, Ashley was sitting on her bed, staring out the window. She turned and took the Coke and the milk.

"I bet Mama was on the phone half an hour," she said. "You know the main thing we talked about? Sears."

"Sears?"

"Mama's excited because they're building a new Sears in Wilmington. It's supposed to be finished next summer." Her voice was expressionless. "It seems strange anyone could get excited about a new store opening." She opened the milk carton and slowly unwrapped her straw.

"Susan told Anna Mae you had hepatitis," I said. "To explain the throwing up."

Ashley sipped her milk with such unruffled calm that she

seemed not to have heard. She lowered the carton to regard us with a serene gray gaze. "I've decided to convert," she said.

"No!" I said, incredulous.

"Oh, Ashley," Susan whispered.

Ashley set the milk carton on the floor. She took a swallow of Coke. "The hardest part," she said, "is going to be breaking the news to Mama and Daddy."

"How will you?" I asked.

"Not on the phone, Ashley," Susan instructed.

"Of course not." Ashley's tone made it clear she didn't need our advice on this matter; in some way, didn't need us at all. "We'll tell them in person. Paco's driving me down next weekend. We'll settle it with my folks, then with his."

Once more I wanted to shout, no! Abort the baby! Or send it out for adoption! Finish school! Live your life! But some instinct said not to. I thought then it was only because I couldn't have stood censure, couldn't have endured coldness from the same frail shoulder that had leaned against mine, mornings as we made our way back down the hall.

"I've already told Mama I'm coming," Ashley said. She raised the Coke to her lips, then lowered it. "I won't say Paco's coming with me until later." She spoke with the authority of someone who had charted her course to the abyss and had no intention of deviating. More chilling yet was her perfect, accepting, bovine calm.

12

Packard's Sandwich Shop was the only restaurant on the main part of Franklin Street that still refused to serve Negroes. According to Tripp, it was also the restaurant that supplied the jail, where the demonstrators had spent so much time. Packard's was the target the Harry's crowd had in mind when they spoke of a public-accommodations law.

Packard's wasn't a popular hangout, just a greasy spoon that catered to a bunch of rough-looking boys who didn't look or act like students, although most of them were. Watching them, I began to understand why Stuart called them grits. They were well-dressed but mean, the kinds of boys you expected to drive old cars with shotguns in the back seat, boys with gritty, flinty eyes.

Every day, every hour Packard's was open, a cluster of picketers marched in a circle the width of the sidewalk in front, holding signs saying, "Serve Everyone Now" and "Segregation is Wrong." During heavy traffic hours, sometimes a second group stood nearby, singing "We Shall Overcome" until they were told to disperse.

All through September and October, I walked on the other side of the street when I passed Packard's, except when I had to buy toiletries in the drugstore next door. I had visions of reporters coming to take pictures of the picketing. I imagined the peaceful demonstrations erupting into violence—police with billy clubs, marchers beaten to the sidewalk and writhing in pain. I worried all the more after I watched one of the Packard's regulars brush roughly against one of the sign-bearers and almost shove him out of the way, mouthing the words "nigger-lover" as he passed.

But the picketers never spoke, even when people shouted or snickered. They didn't respond to hecklers and they didn't exchange greetings with passing friends. The rule was not to talk at all. They did exactly what my mother trained people to do when she gave workshops in places like Greensboro.

If I had to pass by, I would nod to Tripp or Gloria or Laura in the picket line, even though the sight of them embarrassed me no end. In the glaring daylight, Gloria's white-skinned face looked chapped and windburned, revealing her to be the sort of person who ought to spend her life under mellow indoor lamps instead of the harsh sun. I felt sorry for her. She was following her principles, even knowing she'd end up with a wilderness of crow's feet around her eyes. At night in Harry's, when I refused the sign-up sheet she and Tripp passed around, trying to recruit volunteers to picket all the hours Packard's was open, I always felt as if I'd betrayed her. David never signed the sheet, either, but that didn't make me feel better.

For a month I told myself that walking by a segregated restaurant was no crime. I was brainwashed by the propaganda my parents had fed me all my life. I should get over it. Why should I cross the street to avoid a stupid greasy spoon?

Why stare at my shoes as I slunk into the drugstore next door? What kind of coward was I? I should muster the courage to buy soap or toothpaste any time I needed to. And finally I did.

It was the Friday Ashley and Paco left for Wilmington. Between runs to the bathroom, Ashley packed her overnight case, looked at herself in the mirror every thirty seconds, and changed her outfit twice. By the time she left, I was biting my fingernails exactly the way Susan did, down to the sore remains of the quick. As relieved as I was to have her gone, I was worried about her, too. I would do something constructive. Buying shampoo was the first thing that came to mind.

It was too late to escape, or pretend I hadn't noticed, or melt into the sidewalk, when I got in sight of Packard's and saw David marching among the picketers with a placard stuck in the top brace of his crutch, reading, "I'm different, too. Would you deny me a seat?"

I might as well have been hit in the stomach. For a couple of seconds I actually couldn't take in any air. Could this be David? The man who snarled like a wildcat the moment anyone happened to notice his crutches? The same David who never, even for a second, forgot he didn't look like everyone else?

I stood open-mouthed but not breathing, reading the sign over his head: "I'm different, too." Drawing attention to his very infirmity. What was going on? Just the other night when his crutch hit a crack in the sidewalk, he stumbled and nearly fell before he regained his balance, and then was sarcastic to me for an hour afterwards. I had thought he hated me for being there. For observing his lack of grace. For witnessing evidence of his disability. Yet there he was.

Seeing him was like watching a parade for the March of Dimes, seeing the scores of mothers trudging along, bored— and then noticing among them a child with a strange jut to his arms and an odd angle to his walk, his birth defect the very one they were trying to obliterate. In such a moment the parade that had been mostly an excuse to be out in the sunshine grew suddenly darker and more holy—because there was the reason for all the effort, the *cause,* the child incarnate.

So it was with David, who kept to his small circle, dragging himself to match the pace of the others. His hands gripped his crutches, and the wooden stick of his placard was wedged into his arm brace, cruelly drawing the eye. Most people on the sidewalk wouldn't be able to identify a single other picketer afterwards, but every one of them would remember David.

I stood mesmerized for who knows how long. Then Ivan recognized me from a doorway stoop where he was lying and leaped up to greet me. He wagged his tail violently; he licked my hands and brought me back to myself. As my shock receded, I filled up with a clear, icy sense of betrayal.

David was no eighteen-year-old student activist. He was twenty-three, a man who would be in law school next year. Who took me home with him night after night instead of talking desegregation in Harry's because he was more interested in sex than politics. He was so sensitive about his crutches he felt hatred for anyone who noticed them. His marching here was not just incongruous, it was impossible.

But as I stroked Ivan's mottled fur and watched David picket, what frightened me most was not even feeling betrayed. It was that, instead of looking foolish as my mother did, David looked electrifying. He looked as if he were doing exactly what he ought to do. As if he were fulfilling his very destiny.

I forgot about the shampoo. I headed back to the dorm. It was only four in the afternoon. Shouldn't David be at his part-time job in the psych department?

More puzzling, why should I feel so horrified? Why

should I think that what he was doing had anything to do with me?

But it did, just as my mother's arrest had a year ago, even when everyone else insisted otherwise.

My head began to throb, and by the time I reached Alderman I had a blinding headache. I closed the shades, sank onto my bed, and didn't budge until Susan turned on the lights hours later and asked if I wanted to go to dinner. I felt too beaten to say no. After we ate, after Susan dressed and left for her date with Colby Lee, I opened my zoology book but didn't study. I pictured Paco and Ashley being interrogated by her father in Wilmington. I imagined Ashley being sent to her room, Paco being forced out of the house. I remembered the photo of my mother's bare legs exposed above her skirt as police dragged her off from the demonstration. What could possess anyone to draw the spotlight that way? To look the fool. How could David do what he'd done this afternoon and look so noble?

I put on a stack of Susan's records, as many as the spindle would hold. The first notes of "Sugar Shack" began to play. I'd always thought of David's house as a sugar shack, but the truth was, the place was a shack, nothing more. I pushed the lever to make another record drop. The second song was new, not something I recognized. It sounded cheap and tinny, not good for the soul.

Finally someone knocked on my door.

"What?" I called.

"You have a visitor in the parlor."

It could only be David. He'd be wearing his tan suede jacket, arm flung across the back of a silk brocade sofa, crutches perched at his side. The perfect parody of a fraternity man waiting for his date.

"Tell him I'm not here," I said to the door.

Five minutes later, someone tapped at the window. Although Paco and Ashley were in Wilmington, force of habit propelled me across the room, made me raise the blinds. David pressed his nose against the glass, clowning.

I considered turning away, but David's comic expression threw me. David never clowned. I pushed the window up.

"You left before the fun started," he said.

"What fun?" He seemed unfazed that I'd just sent him word I wasn't here.

"Somebody called the cops on Ivan."

"On Ivan. Sure." I crossed my arms over my chest.

"He jumped on some lady."

"He's fanatically friendly, David. He can't help it."

David didn't offer more details. We stared at each other through the screen. The silence lengthened. I grew curious. "The cops?" I asked finally. "What happened?"

"Nothing much. He didn't do any harm, just jumped. The policeman said from now on, either I take him straight to campus or leave him home."

"Where is he now?"

"He's been locked in the house ever since."

"Poor Ivan."

David smiled impertinently. "He's dying to see you."

"Very funny, David."

"I mean it." He was friendly, charming, even manic. This wasn't like him.

"I'll see Ivan some other time," I said.

"Why'd you run away this afternoon? You should have waited for me."

For a minute I wasn't sure what to say. "I was surprised to see you."

"Horrified, I would have said."

"You never picketed before. You never seemed interested." I hugged myself against the cold.

His manic grin grew wider. "I marched in those demonstrations last summer."

"Then why didn't you ever mention it?"

"You never asked."

"You said yourself you don't think a public-accommodations law is going to pass."

"I don't. Integration is a larger issue than just one law. Next time you ought to come with me. Check out the cracks in Packard's sidewalk." He raised his eyebrows at me like Groucho Marx. "We'll go to jail together. It'll be romantic."

"Very funny, David. It's my mother who goes to jail, not me."

He leaned forward on his crutches, hunched against the cold. Inside, the radiator blasted, but the heat had all gone out the window. Why was he acting like this?

"Come on, Beryl. Don't make me stand out here. Let's continue this at Harry's."

"No." He was being much too cute. I wasn't going to be taken in.

"Then come to my place."

"David, no."

"I've known girls before who didn't want to go out with a guy on crutches. I never knew one who didn't want to be seen with a picket."

Could this be the same David I thought I knew? Poking fun at his own infirmity? Maybe he was on some kind of drugs.

"David, who did you think you were helping out there? Who do Tripp and Gloria think they're helping? And Laura and Stuart and all the rest of you? All you do is put yourself in embarrassing situations—and everybody else, too."

"Who else?"

"Everybody. People who want to walk by on the side-walk. People who want a sandwich. Emily Moses." I hoped Emily's name would be the last word; I considered slamming the window. I wondered how Ashley could endure standing here, night after night.

"Will you just come out here and talk to me?" He spoke at

precisely the moment the wind moaned around the corner of the building, calling the elements to his defense.

"Just a minute." I lowered the blinds against him and put on my jacket.

⚛

The instant I got outside, I knew it was a mistake. David's smile was gone. He was no longer cajoling or friendly. He led me to his car. "You should join us at Packard's, I'm serious. Learn to think for yourself. This has nothing to do with your mother."

"Who's us? Tripp and Gloria? Laura? Stuart? Leave my mother out of it."

He started the car and pulled away from the curb with a screech.

"I've been at my share of demonstrations," I said.

"Oh, have you?" Sarcastic. Hateful.

"You don't think so? When I was a kid they were called sit-downs. Before your time." I wanted to add it was just when he was probably too concerned with having polio to be involved in politics; I wanted to pile cruelty on cruelty. In any case, the sit-downs must have happened before his illness, maybe in 1952, I couldn't remember exactly–sometime before my father went to the Hearings, a summer so hot the drowsy heat crept inside our clothes and inside our skin, and there was nothing we could do to escape it except drive to Hains Point late at night and sleep on blankets by the Potomac River. Now David clutched the steering wheel as if it took great concentration to drive, but the more clearly I remembered that long-ago summer, the less his anger offended me. I decided to say my piece, whether he wanted to hear or not.

"At the dime stores in downtown D.C., you could eat even if you were Negro, but you had to eat standing up," I said. "The seats were reserved for whites. We went to sit-downs there all the time."

"Oh, commendable," David said. "She does have a social conscience after all."

"I was little, but the mothers all took their kids in those days. We'd meet these other families and they'd pair us up with little colored kids about the same age we were. Then we'd hold hands and sit down at the lunch counters and try to get served."

David focused on the road, giving no indication that he was listening. I didn't say how much Natalie and I resented being dragged from our paper dolls and the deep shade of our porch, onto streetcars that swayed on their tracks in the thick heat. Didn't say how we hated the bright treeless sun of F Street, where we were introduced to dark-skinned girls in church clothes and patent-leather shoes, girls we didn't know or care about or want to hold hands with. My mother said the lives of Negroes were full of struggle and injustice, but Rayfield's life seemed neither harsh nor unjust to me. In any case, the sit-downs seemed to have nothing to do with injustice, only with sweaty tension among adults both colored and white, with large and fearful eyes.

Inside the dime stores, the only cool place was just inside the doors, where big floor fans made a steady breeze. But we moved away from those fans toward the airless lunch counters, where we sat on swivel stools and absorbed the glares of waitresses in hair nets. We ordered Cokes but were never served. We sat on the stools and perspired and swallowed our thirst.

"One day we were walking toward some store—we hadn't even gotten there yet," I told David, "when one of the little colored girls said she had to pee. The bathrooms all along F Street were just for whites. Some colored lady said, 'The closest place is the public rest room in the National Art

Gallery.' Which was maybe five blocks away. My mother told Natalie to take us there.

"So we went running down the street toward the Art Gallery. The colored girl had on these cheap patent-leather shoes with slick bottoms. Natalie had to hold her hand to keep her from slipping. I was just six and the colored girl was even younger. Maybe not even school age yet. She was making faces and holding her legs together every time we stopped for a light.

"Finally we got there, three sweaty little dressed-up kids. I don't remember if it was air-conditioned back then or if the marble columns and the tiled floors just made it seem cold. Maybe the cool air releases your bladder after all that heat, I don't know. All I know is, while Natalie was asking the guard where the restroom was, the colored kid peed in her pants. It went all over her dress and made a puddle on the nice tile floor of the National Gallery."

"And this is why you won't stand in a picket line in front of Packard's?" David asked.

"Let me finish. I know the lunch counters finally got desegregated. But that day, all I remember is this little kid embarrassed and crying because some do-gooder parent made her go to a demonstration."

David pulled the car up in front of his house but made no move to get out.

"Natalie practically had to drag her back to the dime store, she was so humiliated. Finally we got there, and when her mother saw her all wet and messy, the mother started crying, too. Imagine that—four years old, at some cheap lunch counter in Kresge's or Neisner's or wherever it was, bawling and having everyone stare at you. That's what I remember about civil rights demonstrations. If you were her, what would you hate worse? Having to stand up while you ate? Or crying in front of a big crowd because somebody made you demonstrate where there wasn't even a place to pee?"

154

I didn't add that, afterwards, when my mother tried to take me to the sit-downs, I wouldn't go. I had temper tantrums; I complained of stomach aches. Eventually she began leaving me at Miriam's, where in the oppressive, hot, back room of the tailor shop, Rayfield pressed his shirts and Papa and Miriam sat at their sewing machines, and I spent hours picking through the scrap box tying rags together to help me escape from the high tower where I imagined myself trapped.

"In D.C.," David said, "it wasn't long before the lunch counters were desegregated and the playgrounds and swimming pools and you name it. The busses and schools—"

"The schools were a different issue entirely, years later—"

"And that kid, I'm sure she's all grown up now and doesn't think peeing in her pants was too high a price to pay."

He flung himself out of the car and grabbed his crutches from the back seat, leaving me to open my own door and follow. I caught up to him, yelling. "How do you know what's too high a price? How can you judge for someone else?" He stalked toward the house. "Answer me!"

He pulled out his key, opened the front door. Ivan bounded out from the darkness inside. He was larger than he'd been a month ago, one of those dogs you feared would grow into his feet. David braced himself as Ivan pawed his chest. He kneaded the dog's ears, then edged inside and clicked on the light.

"Jesus Christ," he said.

The two of us stood in the doorway, staring at the shambles inside. The couch was in tatters. The arm and the whole side closest to us had been chewed through. Pieces of batting spewed out. An old blanket, also chewed, had been dragged across the floor.

Ivan sat down, a little to the side of us, as if trying to keep out of our line of sight.

We stared at the mess for a few seconds. Ivan regarded it, too. "It was never a good couch," David said weakly.

"Didn't you ever leave him locked up before?"

David considered this. "I guess I never did. Not for five or six hours."

We turned toward Ivan accusingly. He cocked his head and looked remorseful, ears flopping.

What was left to do? Beat him? Yell?

We began to laugh. David dropped his crutches, and we sat on the remains of the couch. Ivan nuzzled between us. It was impossible to stay angry. Impossible not to lean close and be drawn into mingling scents of dog hair and aftershave. After a time, David slid off his jacket. Underneath, he wore a short-sleeved shirt. I looked at his arm but didn't move away, even when I saw, tattooed into the muscle beneath his elbow, the dark indentation made by the placard that afternoon, where it had been wedged into his skin by the brace.

13

On Sunday night when Ashley hadn't returned from Wilmington, Susan and I were so frantic we almost called her parents to make sure they hadn't mistreated her in some way. Locked her in her room, forced her to drop out of school, forced her to . . . we couldn't imagine.

"Aunt Sally Ann won't be happy about the baby, but she won't fall apart. She'd never do anything to hurt Ashley," Susan said over and over again. "The one it's going to kill is Uncle Toby."

This was at least the hundredth time I'd heard about Uncle Toby's imminent demise. I didn't believe it. Car salesmen weren't that sensitive. Anyway, who cared? Wasn't the main thing that Uncle Toby not kill *Ashley?*

"Why will it kill your uncle and not your aunt?" I asked Susan. "How do you know she won't be as upset as he will?"

"Aunt Sally Ann was raised Methodist. She's already been through this. She went to a different church half her life." She looked at the mournful Keane painting as if for support. "But him, being such a good Baptist—"

"Oh, Susan."

"You aren't Southern, so you don't know. Baptists are so—" She shook her head in exasperation. "You heard how Uncle Toby called Daddy a Whiskeypalian. That's honestly how he feels. He thinks Episcopalians go around drinking liquor and being dissolute."

"Then he's a jerk," I said.

"Yes, but he believes it. He'll bless you out up and down, but just say one thing about *his* religion . . ."

"I know. It just kills him," I said. "He should have been buried a dozen times by now."

Susan bit a scrap of hangnail off her index finger and flicked it off her tongue. "It's not funny, Beryl. Baptists are serious about what they believe. Church twice a week, all that. It's harder if their kids want to convert."

"All religions try to keep their members."

"Not really. You could go to a Methodist service one week and Presbyterian the next and hardly know the difference."

Having never gone to services, I felt powerless to argue.

Susan's finger began to bleed where the hangnail had been. She rubbed it against her slacks. "And it's the social thing, too," she said. "I'm sure he thinks most Catholics are factory workers—"

"Susan, there are millions of Catholics! Paco's father's a diplomat."

"Yes, but South American."

We gaped at each other, spent. What else was there to say?

Susan rummaged through the mess on her desk, found a Band-Aid, and wrapped it around her finger. A record buried in the debris caught her eye. Usually she put her records back in their jackets as soon as she'd played them. She held it up.

"Ahab the Arab," she told me—the song she hadn't played since Ashley pointed out that one of Paco's roommates was from Saudi Arabia. "It really isn't fair," she said, "the way the lyrics poke fun." She dropped it into the trash.

A tap came at our door. I leapt up to open it. A girl from down the hall stood outside. "Paco's here to see you."

Susan and I locked gazes. We bumped shoulders as we raced from the room. We flew into the parlor as if wind-blown.

Paco didn't even look disheveled. His hair was slicked-down, glossy as patent leather. His chinos were pressed. He stood beneath an archway of white-painted molding, devastatingly composed.

"Ashley is not with me because she stays in Wilmington a few days with her mother," he said formally. "To make preparation for the wedding."

After such a disclosure, a big grin would have been in order, but Paco's expression remained neutral. "She asked me to tell you this."

"Is she okay?" Susan asked.

"Yes. Of course. She sends me here so you will not worry."

Always before, Paco's formality had struck me as exotic and agreeable. Now, it was simply enigmatic. Always before, I'd seen him exclusively with Ashley, softened by her presence, holding her hand, gazing into her eyes. Alone, he seemed stiff and not quite real; even his Latin beauty looked painted-on. He offered no details about the scene in Wilmington; he didn't make it easy to ask. He was so remote and unruffled that I wanted to pinch him.

"So they agreed to the wedding?" Susan prodded.

"They are not happy. But they agreed."

"And what about *your* parents?"

"We will contact them when Ashley returns," Paco told us.

"When you get engaged, most people tell both sets of parents right away," Susan said.

"Perhaps—most people," Paco countered.

"But it's settled? The wedding, I mean?"

"My parents, too, will have to agree."

❊

On Wednesday, Ashley's mother drove her up from Wilmington. Mrs. Vance was tall and stately, with Ashley's gray eyes and sharp nose, but without her blonde mane. She hugged Susan, and me, and said she couldn't tell us how grateful she was Ashley lived with girls who looked after her. Then she checked her watch and said she had to get on the road this minute if she wanted to be home by dark.

"The wedding will be right here in Chapel Hill," Ashley told us. She sounded deliberately chipper but looked exhausted. "The Saturday after school lets out for Christmas. At the Catholic Church. I have from now until then to take instruction."

"Instruction?" I stared at her blankly.

"In Catholicism. To convert."

"I guess it'll be easier for you," I offered, "to do everything here."

A ripple of energy crossed Ashley's face. "Easier. But also conveniently out of Wilmington, where the date won't be noted so carefully. And where most of Mama's friends won't be sitting there trying to size up the groom." She managed a wry smile.

"Oh, Ashley." Susan walked toward her with outstretched arms. Ashley backed up and held her off.

"I liked the priest," Ashley said. "That's the one bright spot. I met him this afternoon and he's really nice."

"How often do you take these lessons?" Susan asked.

"Every day. We only have from now till Christmas. Less than six weeks."

"Every *day?*"

Ashley ignored this. "Don't say anything to anyone until

we talk to Paco's parents, hear?" And we knew then that nothing had really been settled.

⁂

There was one other Jewish girl in the dorm, Marilyn Adler, who lived on the third floor. She was a delicate-looking girl, very petite, who wore no makeup. Her voice was as tiny as the rest of her, high and thin like a child's. I'd met her in Harry's, where she went sometimes with Stuart.

In the halls of Alderman, Marilyn had the distinction of being the only white girl who hung around with Emily Moses. She'd often leave for class with Emily, laughing and talking, and return to the dorm with her hours later. The two of them had often been seen picketing together in front of Packard's.

Like me, Marilyn lived in one of the double rooms that had been converted to a triple. Unlike me, she hadn't the advantage of the first floor's high ceilings to make the room feel large enough for three people. Her roommates didn't like her, or she them. The person Marilyn liked was—Emily. Marilyn began asking why she couldn't move out of her crowded triple on the third floor and into the segregated but serene first-floor room with her friend. Mrs. West, the house-mother, said, "Now, Marilyn, I don't have to tell you why."

"Yes, you do," Marilyn responded.

Mrs. West said, "Marilyn, that's enough."

It was probably because of Marilyn that Ashley wasn't kicked out of school.

Ashley hadn't been back twenty-four hours before Anna Mae cornered her. Anna Mae asked her how she was feeling, why she'd been away so long. Ashley said she'd been in Wilmington to help her mother with some important arrangements. She didn't say what.

"Ashley, I'm not sure I quite understand what's going on." Anna Mae tapped a bare toe on the floor beneath a knee-length nightshirt that set off white stringbean legs. "But I understand you've been sick and missing a lot of classes."

"I have been sick," Ashley said mildly.

"With hepatitis?"

Ashley said nothing. Anna Mae leaned toward her, confidential and oily. "Do you want to talk about it?"

"There's nothing really to talk about."

"I'm not sure of that." Anna Mae's voice turned suddenly sharp and crisp. "I think anyone with problems needs to talk them out. If not with me, then with someone else. Maybe you should take this up with the Dean." This was the dean of women, a fearsome woman hated by all.

"I don't think so," Ashley said. Her unsettling calm permeated the room.

"Ashley, whatever you're keeping from me—if you *are* keeping something from me—you have to understand I'm just trying to help you before this ends up before the women's Honor Council."

Anna Mae rubbed her too-short nose and blinked her lashless eyes. I was tempted to blurt out that if it was Honor Council offenses she was searching for, she should look no farther. I myself was breaking the two-couple rule a couple of times a week. But I could see from Anna Mae's displeasure that it wasn't my downfall she was after, only Ashley's. Even gray and worn from stress, Ashley was striking to look at. Anna Mae never would be. Her eyes glinted hard and judgmental, and it was clear from her expression that sending Ashley to the Honor Council was the only power over her Anna Mae would ever have.

"Anna Mae, if I had something I wanted to confide, I would," Ashley said.

"I see."

The women's council indeed! Beside throwing up and going home for a long weekend, what did anyone know for sure that Ashley had done? And even if it came out that she'd

162

slept with somebody, why should that be grounds for cutting off the rest of her education?

"There's nothing they can get you for," I said after Anna Mae left. "You never stayed out late. You never took an illegal overnight. Nothing!"

"I had a pregnancy test at the infirmary," Ashley said.

"So?"

"They could find out."

"Medical records are confidential."

"At a normal doctor's office they are. But here?" Ashley sounded bitter.

"Once you're married, there's nothing they can do to you," Susan reassured her.

Ashley looked at herself in the mirror above the sink and touched an index finger to the dark spots beneath her eyes. "I'd just like to finish the semester," she told us.

So it seemed pure luck when, the very next day, Ashley ceased being an object of curiosity. Something far more momentous had happened. Something unheard-of! Marilyn Adler had dragged her clothes, books, and bedding down two flights of stairs, and set up housekeeping with Emily Moses.

Amazing, how quickly the spotlight could shift. Anna Mae sashayed off to the administration building to report the move to the dean in person rather than on the phone. The dean called Marilyn in for consultation. Marilyn returned to the dorm in tears. Mrs. West, the housemother, was seen conferring with Marilyn in the hall. Rumors abounded of possible punishment, censure, expulsion.

Ashley had her own reaction to the news. "I'm finished throwing up in that shower," she said. "I am. I about got burned to death the other day."

From then on, she vomited loudly into the toilet where everyone could hear. No one cared. A white girl had moved in with a Negro! Had anyone ever heard of such a thing? When a girl across the hall wanted to know why, if Ashley was getting over hepatitis, her skin wasn't yellow instead of so deathly white, Susan shrugged and said, "Did you hear Marilyn had to go back to the Dean's office today?" And that preempted further discussion about Ashley.

Even though attention had shifted, Ashley's dilemma grew more complicated by the day. Paco called his parents in New York, who said marriage to some little North American was out of the question. Think what it would mean for his career. How could he have done such a thing? How did they know the baby was Paco's?

"How could they accuse me of having someone else's baby?" Ashley wailed.

How could Paco tell her everything his parents had uttered?

"They don't know you. When they know you they'll see."

"When they see a black-haired Latin-looking baby, they'll see," Ashley lamented.

Paco agreed to fly home for the weekend to talk to his parents alone. Ashley feared she'd never see him again. For hours she sat mournfully by the window, watching the falling leaves. I sympathized, but the mood in our room grew so cloying and claustrophobic that it was impossible even to read. David and I weren't getting along, hadn't been ever since we'd disagreed about his picketing. But when I needed to escape from Ashley, where else was there to go except Harry's?

I found him alone in a booth after supper, sipping a beer. Maybe a little drunk, although it was early. He didn't normally drink so much. I glanced at his crutches, propped against the booth.

"Looking at something?" he asked.

"Nothing special."

"Could've fooled me."

"Don't be so sensitive, David."

"Who's sensitive?"

"Oh, for Christ's sake."

His eyes were black marbles without sparkle. I had believed—mistakenly—that handicaps made people more noble. That was the lesson my family had tried to teach. How naïve we all were! Handicaps didn't produce nobility, they produced bitterness and cynicism. I was a fool not to have seen it before.

The door swung open and a gaggle of people swept in— Marilyn Adler, Laura and Fran, Stuart, Emily Moses, Gloria. They were buoyed up, excited, flinging their jackets over the chairs. They almost wiped out David's aura of gloom.

"The women's Honor Council wants to prosecute her for an illegal move!" Gloria shouted, sweeping her wool cape in Marilyn's direction. "Can you believe it?"

"I was with the dean of women *two hours*," Marilyn said. "Two *hours*. Other girls move from one room to another all the time."

"But always 'with permission'," Emily pointed out archly.

"What I don't understand is, why does anyone care?" Laura asked. "It's a double room, isn't it? With two beds."

"And an empty room next to it," Emily added.

Marilyn opened her slits of eyes as wide as they'd go. "The extra *study lounge*." She chuckled mirthlessly.

"Marilyn and I are the only ones who study there," Emily said, and everyone laughed. I laughed, too, though the only study lounge I'd ever used, myself, was in the basement.

David bent close, lips to my ear. "You see what they're going through," he whispered. "You see their bravery."

Bravery! His voice was so low, his breath so gentle that everyone at the table must have thought he was making a proposition.

I straightened up and rubbed my ear. He was right. Emily and Marilyn were brave. I wasn't. Emily and Marilyn were friends. Emily and I hardly knew each other. Even sitting across the table, not paying a bit of attention to me, Emily made me as uncomfortable as the little girls had at those lunch counters in D.C. when I was six. Colored people had always made me uncomfortable. Even the ones my mother brought home were only people involved in the movement–the movement!–never really friends. In high school, after integration, the schools west of Rock Creek Park, including mine, had only a few Negroes. I never knew any of them. The only colored person I'd ever known well enough to care about was Rayfield the presser.

"I wish you could get a look at the inside of Alderman," Emily said to Stuart and David. "A couple of those rooms on the third floor are so packed that one girl even tried moving her desk out into the hall to get some space for herself." Emily's voice was smooth and unaccented. She talked exactly like a television reporter–deliberately, properly, anonymously. Nothing marked her. With her hazel eyes and tan skin, she hardly looked Negro. What was I supposed to make of her? I listened to Emily and then to Marilyn until my face actually ached from the effort of trying to be pleasant.

"Ridiculous!" Gloria shouted again. "When there's an extra room just sitting there!"

David's eyes told me to say something. What did he expect? For me to announce I was dragging my clothes across the parlor and claiming the unused study lounge as a bedroom? Not likely! What gave him the right to stare so accusingly? He was guilty himself: of not knowing a single name of any of his colored neighbors who walked down the road by his house, heading for their shanties on the next block. Did he care that they couldn't rent the house next door to his? That they could only rent the ones in colored-town? Who did he think he was?

I stared back at him. He dropped his gaze before I did.

"About the Honor Council—what will you do?" someone asked.

"The almighty Honor Council!" I said without thinking. Everyone looked surprised. But it wasn't Marilyn or Emily I had in mind, it was Ashley. Powerless before the Honor Council's definition of what it meant to be a lady. Powerless to argue if it expelled her from school because she didn't fit. Lady: a virgin white girl who doesn't live with coloreds. Who doesn't sleep with boys.

"My parents are coming to Chapel Hill tomorrow," Marilyn said. "They're going to see the dean."

"They'll say they don't understand why it would be illegal for Marilyn to move into a double room instead of staying crowded in a triple," Stuart explained, blanketing the table in a vast exhalation of cigarette smoke. "They're going to use something the dean isn't familiar with. Reason and logic."

For once, I agreed with him. What would they prosecute Marilyn for? For moving into a better room? Would they go after Ashley for throwing up too often in the first-floor bathroom? The restaurant felt stuffy and hot. I could have strangled the dean of women with my bare hands. I was so involved in the general sense of outrage that for a moment I actually forgot that Emily Moses was a Negro.

The conversation lost energy then. David went to the men's room. Stuart, Marilyn, Laura, and Emily left for a meeting. Only Gloria and I remained at the table. A strand of her long hair had fallen onto the wood, a long jagged curlicue glowing red in the light. I tried not to stare at it. The detached hair seemed intensely personal and intimate.

"David had a fit before because he thought I was looking at his crutches," I found myself saying. "Not that they're easy to miss. He has to know people notice."

"Yeah, he was always like that," Gloria said, plucking the

last cigarette from a pack Stuart had left behind.

"He was always like what?" I asked.

"A moody little buster. Even before he had polio."

"Did you know him pretty well? I mean—before?"

"Huh?" Gloria shifted her shoulders and tugged at the bra beneath her sweater. Whenever she wore ordinary clothes instead of her loose, flowing, costumey ones, they looked ill-fitting and unsuitable.

"David," I repeated. "Did you know him pretty well before he got sick?"

"I guess. He lived a couple of blocks away." She looked at Stuart's cigarette as if debating what to do with it. I'd never seen her smoke. She spotted a pack of matches on the table, lit one, and held it dangerously close to her hair. When the cigarette caught and she blew out the match, I realized I'd been holding my breath.

"We went to the same schools," she said. "We were in the same classes." She inhaled, then turned her head so as not to blow smoke in my face. "He used to play baseball. He was the catcher, and he could hit, too. But, you know, we were kids, the girls didn't care that much about Little League."

"Little League?"

"Yeah, sure. His father used to coach. Yuck." She frowned and stubbed the cigarette out. "Like I said, David was the same as he is now, up one day and down the next. A kid like that, it's hard if he gets polio and can't play. But he wasn't easy to take, even before."

"I can't picture him—you know. *Before.*"

"He was the great athlete, going to be the next Mickey Mantle. A real arrogant little guy. Drove everybody crazy." She reached down and tugged again at her bra. "Still does," she said, and grinned.

So maybe that was why he was so bitter.

David was more cheerful when he returned to the table. Down one minute, up the next. He balanced on his good leg and put down a crutch while he got his coat. Look, everyone, the man can do anything! Now that I knew he'd been an athlete before fate cut him down, I supposed I'd have to feel sorry for him as well as just annoyed. Spending the evening with him would be exhausting. But beneath the fabric of his shirt, David's muscular arms were rich with the olive smoothness of his skin, and when he asked if I wanted to go back to his house for a while I said sure, why not. So what if our relationship was built on desire tinged with rage? I still wanted to touch him.

In David's backyard, Ivan had managed to tangle himself thoroughly in his rope. The rope was tied to the oil tank, and Ivan was so wrapped up in it he couldn't move. Ever since the warning from the police at Packard's and the chewed couch afterwards, David had been leaving Ivan in the yard if he was going to be downtown very long. But Ivan never adjusted. He carried on until he was too tired to bark. He exhausted himself trying to protest the insult of being confined. That night he must have been at it for a long time, because he barely whimpered as we approached.

"Poor fella, he plumb wore himself out," David said. He set his crutches on the ground and kneeled, balancing on his good right knee while he worked to release Ivan from his knots. In the glow of a distant street lamp, his expression was as concentrated as if he'd been performing surgery. He untangled the rope, undid the hook. Ivan realized he was free. Renewed energy infused him. He pounced and practically knocked David over. I held my breath, waiting for David to grow angry with me for being there to see his show of weakness. But he laughed. He scratched Ivan's ears. The dog had restored the sweeter part of his nature. For long moments, Ivan lavished uncritical love on him with his slobbery tongue. I reminded myself, as I'd been doing ever since the incident at Packard's, that it was impossible to hate a man who was as good as David was to his dog.

14

Paco did return from his trip to New York. His parents were upset, but what could they do? Paco was of age. He was fathering a child. He had ruined his life.

What they could do, it turned out, was refuse to come to the wedding.

The sixty-four-dollar question was: would Paco go through with the marriage without his parents' blessing?

"They'll come around," Susan maintained. "Give them time to settle down. Then get your mother to talk to his mother. It'll be fine."

"I don't think things will ever be fine," Ashley said.

All the same, in a small way, she began announcing her engagement. Though the ceremony would be at the Catholic church, the reception would be at the Carolina Inn, the elegant hotel at the edge of campus. Punch and cake. No liquor, of course.

Word got around that Ashley was not getting married out

of choice. Pregnant, someone whispered. A Wilmington Vance and pregnant! Ashley pretended not to hear. Graciously, she accepted everyone's congratulations.

Every day after class, she went to the Catholic Church for instruction. Back when Mr. Vance had said church had been a pleasant experience for Ashley, growing up, he probably hadn't meant just any church. But Ashley didn't complain. A stack of pamphlets about Catholicism sat on the corner of her desk. In her low moments, she often consulted them. They seemed to make her calmer.

While Ashley studied and prepared herself, Paco kept trying to win over his parents. He was having no luck. Ashley was sure they'd cut off his funds for school if he married without their blessing. This was not good news. He had a little inheritance, but not enough to live on.

"I can always get a job," Ashley said. "Someone will hire me."

But who? By the time the wedding was over, by the time the holidays had passed and the new semester started, Ashley would be showing. Susan and I weren't at all sure that, if his money was cut off, Paco would go through with the wedding.

In public, Ashley was stoic. She'd walk slowly to the room, past the inquiring eyes of her friends, smiling and answering questions, expression composed. Then she'd close the door to our room, lean back against it, and let the tears escape. Sobs would rack her chest. Nothing was going as planned! Paco's parents remained adamant. Ashley's father wouldn't speak to her. Even her mother was causing problems. The two of them couldn't agree about her wedding dress.

"What do you mean—couldn't agree?"

A new flood of tears cascaded down her cheeks. "She says wait until Thanksgiving for the fitting. You know what she's thinking—she doesn't know what size I'll be." More sobs, then sniffles.

Susan handed her a tissue. Ashley blew her nose.

"I just wanted this to be nice," she said. "All my life I just expected my wedding to be *nice.*"

I wondered why, under the circumstances, she should expect that. Then I felt treacherous and held my tongue. It was Ashley's life, not mine. And sometimes, in spite of everything, we were all as carefree as we might have been if Ashley had stayed a virgin.

A song came out by a group called The Kingsmen. "Louie Louie," pronounced Louie, Lou-AYE. It was banned by almost every radio station in North Carolina because the lyrics were thought to be obscene. Susan bought the 45 just before the record stores took it off their shelves. We played it over and over again. We turned the speed down to 33 to hear the words more clearly. Girls came from all over the dorm to listen. We wrote what we heard on a torn-out piece of notebook paper and then read our interpretations to the group, trying to get a consensus about what The Kingsmen were really saying.

Penny Blankenship said she could make out the F-word, she was surprised the rest of us couldn't. Marilyn Adler said the words seemed pretty normal, maybe The Kingsmen themselves spread the rumor about obscenity just to get publicity. Once, Emily Moses came in to hear the record. One girl left when she saw Emily, but the rest of them stayed.

We huddled around the record player, sometimes five or six of us at a time. So intent were we on deciphering the language that Ashley's predicament grew hazy, David's dark moods unimportant. In the throes of "Louie Louie," we were awash in nothing beyond the mystery of the lyrics. It was a wonderful, clear state of mind, the perfect distillation of college life. After a dozen replays, we all concluded it was impossible to understand the words of "Louie Louie" at 33 or 45 or any other speed.

That decided, Susan took "Louie Louie" off the turntable and stacked up a couple of Beach Boys hits that Penny Blankenship liked, along with "Donna the Prima Donna" for Donna Manning on the second floor. We listened and ate the potato chips somebody had brought. We sang along and talked until midnight. Then the room emptied except for Penny, who sat trying to get some spilled Coke out of one of her cashmere sweaters.

"Daddy brought me the car last weekend," she said to Susan as she pressed a wet washcloth into the stain. "I've got it here if you want a ride home for Thanksgiving."

"Thanksgiving?" I asked. Despite Ashley's tears over having to wait until then for her dress fitting, I hadn't given a thought to the fact that the holiday was only a couple of weeks off. Time had whipped by since my arrival. I might have entered the dorm for the first time ten minutes ago, or I might have lived there forever.

"I'd love a ride. Even with you," Susan teased. "Better than the bus."

Both girls giggled.

"What about you, Beryl?" Susan asked.

"The bus, I guess. It's that or ask Stuart Gershner who he's riding with. Or else ask my father to come get me." I made a face.

What was I thinking? This was a college campus where my father couldn't give a lecture even if asked. Hadn't my mother pointed this out? Hadn't she wanted me to feel guilty for coming to Chapel Hill and thereby casting aspersions on his honor? The sweet, bubbly aftermath of listening to music evaporated.

Susan must have read my mind. "It's a long way to D.C., and you'll see them in a month at Christmas," she said.

"Thanksgiving's just a long weekend. Why not come home to Winston with me?"

Why not? What relief! Winston-Salem! At home, I'd get my mother's political intrigues along with the turkey. I'd get her personal litany of the guilt I should feel for coming South. I'd be brainwashed for ninety-six hours, four days. There was no telling whether I could stand it.

"I'd love to see Winston-Salem," I said. And before Susan could change her mind, I rushed into the hallway to call home.

It took Miriam less than forty-eight hours to respond. Like my mother before her, she arrived in Chapel Hill without warning. Instead of coming into my room, she sent the first person she saw in the parlor to fetch me. I found her sitting on a flowery sofa, Aunt Gussie perched beside her, each in a black coat and sensible hat, each clutching a large pocketbook in her lap. My first thought was: Good Lord, I come from a family of midgets.

Maybe we live with our families for so long that we don't see them objectively until we emigrate to another country. Before then they're too familiar to us—generous mouths, high-bridged noses, square chins repeated in sisters and brothers and cousins, so many variations on a theme that we don't notice them at all. Ever since Papa's death, Miriam had cooked my meals and cleaned our house and ordered me around. She'd seemed large and powerful. I'd never once noticed that when she sat back on a couch, her feet didn't touch the floor.

Gussie's, either. Neither one of them could have been more than four feet ten.

"Miriam! Aunt Gussie! What are you doing here?" I exclaimed. Both of them shifted in their seats and then in one lurching movement propelled themselves forward and up. Miriam advanced toward me for a hug.

"Who brought you?" I asked when we had released each other.

Gussie cuffed me on the arm. "What—who brought us? You think we couldn't bring ourselves?"

"A bus," Miriam said. "Trailways."

"It takes all day, a thousand stops," Gussie added. "And such little aisles, you can't hardly stretch your legs. What we went through to see you. *Oy.*"

Neither one of them had ever learned to drive. I envisioned them in the dismal Trailways terminal in Washington, offering Lifesavers to winos and derelicts.

"Tomorrow, we go back," Gussie said. "An adventure!" She grinned. Her hair was blue enough to indicate a recent stretch of madness.

"Your mother, she wanted to come but couldn't. So she found us a guest house to stay," Miriam told me. "We took our satchels there already."

"By taxi," Aunt Gussie added. "The owner, she recommended us a place to eat. The Rat. You know this place?"

"Sure, I—"

"It's some Southern tradition, naming a restaurant after a rat?" Gussie pressed.

"The Rathskellar," I said, recalling how I myself had once thought Lenoir Hall was a person named Lenoir.

"I told you," Miriam said to her sister. "It wasn't named after no rat."

During the summer, a fire had burned the Rathskellar and the gift shop next door, but the restaurant had been repaired and reopened shortly after school started. We clumped down the concrete stairs leading from the street into the darkened, cavelike interior.

Aunt Gussie was delighted. "Imagine, a restaurant under ground," she said. She draped her coat and purse straps over the back of the chair and arranged her dress, a dress of such pale blue, so exactly the UNC school color, that I wondered if she'd chosen it on purpose. It also very nearly matched her hair. She took her glasses off and cleaned them with the napkin, then began poring over the menu.

"Such food," she said over and over.

"She never eats nothing," Miriam told me.

Gussie tapped the menu with her finger. "Food I know what it is, I eat."

"Try the lasagna, Aunt Gussie," I suggested. "It's a little like blintzes. You like blintzes."

"She likes blintzes but she don't eat them. She wants to keep herself thin," Miriam told me.

"*Nu?* It's a crime that I never let myself get heavy?"

The two women glared at each other. When Aunt Gussie was well, they would fight over anything. I convinced them that they should both try the lasagna. "I'll have it, too."

The waiter had no sooner turned away than Miriam and Gussie fixed me with identical expectant stares. "Well?" Miriam asked, pronouncing it *vell.*

"Well?" I replied. "Why did you come?"

"Why did we come?" Gussie asked the ceiling. "Did she give us a choice? Why did we come?"

"You go to visit Susan at Thanksgiving, no?" Miriam asked. "You don't come home, so we have to come here to see you."

"Oh. The mountain going to Muhammad," I said.

"*Nu?*" Miriam persisted.

"I'm fine. Everything's fine."

We went through the standard recitation of family news. How was Uncle Abe? Good, good. The dry cleaning business? Like always, what could you expect, from dry cleaning you didn't make a fortune. My mother? Back in town for a change.

I knew this from phone calls and letters. Natalie?

"How can I tell you about Natalie?" Miriam sounded offended. "Natalie lives in New York."

The salads came. Miriam and Aunt Gussie both believed vegetables should be cooked. They nibbled politely until the waiter appeared with the lasagnas, each in a brown crock set on a larger plate.

"Two plates," Aunt Gussie noted.

"Very hot," the waiter told her, indicating the crock.

Aunt Gussie gave an approving nod. Food should be hot, no? She turned her attention to separating the layers of lasagna with her fork, to see what they might contain. When she spoke, she might have been addressing the noodles. "Your mother says you go out with a boy on crutches," she said.

Aha, I thought.

Miriam addressed her own plate of noodles. "You're seeing this boy a lot?"

"Sometimes. Why?"

"The boy's a cripple," Gussie noted, looking up.

"He had polio when he was twelve," I said. "He gets around all right. He does everything."

"Better you shouldn't get involved with a cripple," Aunt Gussie said.

She was about to put a forkful of lasagna into her mouth, but a long string of cheese refused to detach itself from the dish. "A cripple, he might be more trouble than it's worth." She jerked her fork up and to the side. The string of cheese suddenly broke free and hung in the air.

I wondered if Uncle Abe would be able to tug at defiant cheese with his mutilated fingers, or if Aunt Gussie would have to help him. I wondered if Uncle Abe was her model for thinking a cripple might be more trouble than he was worth. I pictured Uncle Abe's amputated fingers rotting in the Jewish cemetery. Yet, besides a lack of fingers and a functioning left leg, what was actually wrong with David or Uncle Abe, either one?

"David really isn't a cripple," I said. A moody, difficult person, yes. Possibly an activist. That was all.

"Anybody can't walk without crutches, you got to say he's a cripple," Miriam corrected me.

"So?"

"Better you shouldn't get too involved," she repeated.

But wasn't that what we in my family *did?* Didn't we consort with Negroes and cripples and other underdogs in order to better their lot? How could they tell me not to get involved with David?

"It's only his left leg," I said. "The right is fine."

Gussie rolled a bite of lasagna around in her mouth. "So rich," she said. "Not like blintzes. More like—I don't know."

She looked confused. Maybe it was true she'd always resented Bubby Tsippi for hiring the matchmaker who'd fixed her up with Uncle Abe. Maybe it was true Bubby Tsippi had sold Gussie into marriage so she wouldn't be an old maid. The way Gussie chewed and played with her food, anyone could see she wasn't normal. Maybe, as Mother had said, Bubby Tsippi had ruined her.

Miriam turned to me. "What you should remember is, you're here to go to school. Not to get mixed in with some boy."

"Mixed up, not mixed in," Aunt Gussie corrected.

"Mixed up, mixed in, she knows what I mean." To me she added, "I told Natalie the same thing. What does she do, she gets married anyway. But I told her. She shouldn't get mixed up too early. Better wait a while."

"You told her that?"

"Better she should go live with him first. It wasn't necessary she should get married."

"You told her she should live with him?" My voice came out a squeak.

"*Nu?* She could take that pill. We didn't have it back then. What's the harm in living together?"

I took a sip of water. No one's grandmother talked like this.

"You were younger than Natalie when you married Papa," I managed.

"Beryl, listen for a change. What I'm saying is, today it isn't necessary."

"I never said I was getting married," I told her.

"Not you," Gussie seemed compelled to explain. "Natalie."

Miriam pointed her fork at me. "I married, sure. But not until I decided I would stay with somebody." She drew herself up. "You think I married the first boy I saw? You think I decided some rabbi should tell me with whom I should sleep?"

"What—?"

I couldn't finish. I lifted my water glass to my cheek to cool it. Miriam and Gussie had arrived in this country in 1914. Miriam was fifteen. My father was born five years later. Between coming to America and settling down, that gave Miriam—what? Four years to play around? I couldn't imagine it. My own grandmother, a loose woman.

"In those days you married when you decided you would have children. Own property. What I'm saying is, today it isn't necessary."

"When you own property, you don't want it to go to some man," Gussie said, drifting. "In Russia, a woman couldn't own property. Our brother Reuben had to write a note giving our mother permission to sell it."

With a slight shake of her head, Miriam signaled me to pay Gussie no mind. "Nineteen, twenty, today it's too young," Miriam told me. "You! Not even eighteen yet, and all of a sudden you can't come home for Thanksgiving? All of a sudden you have to visit Susan in Winston-Salem? Maybe all of a sudden you're really going to spend your time with the cripple—no?"

Ah.

"No, Miriam," I said.

"No? Good." As if for emphasis, she dropped her fork in the lasagna crock and began to butter a roll.

Aunt Gussie leaned in my direction. "When we were on the boat from Russia, I cut my hair," she said.

"Huh?" I looked again to Miriam for confirmation that Gussie was losing track of reality, but Miriam pointed to Gussie's waist with her butter knife, as if everything were proceeding as expected. "Her hair was down to there," she said.

"Our brother Reuben went second class," Gussie told me, "but we girls had to go steerage. All we had to eat was herring and potatoes and bread." She gestured toward the rolls. "Once the whole trip they gave us hard-boiled eggs."

"Why are you mixing hard-boiled eggs and the story of your hair?" Miriam asked her.

"I'm not mixing nothing," Aunt Gussie said. "The first few days, the sea was so rough the cabinet with the dishes fell over. We were all sick. *Ach!* Then we got better. That's when I cut my hair." She touched her hand to her blue-white hairline.

Miriam warmed to this. "All of a sudden Gussie takes a scissors and cuts off her braids. Just like that." She put down her roll and snapped her fingers.

"Just like that," Gussie echoed. "I was going to save my braids for a scrapbook, but one of the children on the ship unraveled them and they were no good. So we went by the side of the boat and I threw them over."

She made a throwing motion, which made the waiter look our way.

"She was a little sad when we watched the braids sink under," Miriam said.

"Not so sad," Gussie corrected.

"So I said to her, 'See, you throw your hair into the water and we start a whole new life.'"

"I always kept my hair short from then," Gussie said.

"And you had a whole new life," I concluded.

When people are old, it's hard to imagine them young. I couldn't picture Gussie a young girl with beautiful dark hair, in love with the boy she would have married if he hadn't been killed in the pogrom. I couldn't envision her suffering from depression for four years, her long hair so heavy it weighted her down. I had heard that she dreamed night after night of Cossacks on dark horses, galloping through the streets of the town, striking down Jews with whips and swords. I couldn't conceive of any of that.

But I could see her perfectly, watching from the ship as her braids disappeared into the waves. I could feel the fresh wind blowing her short new locks away from her face, and I could almost hear her laughing, and Miriam laughing, too.

Aunt Gussie smiled and studied the transparent air between me and Miriam, as if viewing images lost on the rest of us. I felt suddenly full and sad.

Aunt Gussie's eyes found my face and focused. "Better you should spend your time on your studies," she said.

Both sisters nodded, as if something important had been settled. I wasn't sure what.

15

By the time we finished eating, Aunt Gussie could hardly keep her eyes open. I glanced at my watch. Just after seven.

"She don't like to stay up after dark." Miriam jutted her chin in her sister's direction. "Better she should get some sleep, she shouldn't get crazy again."

Gussie jerked herself awake. "What, crazy? After a six-hour bus ride, I'm not entitled to be tired?" Gussie waved a hand to dismiss the talk of infirmity, but she looked every minute of her seventy-two years.

"Tomorrow, we stop by your room," Miriam told me. She gathered her purse and coat and gestured for Gussie to do the same. "Then we go to the bus."

The idea of Miriam and Gussie meeting Susan and Ashley did not appeal to me. They'd been kind to me all this time. What would they think once they heard how my relatives talked? Once they saw their old-fashioned clothes?

"Are you sure you have time to come to the dorm?" I asked. "Maybe you should—"

"Maybe nothing," Miriam said.

We waited for the cab to take them to their guest house. Then I debated going to Harry's, decided not to, and started back to the dorm.

Until I walked into the parlor and saw a girl attaching a corsage to her bosom with the help of her date, I'd forgotten it was the night of the Interfraternity Ball. Ashley wasn't having anything to do with it, but Susan was going with Colby Lee.

I often teased her about how much it pained me to have to remember two names for him—indeed for everybody's dates here in North Carolina, not just one name like back in D.C. I laughed when Susan replied with mock gravity, "Colby's a family name from his Daddy's side and Lee from his Mama's side, Beryl. We have to call him by both names or the Lees might cut him off." She winked, but I thought she was trying hard not to be impressed by his illustrious family connections.

Other than that, I wasn't sure if she liked him or not. She never seemed to care if he didn't call, never talked about him, never mooned or emoted. "Are you really dating him, or is this just an arranged marriage?" I sometimes teased her. "A convenient way to make the social scene?"

"Arranged," she'd shoot back.

But I was never certain. And even less certain that night.

Susan didn't normally fuss much with her appearance, even for dances. Her natural well-scrubbed look wasn't flashy like Ashley's, but she was pretty enough, with even features, healthy brown hair, a firm chin.

That night she was someone else entirely. She stood in front of the mirror in full battle dress, dabbing her lashes with mascara. A thin black streak of eyeliner accented her eyelids, and her lips shone with an unaccustomed sheen of magenta lipstick. She turned from the mirror and pointed to her face. "What do you think?"

"Terrific." Lashes thick as a movie star's, skin shimmering with powder and blusher.

She spun around to show me her dress.

"Like it?"

I did! A three-quarter-length semi-formal of palest pink, with a shiny, satiny underskirt and an overskirt of organdy that burst into ruffles just below the knee. Susan usually wore more forthright colors—greens and reds and yellows—and the pink quilt that sat rumpled on her bed always seemed like something from somebody else's room. But tonight, pink suited her perfectly. The bodice of the dress was held up by lacy spaghetti straps, delicate against Susan's white shoulders. The underskirt hugged her hips; the overskirt muted the effect so that it suggested her shape but didn't shout. I stared with admiration and a pang of envy. I had never owned such a dress. It was unthinkable! Mother would have taken one look at it on the hanger in the store and labeled it a *shiksa* dress, out of the question, unsuitable for nice Jewish girls.

All through high school she'd steered Natalie and me toward sensible tailored sheaths we could use again—though we never did. I always wondered why it was so important to her that we might.

As always, a stack of Susan's records played softly in the background, the volume low to set the mood. Susan hummed to the strains of Bobby Vinton's "Blue Velvet" and put a few items from her purse into a sequined clutch. She might be wearing organdy instead of velvet, but the song was right for the occasion—dressing up, applying three coats of mascara, waiting for a boy named Colby Lee. I envied her. I ached with jealousy.

In our family we went to dances not just for fun but because they were "part of our social development." We went in sensible outfits and we listened to serious, enlightening music while we got dressed, Beethoven's *Fifth* or Verdi's *Aïda,* never Bobby Vinton. We were not that silly.

Life was serious. People were being oppressed, causes required our attention. Being normal and having a good time were not the goals that mattered. What counted was having some purpose to every day, every minute, every piece of clothing.

The more I thought about this, with Susan standing before me in all her ruffled pinkness, the more upset I felt. What was wrong with being purely ornamental once in a while? What was wrong with enjoying yourself? By the time the runner who announced dates knocked on our door, I was blinking away angry tears. As I waved goodbye and watched the door shut before me, I felt exactly like Cinderella.

I knew then why Aunt Gussie and Miriam had warned me against getting involved with David. The idea was not so much to avoid cripples specifically as to beware of pleasant distractions in general. Boys, crippled or otherwise, might lure me off my path. I was not here for pleasure; I was here to get an education, to prepare for a purpose, even if none of us knew yet what it might be. I wasn't expected to be irresponsible—even here, in this alluring new country.

I sank onto my bed and stared at the ceiling. "Blue Velvet" finished and another record dropped, but I lifted the needle before it began to play. This is what we were not allowed in my family: moments of rhyme rather than reason, moments of mindlessness, as when a group of girls crowded around a record player trying to figure out the words of a song called "Louie Louie." Words that might be filthy but thrilling.

Still fully dressed, still staring at the ceiling and meaning to get up, I fell sound asleep. I didn't hear Susan or Ashley come in from their dates. I didn't know anything until I began to have a vivid dream of myself at the Interfraternity Ball. I wore a pink ruffled dress and swayed belly-to-belly with a faceless boy with a thick Southern accent. I leaned my head against his shoulder and listened to Bobby Vinton. I had a wonderful time.

It was morning when I opened my eyes. The first thing that came into focus was Susan's pink party dress lying in a heap beside her bed. She was sound asleep, with her makeup still on and her mascara smudged down her cheek. Ashley was sleeping, too. I bolted up. My body felt heavy, which puzzled me until I realized I still had all my clothes on.

"Get up," I demanded. "My grandmother and great-aunt are coming to see the room."

Susan and Ashley groaned but complied. Ashley trotted off to the bathroom but wasn't gone long. With enough practice, it was possible to be efficient even about morning sickness. I went downstairs to get her a carton of chocolate milk and a Coke. Susan opened the box of saltines we kept in Ashley's dresser. In half an hour we had her looking and feeling presentable.

We straightened the room as we always did before family visits—quickly and thoroughly, a team effort. Susan swiped her dress up from the floor, then noticed what she was doing and stopped, held the skirt in her hand, looking thoughtful.

"Does this mean it was a sterling evening?" I asked.

A mix of emotions crossed her face as she glanced furtively toward Ashley, who was making her bed.

Miriam and Gussie arrived on the dot of nine, an hour before their bus was due to leave. Gussie looked calm and well-rested. Miriam looked harried. Each of them lugged a huge shopping bag in one hand and carried her purse in the other. They looked as if they'd just gotten off the boat, so foreign and inept that I dreaded having to own up to them.

"Didn't you bring suitcases?" I asked.

"Our satchels? Sure," Aunt Gussie said. "Out there." She pointed toward the parlor. "They can sit for a while, no? Nobody will take them?"

"No," I said. "They're safe."

With deep misgiving, I introduced them to Susan and Ashley, whose expressions I couldn't read. Polite pleasantness, of course. But also amusement?

"Here." Miriam thrust one of the shopping bags at me, then swept her hand toward the others. "For all of you."

Gussie set down the other shopping bag and mimicked Miriam's sweeping motion.

No one moved.

"Well?" Miriam asked. It came out *vell*. She reached into one of the bags and plucked out a sack of bagels. She held one up for us to see.

"Doughnuts?" Susan asked.

"Just a kind of roll," I managed. "Hard. Not sweet."

Ashley narrowed her eyes.

"Nothing religious," I told her.

Miriam brightened and lifted a challah from the bag. "Bread for Friday night. The Sabbath." As if we observed the Sabbath!

"Come! Look!" Miriam exclaimed, beckoning Ashley and Susan to empty the shopping bags themselves. Obediently, they began lifting out the food, item by item. They turned over the breads and sweets in their fingers; they examined them as if they had come from China. For each new delicacy, they looked to Miriam and Gussie and me for an explanation.

A rye bread.

A dozen *rugelach*.

A square of halvah wrapped in butcher's paper.

"Sesame candy," Aunt Gussie explained. "Very good. Very rich. Not that I eat sweets so much."

Miriam nudged Ashley. "She don't eat right, never mind just sweets."

"What, don't eat right?"

Miriam ignored that. "It wouldn't hurt you should eat a little of this," she told Ashley. "Put a little meat on your bones."

I cringed and pretended not to hear. Ashley only smiled. She was still intent on unpacking food.

At the bottom of one of the bags was a cooler filled with ice. A cooler! Brought on a bus from Washington, stashed in a guest room overnight! Inside was cream cheese and lox, a whitefish, a container of gefilte fish, another of chopped liver, a thermos of chicken noodle soup.

"We thought you can't buy these things in Chapel Hill," Miriam said.

"I'll say." Susan sounded delighted, as if she'd been yearning for such treats all her life.

I began to feel ashamed of feeling ashamed. I pulled out a Tupperware container, lifted the top. "Not *flumen*. Oh, Miriam, not *flumen!*"

"*Nu?* What's wrong with *flumen?*" Miriam turned to Ashley and Susan. "Stewed prunes and raisins. Also little of the juice. Very good to keep you regular."

"I'm surprised you didn't make matzoh balls and farfel," I joked nervously.

"What do you expect from two days' cooking?" Miriam asked. So: she and Aunt Gussie had been cooking ever since they'd learned I was going to Susan's for Thanksgiving. "No farfel," Miriam said, "but look—you'll be satisfied with this." She brought out a casserole dish from the cooler, lifted the top. The scent of cinnamon wafted up. "Kugel."

"Noodle pudding," Gussie explained. "Raisins, cream cheese, sour cream. Very fattening."

Again, Miriam reached for Ashley's arm. "You could use

it." She wrapped her thick fingers around Ashley's wrist bone, feeling its frailness.

Ashley giggled.

Gussie pointed to Susan's clock. "We got to go."

"Already?" Ashley asked.

"I'll come with you to the bus," I said.

"No, we go by taxi. You stay here," Miriam ordered. "You'll get some girls together. Eat. It shouldn't spoil."

There was no point arguing. They let me walk them as far as the low stone wall at the edge of the quad, to help them carry their suitcases.

"This was the Ashley who's getting married?" Miriam asked as we waited for the cab.

"What other Ashley did you meet, Miriam?" Gussie asked. "What do you think?"

Miriam shook her head sadly. "Blonde," she said. "Very frail."

Gussie nodded. "Too young." A chipmunk ran in and out of an opening in the low stone wall, but neither sister noticed. "Five years from now she could marry, it would be soon enough."

"Not even out of school," Miriam added, eyeing me. "A pretty girl, too. I don't want you should get any ideas."

The exchange seemed rehearsed, a stand-up comic act. The Two Sisters from Slobotsky. They couldn't be the task-masters I'd imagined last night. Maybe, after all, the only reason they'd come to Chapel Hill was to feed me.

Back inside, Ashley and I set out platters in the kitchen while Susan spread the word we were having an impromptu brunch. In minutes, girls began appearing from all over the dorm. Donna Manning stuck a big wad of lox in her mouth, squealed, and spit it into her hand.

"Don't eat it straight. Look." I made her a cream cheese and lox sandwich on a bagel. I opened the jar of horseradish Miriam had brought to go with the gefilte fish. If Miriam and

190

Gussie had seemed foreign before, now I was the foreigner. Instead of being embarrassed, I enjoyed it. I was the hostess. I was serving international cuisine.

"They look like meatballs, but they're fish?" Penny Blankenship eyed the gefilte fish and wrinkled her nose. "And you eat them cold? I'll pass."

"It's an acquired taste," Marilyn Adler observed in her small voice, as she came into the door.

"Try the *flumen,*" Susan said to Penny. I was surprised she remembered the word.

Penny looked into the bowl. "Ugh. Prunes."

"It'll keep you regular." Susan winked at me.

The bagels and challah were a big hit, and especially the kugel. Reaction was mixed to the halvah, and there was a general aversion to the whitefish.

"It's something you have to grow up with," I said. "Like okra."

"I thought you liked okra, Beryl."

"Fried, yes. But the other night when they boiled it? Ugh. Like boiled slime."

"An interesting perspective," someone said.

About halfway through the feast, Emily Moses appeared in the doorway, curious. We'd all been waiting for her, somehow. The kitchen was directly across from her room.

I held my breath. "Come on in," said Marilyn. "Try this." She held out a piece of rye bread spread with chopped liver. No one objected. No one moved. Emily tasted and chewed.

"Reminds me of something," she said finally.

"Chitlings," said a voice.

Emily smiled, not insulted. "Maybe so. What else you got?"

"Halvah, *gefilte* fish, kugel." Ashley pointed. Susan pronounced the words with a flourish. Someone handed Emily a paper plate. "Be careful of the *flumen.*"

By the time we'd cleaned up, I was tired and content. I found myself humming the strains of "Blue Velvet" as I walked back to our room. It didn't dawn on me until later that Gussie and Miriam must have brought their elaborate, ethnic feast not to make me popular with my dormmates, but to remind me who I was.

16

David and I were fighting every evening. We argued about his moodiness. About his abrupt about-face on civil rights issues. His frequent presence in front of Packard's. He began to make fun of my haircut and my clothes. If I got a good grade on a test, he reminded me I was only a freshman and freshman classes were easy. I told him the only reason he picketed was to goad me. He told me I was paranoid.

"If it offends you, don't come by," he said. "Don't watch."

"I try not to." After all, nonviolence bred violence; it led to going to jail for no good reason, to being a public fool. Hadn't we discussed this many times? Our relationship was like cloth being shredded, a Band-Aid being pulled off so slowly it took skin and hair. "Believe me, it doesn't become you, wedging signs against your arm so they make bruises. Who are you trying to be, some holy wounded martyr?"

"On the contrary."

"Not to mention that I think your motives are a little

suspect." Goosebumps erupted on my arms, but I kept my voice even. "It's clear who you're trying to hurt. Yourself. Your chances for getting into law school. When did you become a masochist?"

"Drop it, Beryl," he said.

"No. It's clear who you're hurting. The question is, who are you helping?"

"The whole Negro race," he replied blandly.

"Not that I can see."

He leaned close, fixed me in the spell of his onyx eyes. "You don't think so? Let me tell you about it. Remember when you were ten and you got sick and your mother told you you go to sleep, when you woke up it'd be all better? Every morning I wake up and for a second I'm ten years old again, getting out of bed with two good legs."

"Great, the polio lecture again." I tensed, but David brushed my cheek lightly with the back of his hand, a parody of the gesture I remembered as endearment.

"Then I almost fall flat on my face," he said, moving away. "Every morning."

A ripple of tension ran through his face as the muscles in his jaw worked, but his tone was flat. "That's when I remember. I was born too soon to swallow vaccine in a sugar cube. I went to the wrong swimming pool on the wrong day. Well, hell, that's the breaks. Bad luck. I'm never going to wake up being able to use both legs." He didn't move, didn't blink. "And this is why I picket—because people like Emily Moses are never going to wake up white."

"How cryptic, David."

"Not cryptic at all."

"Why didn't you picket before, then? Why now? Just to make me angry?"

"I picketed all last summer. I stopped for a while because of you. I was wrong. Don't be an asshole, Beryl."

I began to see no future for us, and it was like being

pushed out of a plane without a parachute. An adrenaline rush in all the limbs. A sense of free-falling. Flashes of our little life together in pieces. I hated him, but I couldn't stand to lose him.

Practically everything I'd done with him was a first. The hours I'd spent alone in his house at the risk of being expelled from school. The long stretches of not-quite-consummated sex. The way I'd learned to drink just enough beer to get a buzz without getting drunk or losing control—a lesson mastered not in Harry's, where I was underage, but from the six-packs in David's refrigerator, black and gold cans lined up neatly on a shelf, next to an opened package of Arm and Hammer baking soda. All my life when I thought of drinking beer, that's what I'd remember.

Every night after I got back to the dorm, and in the daytime in my classes, I thought about David more than I ever had when we weren't fighting. He became an obsessive vision. Walking across campus beneath the bare old trees, or sitting in Graham Memorial deep into my chemistry book, suddenly my concentration would wane; I would conjure up his image, he would be all I could see. The crispness would vanish from my mind and I would be left shaking.

Irritating as he was in front of Packard's Sandwich Shop, in private David was a league apart from the high school boys who'd once fumbled under my sweaters in the backs of cars. He knew more than they did, and he was kinder. Each night, he took off the clothes above my waist and groped inside my underpants, but never insisted I take them off. He invited me to his bedroom but accepted my refusal graciously. He lay with me on his lumpy living room couch, kissing and stroking so expertly that I was always surprised to open my eyes and find us flanked by John F. Kennedy on the wall above us and Ivan on the floor below.

Here was the measure of David's patience: It wasn't until November, when we were deep into our fights, that he guided my hand to his crotch, so slowly and smoothly that I never realized I was supposed to have thought of this myself. I thought I would faint, but I didn't let go. My stomach actually seemed to turn over. I was holding a *man's penis*. It was wrong, but amazing. He slid his hands between my legs. For a full hour, he made not a single sarcastic remark.

That was the sweetest chapter we wrote, the one I didn't want to let go of, even as I felt myself careening closer and closer to the uprushing ground.

Our relationship kept deteriorating. David went to public-accommodations meetings—the very thing he'd once made fun of!—and told me about them with a wicked smile. Unlike the Noble Downtrodden my family was always trying to help, he seemed angry at me for being better off than he was. He seemed proud of making me feel guilty. He wielded his help-lessness like a weapon.

His bad leg. His crutches. The fact that he was followed around by a maniacally friendly dog. The more he picketed, the more he left Ivan tied up in the yard so the dog wouldn't jump on some stranger again and attract the renewed attention of the police. I'm picketing, he'd seem to say. You aren't. I've tied up my dog, which he hates, which *I* hate, to answer this noble calling. What are you doing to earn your keep in the world? He touched the little sore spot over and over again; he jabbed and jabbed.

I did go to one meeting with him, about Marilyn and Emily and their battle with the dean of women. I felt obligated to be there not because of David but because the girls were dormmates, compatriots. Both of them had been campused for a week because of the illegal move. This was nothing serious, nothing they couldn't live with. The meeting was not a call to action, just an update on their situation.

David and I stood in line, waiting for someone to show up with a key to the vacant office where the meeting was to be held. There must have been nearly thirty of us. A couple of boys walked by, one of them from my chemistry class. As he took in the scene—girls with long hair, boys in unfashionable flannel shirts—his eyes raked across me, pausing in recognition. He said to his friend, indicating all of us in general: "Beatniks." I felt dirty, unkempt.

Inside, Marilyn reported in her small thread of a voice that her parents had come to Chapel Hill to defend her actions. She told us the dean of women had made a rule that, from now on, white students would need parental permission slips signed in advance if they wanted to move in with a Negro.

The Negro did not need a similar permission slip to live with a white.

"They didn't report this in the *Daily Tar Heel*," someone said.

"It doesn't matter," Emily assured him.

"Doesn't matter!" a voice cried. "Sure it does!"

"We should have a demonstration at the dean's office," a boy suggested.

"Good idea," David agreed. He turned to me, smiled, his eyes daring me to protest.

The room felt warm and prickly. I could feel the tension building. "I'll meet you at Harry's," I said. The advantage of dating someone on crutches was, it was easy to stalk off and leave him behind.

Tripp and Gloria were already at a table when I came in. They hadn't been at the meeting. They looked preoccupied, perhaps the aftermath of a fight. Instead of talking nonstop, Tripp was studying the menu and Gloria was studying the tabletop. They looked up idly and motioned me to join them. Stuart came in and took the seat beside me.

"I'm solo tonight, as you'll notice," he said. "Marilyn's got a waiting list to see her." His voice was thick with pride. Tripp and Gloria said nothing. I felt I had to respond.

"The romance sounds hot and heavy," I told him.

"Yours, too?" He took out a cigarette and tapped it on the table.

"Not really. David and I don't agree on very much—or haven't you noticed?"

Stuart lit up and leaned toward me, big-brotherly, the math scholar enamored of psychology courses. "It doesn't have to be that way, if you care about him. You could start agreeing."

"Even if I don't? No, thanks."

Tripp glanced from one of us to the other like a blind man following sound, not really seeing either of us. Gloria glanced at Tripp and then back down at the table, her face tight as if she were trying not to cry.

"What difference does it make in the end?" Stuart asked. "You want to end up washing his dishes, right?"

"Wrong. My mother didn't want that, either." I waved away his cigarette smoke.

Stuart smiled and pointed at me. He laughed. "Got you going, didn't I?"

Tripp took Gloria's hand. She let him hold it. Maybe they were making up after their disagreement. "Don't mind David," he said to me, pulling Gloria's hand closer to him. "He's finding himself, that's all."

"Finding himself, hell," I said. "He blames the whole world because he got polio and it made him a cripple." I nodded toward Gloria. "You might think he was always that way, but I don't believe it."

She shrugged, aimless, distracted.

To Tripp I said, "How can you say he's finding himself? Anyone twenty-three years old and getting ready to go to law school is found."

"Who told you that?"

"That he was found?"

"That he was going to law school," Tripp said.

"David told me himself. He's taking a couple of courses so he can go next year."

Tripp let go of Gloria's hand, and both of them focused on my face.

"Well, isn't he?" I asked.

"Not that I know of," Tripp said.

"Not that you know of?" I stared from one to the other. Tripp shrugged. Stuart stubbed his cigarette out, paying strict attention to the ashtray. The sense of falling overtook me again. "I guess this explains why I never see him on campus anymore," I said.

No one spoke.

"Why the books on his shelves are always lined up so neatly." I spun downward toward fields, roads, an entire universe. I couldn't believe all of them were sitting there so passively.

"He dropped out after the first month of school this year," Gloria said weakly.

"And now what does he do?" I asked.

"He has that job in the psych department," Stuart said. "You knew that."

"That's *all?*" My voice rose a notch, a squeaky treble.

Tripp set his minister's features into a calm-in-the-face-of-crisis pose. "His parents send him some money," he said.

"The parents he never goes home to see?" I screamed. "Why would he lie to me about school?"

"He lies to everybody," Gloria said. She'd grown pale. Embarrassed by my yelling? Guilty for not telling me the truth? "That's how he is," she said. "He always lied."

I turned to Stuart. "He lies to everybody—and you don't set me straight?" Rage pounded at my temples like a dark fist, canceling out my sense of falling. "I've known you ever since I can remember, and you don't say a word?"

"I didn't know you didn't know," Stuart mumbled.

"If it's general knowledge that he lies to *everybody*—"

"He would have told you sooner or later," Tripp said, low. Gloria's mouth set itself into a tight, chapped line, as if she were in pain. They all looked away, even Stuart, afraid I'd make a scene. Weren't these the very people who loved scenes the most? Why the sudden silence?

I opened my mouth to protest, angry enough to sputter. But everyone's attention slid past me, toward the front door. When I turned around, David was hobbling toward the table.

"Lying bastard," I said before he was close enough to hear.

Gloria reached over and clutched my wrist. "Beryl. Come to the bathroom with me."

I didn't look at her. I faced David.

Gloria dug her fingernails into me. "Beryl. Please. *Now.*"

She stood, still holding my wrist. I didn't understand why she was so intent on distracting me. I shifted my attention from David to her face. It was knuckle-white.

"What's wrong? Are you okay?"

"No."

She clung to me. If she was sick, she was also strong; she pulled me with her toward the ladies room, making nail marks in my wrist. She didn't let go until the door closed behind us.

"What is it?"

In answer, she disappeared into one of the stalls and moaned.

"Gloria!"

Her feet shuffled beneath the door, then stopped in front of the toilet, facing out. Dirty saddle oxfords. White socks. Her skirt dropped and hid the shoes. She must have pulled it down. Pulled it *down?*

"I can't help you if you don't tell me," I said.

"I think I'm having a miscarriage."

"My God!"

She made another sound, almost a grunt. It echoed the

moan of demons and the God who'd struck down Bubby Tsippi. My throat clutched tight as if I'd swallowed a stone.

"I'll call an ambulance," I said when I could speak.

"*No.*"

I started to go out anyway. Gloria grunted again, and something splashed into the toilet. Not a gush, no normal bathroom sound, not diarrhea or vomit. Just a single, undignified plop.

"Gloria?" I rattled the door. "Gloria!"

"I'm all right."

"What happened?"

I heard her pull off toilet paper, heard her arranging herself, saw the bottom of her skirt rise. The door to the stall swung open. She stood beside the toilet, looking in. She pointed.

The water was tinged red. In the middle was a deeper red mess. An object. It might have been a turd or a blood clot. A strand of toilet paper swirled to the side.

"How far along were you?" I asked.

"Five weeks."

We looked at the thing floating in the water. Gloria seemed mesmerized, transfixed.

"I was having cramps and spotting all day." She didn't avert her eyes from the toilet. "Finally I just couldn't stay home." Her voice was flat and disengaged. "Tripp said let's go to Harry's. It was the only thing we could think of."

She stared into the bloody water longer than I thought she should. I put my arm around her shoulder to lead her off. She shrugged me loose. She bent over, stuck her hand into the water, and plucked the bloody wad from the toilet. She held it over the bowl, dripping.

"Gloria, don't—"

She examined it; she didn't respond.

"Gloria, don't be—" But I was studying it, too. It was not much bigger than her thumb.

She held it for a long time. I let her. I watched. Then she turned and held it out to me.

Flinching, I closed my hand around it. Beneath the slime of blood, it was not soft but surprisingly tough. The consistency of a chicken gizzard. The likeness didn't disgust me. It just—was.

An expression of sadness and resignation crossed Gloria's face. She placed the mass carefully back in the toilet. She looked at it a while and then flushed it down.

She washed her hands and I washed mine. We didn't speak. Her hands were slick and soapy when she started shivering. A little shudder at first, then all over, as if she had a fever. I put my hand to her forehead. It was moist and cool. Still trembling, she rinsed her hands and dried them. She locked her jaw, clenched her teeth. She was shaking all over.

She laughed a little, embarrassed. "Nerves, I guess. They say it catches up with you after."

I put my arm around her again. "You're cold," I said. I was no doctor, I wasn't even Susan, but I knew fear, I knew shock. I gathered her to me, and when she didn't resist, I opened the door and led her out of the restroom.

The bustle of the restaurant seemed exceptionally noisy, the lights unnaturally bright. I held her tight, thinking she might fall, but her step was steady. By the time we reached our table, the trembling was a little less. She bent to Tripp and whispered, "I lost it. It's over."

Tripp leapt to his feet. The alarm on his face was unmistakable.

"What's wrong?" Stuart asked.

"She's sick," I told him.

Tripp circled her shoulders with his arm, clutched her hand tight. Gloria didn't speak.

"She has the chills," I said.

"I'll take her home," Tripp told us. "I'll get her under some covers."

"Hope you feel better," Stuart said.

"See you tomorrow," David called.

A bloodstain on the back of Gloria's skirt shifted back and forth with the fabric as she walked away, a jagged oval, not new blood, old and dry. The fabric was green, not dark. The blood must have been there from earlier. David and Stuart saw nothing. They turned back to the table, business as usual.

I remained standing. David reached out to draw me into a chair. I pulled away.

"I can explain," he said.

"About what?"

"About not being in school."

Stuart got out another cigarette, interested.

"You can't."

David patted the chair next to him. I looked through the glass window and focused on a streetlight so the room would stop spinning, so I could walk without swaying. And by the time I got myself to the front door and out, I knew I'd never set foot in Harry's again.

17

I walked, stunned and aimless, for more than an hour. Past Graham Memorial, past the Old Well. I kept seeing the patch of blood on the back of Gloria's skirt, jagged and dark like an ink blot on the Rorschach test, and the grisly wad of tissue in my hand. I had witnessed—what? Another death.

And David. Lying to me all along. I wasn't entirely surprised.

I took off my jacket, amazed that the North Carolina weather could be so warm and balmy in November, even if only for a few hours. I wandered past Wilson Library, past the Bell Tower, into the woods beside the stadium. A sliver of moon cast everything into stark shadow. No one was about. It was seventy degrees, maybe more. Under my clothes, I was slick with sweat.

On the way back, I remembered I'd been warned against walking through the arboretum alone at night, but I did. I didn't care what happened. In a single night, what were the odds? Nothing made sense. If a baby was that easy to lose, why not Ashley instead of Gloria? Why should the earth mother miscarry? The married fertility goddess who could have cared for a child?

Inside the parlor, bright light shattered my vision like a blow to the head. Seeking dimness, I swung open the door to our hallway, and was greeted by a cacophony of noise, *Louie, Louie,* blaring from our room.

There was the usual crowd. Susan at the record player. Donna Manning from upstairs on Susan's bed, her roommate Nita on mine. In the middle of the floor Ashley sat with her elbow on her knee and her chin in her hand, a piece of notebook paper in front of her. She'd written down a few words, her version of the lyrics.

"Hey," Donna called.

"Sit down, Beryl."

"Come help us."

"I thought we were finished doing that," I said.

Susan shrugged.

"Play that part again," Ashley told her.

Susan lifted the needle and did.

A silence, then *Louie, Lou-aye,* mumble mumble mumble. Ashley strained to hear. I went to my closet, stripped off my sweaty clothes and dropped them in a heap. I put on my bathrobe. No one asked where I'd been.

Louie, Lou-AYE. When I'd left earlier, Ashley had been weeping because her father wouldn't speak to her on the phone. Now she shimmied her shoulders and mouthed the words as if she finally had them.

Enough! I wanted to shout. There was no deciphering those lyrics. The song was recorded in a garage, full of echoes, impossible to tell what was said. Why wasn't Ashley thinking about the baby she carried in her belly? About the South American boy whose parents were refusing to come to her wedding? About the possibility there might be no wedding at all?

Ashley kept time with her shoulders and jotted a few more notes, her head apparently empty as air. Hadn't I helped her down the hall many mornings? Hadn't I stood guard at the shower? Weren't we, somehow, kindred? Shouldn't she see I was upset?

"Turn it off," I said.

"Huh?"

No one even heard me. "Never mind."

I watched the rhythmic rise and fall of Ashley's shoulders and thought of Gloria shivering, of Tripp with his arm to her shoulder as he led her out.

Susan lifted the needle again. Ashley picked up her notebook paper with the words she'd written and laughed. "I don't have any more idea what they're saying now than before," she said. "Maybe Paco should have a go at this."

She was carefree, happy. In spite of all her emoting, she was moving implacably toward marriage–wasn't she? On every issue she cared about, she had given in. Paco was what she wanted, and if this was the way to get him, well–

"One more time," she said to Susan, who lowered the needle again and upped the volume.

I stalked out and headed for the shower. In the cheerful hubbub of the room, no one even heard me slam the door.

I didn't see David for two weeks, though he came to the dorm a couple of times looking for me. I avoided Harry's. I asked Marilyn how Gloria was, and she told me she was all right. The whole Harry's crowd knew what had happened, everyone always did. Gloria was lucky, she said. She never had much bleeding. Never needed to see a doctor. "You know how much Gloria hates doctors."

I wished I could complain about David's treachery to someone—to Susan and Ashley in particular. "He's not even in school!" I wanted to say. "He lied to me straight out!"

But the most I'd ever revealed about David, after Susan saw me get out of his car one night, was that he was in one of my study groups and always drove me home. My own brand of lie.

For balance on days when I felt myself falling apart, or falling out of the sky, or whatever I'd chosen to call it at the moment, I went out with Seth Pearlman, an admirer from the TEP house. We studied together; we ate dinner. But I couldn't work up much interest.

It didn't help that Ashley cried incessantly those two weeks. Almost every evening, phone calls went back and forth between Chapel Hill and Wilmington about Paco's parents and the wedding. Paco's father refused to come, absolutely. His mother was vacillating. In an effort to move matters along, Ashley's mother called New York for a woman-to-woman chat. She reported afterwards that Paco's mother was polite but distant, and that her thick accent was almost impossible to understand.

Would Paco go through with the marriage if his parents remained adamant? Would the arrangements for Ashley's dress ever be completed? For Paco's tux? For the florist? Would Ashley ever find a job for next semester? And where, oh, where, would the newlyweds live? As the soap opera continued, I saw it ever more from a distance, locked as I was in mid-flight, plummeting toward the ground.

Seeing Ashley's distress, one of her friends lent her a car so she could search for an apartment on afternoons when Paco was still in class. The first place she found was so far out of town they'd need two cars. The next would have been fine except that a friend clued them the heat didn't work. The third was perfect, sunny and inexpensive, until the widow who owned it took one look at Paco and said it was no longer on the market.

Ashley returned with her face puffed and red. "She didn't want him because he was a foreigner! Can you believe it?" She burst into tears anew.

What planet had she been living on? Hadn't she ever heard of discrimination? Hadn't she been watching Emily Moses? Perfect teardrops clung to her lashes. Susan handed her a tissue. I turned away. For all the little glitches, Ashley's life was on course toward a predictable future. I, on the other hand, was about to crash any second. I hadn't seen David; I hadn't even caught a glimpse of Ivan. I was falling through air so thin that a constant harshness nagged the base of my throat, as if my tonsils were being massaged by sandpaper.

Compared to that, what was a little uncertainty? A little morning sickness? Whatever happened to Romeo and Juliet?

They did find an apartment. They did rent Paco's tux and decide on a florist. Ashley's mother drove up and took her to Raleigh to shop. Ashley wore a gray wool skirt and melon-colored sweater, accented by gray high heels and purse. At Belk's, she chose patterns for china and crystal. She selected silver and everyday glasses. She picked out a pattern for the wedding dress a seamstress in Wilmington would make, the woman who wouldn't fit it until Ashley was home for Thanksgiving, to leave a little room for expansion. Except for a few variations, it was every wedding in the world.

Each day, faithfully, Ashley went for instruction at the Catholic Church. She spoke of catechism and rosary beads, of saints and occasions of sin. I didn't know what most of these terms meant. Ashley didn't explain, but she talked on as if everyone understood.

"Now that I'm schooled in Catholic doctrine, I'll be guilty of sin whenever I do something the Church says is wrong, whether I know it or not," she intoned.

"Sure, Ashley, even if you don't know you're doing it." I hadn't grown up in the Rosinsky household for nothing. I knew religious mumbo-jumbo when I heard it.

"Oh, yes, Father Zimmer explained it," Ashley said. "If you say a thing's okay when it isn't, you're responsible for the bad action because you should have had a right conscience."

She hadn't heard my sarcasm; she was perfectly sincere. "The point is, I should have known, I could have known," she continued.

Her words hit me hard. They were my mother's words exactly, when she'd come to Chapel Hill to tell me I should have known about the gag law that barred my father from speaking on campus. If Ashley was right, then I also should have known the difference between a meat dish and a milk dish last summer. But I hadn't. What kind of law would hold a person responsible despite her ignorance? Could an innocent mistake warrant burning in hell forever? I wasn't sure what religion God was, Catholic or Jewish or Baptist, but whatever the case, I didn't believe He would be so unforgiving.

Ashley looked at herself in the mirror so absently that I knew she wasn't assessing her physical appearance, only her spiritual one. Her expression was dreamy, stoic, noble. She looked exactly the way she had straining to hear the words of "Louie Louie."

I ran into David again finally on a chilly, sober-looking Friday. I'd spent the week taking midterms, filling up one blue book after another. Walking back to the dorm after a ten o'clock quiz, I ran into Penny Blankenship, who asked me if I wanted to drive out to Eastgate shopping center to pick up her cleaning. The football game against Duke was coming up, and her sorority was working on a float for the "Beat Dook" parade. She wanted to run her errands before she joined her friends.

I was so stunned that Penny wanted to spend time with me that I said yes. Besides, after all those tests I was glad for a chance to get off campus. I didn't say I had an abiding interest in dry cleaning establishments, or that I always compared my father's store with those of his competitors. When we arrived at Eastgate, I looked through the window to whitewashed walls and slow-moving circular racks of garments, swishing along at the push of a button. The set-up was more elaborate than anything the Rosinskys had ever owned. I couldn't make myself go in. I leaned against the hood of the car and said I'd wait.

The moment Penny left, David came out of the hardware store. His hair was longer than before, flopping onto his forehead. He hadn't shaved. David Lazar disheveled? Because of our breakup? I considered slipping into Penny's car to hide. I tried to think of a snub. Instead, I was so overcome by my sense of moving at terrible speed that I leaned harder against the hood to stop the motion.

David hobbled over. "I came to the dorm," he said. "Twice."

"I know."

"How've you been?"

"Fine."

"I wanted to explain—about not being in school." His voice was hoarse with what I thought was emotion until I realized he had a cold. His nose looked red from rubbing.

"There's nothing to say," I told him.

"Maybe not."

Neither of us seemed capable of more than short, clipped, phrases. We stood in silence as a woman walked by and David stepped back to let her pass. I followed him onto the sidewalk. We leaned against the brick wall between the dry cleaner's and the hardware store.

"I just didn't think that was who you were," I said.

"A non-student?"

"A liar."

"Who did you think I was—Joe College?" He gave an uneasy, infected-sounding guffaw. "Joe College is a guy who, if he drops out, has to worry about the draft." He rattled his crutches. "As you see, that's not one of my problems."

"Don't, David."

We looked out beyond the shopping center to a distant rise of trees against the clouds. The pretty maples had already shed their leaves, and the foliage on the remaining trees was brown and dead-looking. We surveyed the metal sky, the pavement beneath us, the tops of our feet. My right Weejun was scuffed, a long streak of burgundy finish rubbed off entirely. I struck a pose so only the left shoe would show. "Where's Ivan?" I asked.

"No longer with us."

"What do you mean—*no longer with us?*" I crossed my arms.

"Just that."

"Cute, David."

"You know how he hated to be tied up," he said. "I probably should have given him away as soon as the police got interested."

"What did he do? Run away?"

"Remember how warm it was on Wednesday? I tied him in the yard. I was only gone a couple hours." He looked across the pavement and spoke to the fender of the car. "He hung himself on the rope," he whispered.

I didn't believe him; I hated when he played for sympathy. I straightened up and pulled my face into a frown.

"I think he was just trying to get loose," he said, his voice gravelly and nasal. "He hadn't been dead that long. He was still warm."

"Hey, y'all," Penny said, coming out of the cleaners. We said hey but didn't move. Penny stood at the side of my vision, clean skirts draped over her arm, encased in transparent plastic bags.

"You coming?" she asked me.

"Go on ahead," I said.

I stared at David until I made him look up. His eyes were bloodshot and swimmy. "Is this true?" I asked.

Penny opened her car door, laid her skirts in the back seat.

"I wish it wasn't," David murmured.

Penny closed her car door. "See you later!"

We watched her back up. I closed the gap that separated us and curled my hand around his fingers on the handgrip of his crutch. David's face was so taut he might have been grinding his teeth. Finally, he pulled me in to him, crutch and all, and I wasn't free-falling, I was perfectly suspended.

His house was so neat it felt empty, felt like you could locate any given item by touch without bumping into another one en route, felt like the gray light coming through the windows had painted the walls and lit the mood. A blanket tucked around the corners of the couch hid the holes Ivan had chewed. The little rug Ivan always slept on was gone.

When I looked closer, I saw the neatness was deceptive. A fine layer of dust covered the tidy shelves, tidbits of paper and crumbs littered the floor. In the kitchen someone had spilled Coke and made only a halfhearted swipe to mop it up. Dried liquid clung to the linoleum in crusty patches, an uneven bruise, different shades of dark.

Usually I was there at night. Maybe the place was always like this, neat but not really clean. I didn't think so. I thought I was seeing the result of neglect. David's house had never felt so unlike the sugar shack in the song, so sour and sad.

"Want a beer?" David asked.

It was barely lunchtime. I shook my head. Heat radiated out from the space heater in the middle of the room. Close to the heater it was too hot; farther away in the kitchen, too cold.

"Come to the bedroom?" David asked. His standard invitation. I always refused.

"Sure," I said. "Why not?" I didn't care that he'd lied to me about being in school. If I couldn't bring Ivan back, maybe I should try to fill up the house the only way I could.

David didn't move.

"Well?" I asked.

"Wait a minute."

He went into the bathroom and ran the water a long time. He came out shaved. It seemed an odd, false thing to do. He smelled of some new, strong cologne. I guessed it was too late to change my mind. He took my hand and led me toward the bedroom. Except for my one short glimpse of it on my first visit, I'd had only a view of the closed door. When he opened it after all that time, I expected something grand.

The room was as neat and bare as the rest of the place, white chenille spread pulled carefully over a double bed, not even a throw rug on the floor. I imagined David getting up on cold mornings, with the space heater a whole room away, his good foot shocked into winter the minute he stood.

There was a chair. A dresser. No mirror. In a far corner was a weight bench, the only surprise. A barbell hung on a rack above it. Different-sized weights were stacked beside it on the floor. The first time I'd met him, before he ever stood up, I'd thought David was a weight-lifter. Then I'd seen his crutches and assumed his strength came from hefting his own bulk. The weight bench cheapened that somehow. It was like discovering another lie, finding out he'd gotten his thick arms and bulky chest in the most common, most traditional way.

David was patient; I expected no less. It took us maybe an hour to do what we did, and we did a lot. I liked what led up to it, but not as much as usual because I knew what was coming. I didn't like the grand finale much. The first time, girls didn't, I'd been told. Not that it hurt. And not that there was very much blood. Because there wasn't. It was just that once he got inside and the scary part was over, I couldn't concentrate enough to get beyond the mess that was running through my mind.

This is it, I thought. Goodbye, virginity. I opened my eyes. Nothing was right. We weren't on the couch. Ivan wasn't watching and John F. Kennedy wasn't smiling down from the wall. The weight bench gleamed metallic in the corner. Beneath the strong scent of David's aftershave, his too-long hair smelled greasy.

He moved up and down, up and down. I was naked and David wasn't, which seemed unfair. He had taken off his shirt, but not his pants. He'd pulled them down just a little, just enough. I knew why. He didn't want me to see his bare leg. I lay beneath him and imagined him nude. Imagined the leg uncovered beside me, heavy but shriveled, pale from never being in the sun, covered with fine black hairs. I felt almost tender toward it. Engaged as we were in the most intimate possible act, I'd have to accept his infirmity completely. But how could I accept what I couldn't see? As long as his leg was covered and hidden away, it was as dead to me as the weights in the corner of the room.

David seemed to take forever. Up and down, up and down, like pushups. Then he swallowed hard, close to my ear, and it was finally over.

We left the bedroom as soon as I got dressed. He asked me again if I wanted a beer.

"I haven't even had lunch," I told him. He didn't offer

lunch. There was such an empty feeling in that house, it was impossible to imagine anyone sitting down there to eat a meal.

He drove me slowly to the dorm. We watched the bleak landscape. We didn't talk. There was nothing to say. Maybe what we'd both wanted was not each other, but the departed cheerfulness of a dead dog. I was no longer suspended. I clutched the armrest and heard the wind as I fell.

David walked me all the way to the parlor, ceremonial, though it was the middle of the afternoon. The sky had grown darker, and a soberness hung in the air. In the distance, bells were ringing in the Bell Tower. They didn't usually, at this time of day. They made the day seem bleaker. The ringing stopped.

If it's not for real, my mother always said, you'll feel cheap. I supposed what I felt wasn't gloom or unnatural soberness. It was just cheapness. I was cheap.

Ashley was sitting on her bed by the window, looking out. She was crying. The radio was on, so soft the announcer sounded like background noise. What could her problem be now? Another job interview gone bad? Paco's mother recalcitrant? I wasn't sure I had the energy to care.

"I guess you heard," she said, not turning. Silhouetted in the window, in the gray light, her wet lashes seemed transparent.

"Heard what?"

"The president was shot."

It didn't register. I took my coat off and draped it over a chair. "What?"

"The president."

President of the school? "President Friday?"

"President Kennedy." She rose and turned up the radio.

I heard the words *Dallas* and *motorcade.*

"He's dead," Ashley said. "They killed him."

"Oh, no! The *president?*"

I listened in disbelief. Shot in the head. Rushed to the

hospital. Pronounced dead. The radio announcer repeated it twice. I knew I'd be hearing it the rest of my life.

I ran out of the dorm and caught David halfway to his car. He spun around but didn't look pleased to see me. "What?"

"President Kennedy's been shot."

Anger flashed in his eyes. "I don't believe you."

Tit for tat.

"It's true. I didn't believe it, either. But it's true."

We stood next to the low stone wall at the edge of the quad. I told him what I'd heard. For a while we didn't move or speak. I hadn't put my coat back on, and we stood there long enough to get cold.

David said, "While we were fooling around, he was dying."

"Yes."

"Shit." His jaw worked the way it always did when he was getting angry.

"What's the matter?"

"Shit," he said again. His gaze was malevolent. "Poor David, he lost his dog. Thought you'd give me a little Southern comfort, didn't you? The guy tied up his dog, but hell, let's be a little forgiving, make him feel better. The guy's a cripple, after all."

"What's being crippled got to do—"

"Don't give me that. I left Ivan in the yard so I could picket at Packard's. So I could fool around." He spat the words. "That's what you'd call it, isn't it? Fooling around."

So: he'd been picketing the day Ivan died. Fooling around while Ivan struggled so hard to get out of his bonds that he hung himself. And fooling around in bed with me while Kennedy died. As if they were one and the same.

"You little bitch," he said.

He glared at me as if I were responsible for everything. His knuckles were white, his eyes black and hateful. If his hands had been free of his crutches, he surely would have hit me. But I didn't flinch, I held his gaze. By the time he finally turned and walked away, I knew Miriam and Aunt Gussie were wrong. The reason I shouldn't see David wasn't because he was a cripple. It was because he was a jerk.

18

The weekend passed in a blur. The "Beat Dook" parade was canceled. So was the game itself. Friday night most of the girls in the dorm broke their dates and went home, or else sat with the rest of us around the television in the parlor. Everyone seemed to be moving in slow motion or talking in whispers.

Over and over, we watched the film of the president's motorcade inching through the streets of Dallas. Over and over, we saw him slump, saw dignified Jackie crawl over the back seat of the convertible in search of help.

Sitting in front of the TV, several pairs of roommates actually joined hands as the fateful moment replayed.

We went through boxes of tissues. We watched Lyndon Johnson take his oath on the plane. We cried for Jackie, the young widow standing beside the ungainly new president.

Despite what had happened to me earlier that day, I didn't think of David.

Everyone called home, even those who hated Kennedy and everything he stood for. We lined up, polite and courteous, to use the phones that would briefly connect us with the comfort of our families. Without being asked, we all kept our conversations short.

"In this country, you wouldn't think such a thing could happen," Miriam said.

"A terrible thing," Dad echoed.

My mother took the phone. "Beryl, are you okay?"

"Sure. Are you?"

"Listen," she said. "You're never all right after these things. Not at first. But soon you are. These tragedies are exactly what precipitate change."

"I know, Mom." Even when she was trying to offer comfort, it sounded like a political speech.

"Beryl, do you want to come home? They say the body will lie in state. You could go with us to pay respects. You'd only miss a few days of school before Thanksgiving."

"I can't," I blurted. I wasn't prepared for this. "I mean, I told Susan I'd come to Winston-Salem. Her parents are expecting me."

"You wouldn't have to sleep in your room," she offered.

"Mom, it's not that. It's—"

"I know. You feel honor-bound to go. I know the feeling."

But I didn't feel honor-bound. I just didn't feel like facing her. Yet if she'd insisted, I would have gone.

Emily Moses left to spend the weekend with her family in Greensboro. People asked where she was. No one had done that before. But now, considering Kennedy's position on civil rights, her absence made us feel incomplete.

On Sunday, girls wandered in and out of the TV parlor throughout the morning and early afternoon. They washed underwear, read a few pages of history, then came in to check on the TV coverage of the throngs waiting to file past the President's body in the Capitol rotunda. I tried to find my family in the crowd but couldn't.

I was sitting on the couch, feeling lonely and wounded, when the cameras pulled away from the scene in D.C. to show Lee Harvey Oswald being brought out of jail to be transferred. I wasn't paying full attention. Then, as casually as if he had rehearsed, Jack Ruby stepped out of the crowd and shot Lee Harvey Oswald dead.

At first no one was sure what we were seeing. Most of us were too dazed to register another murder. When we did, the horror started all over again.

By Wednesday, when Susan and I loaded our luggage into Penny Blankenship's car for the drive to Winston-Salem, any journey out of Chapel Hill, away from the nightmarish weekend and days that followed, would have seemed joyous and liberating.

The foothills around Chapel Hill grew steeper as we traveled west. Sun glistened on the bare trees, and the sky grew the exact Carolina blue of the T-shirts they sold on Franklin Street. Less than two hours later we were in Winston-Salem, and it really did feel like Thanksgiving.

Susan's house sat on a hill under big trees, exactly as I'd imagined, laced with ivy crawling up the brick to dormer windows on the second floor. Inside, her brother, Ned, was watching TV—a goofy, pleasant high school boy—and her mother was in the cinnamon-scented kitchen, covered with flour from pie crusts she was rolling. She looked down at her whitened bosom and laughed at herself, then wiped off as best she could and hugged us both.

Moments later she led us upstairs into a spacious bedroom with dormer windows, vaulted ceilings, and a window seat piled with old dolls and stuffed animals. There was flowered wallpaper—pink, with tiny white flowers—and bedspreads to match. It was the exact room every little girl wishes she could grow up in.

Mrs. Tillery brought me towels, showed me the bathroom, asked if I needed anything. At home, the task of showing strangers around had always been delegated to me and Natalie. Mother declared herself too busy. "If there's one thing you don't want, it's to end up forty years old with no personality because you're stuck making brownies and entertaining guests. Let's hope by then you'll have something more important to do." But Mrs. Tillery was so natural and unassuming that these remarks seemed not to apply.

Dr. Tillery didn't come home until dinner was ready. Mrs. Tillery held the meal another half hour while he drank a bourbon and 7-Up and started a second.

"He always needs a few minutes to relax," she declared.

The next day at Thanksgiving dinner, Dr. Tillery drank four glasses of wine with his meal and refused pumpkin pie. He had a final glass of wine instead, and then retreated to the den for a nap.

"He's not on call, for once," Mrs. Tillery explained. She shooed Ned away, although he hadn't actually offered to help us clean up. She and Susan and I did the dishes. Dr. Tillery woke up in time for the ball games on TV and a couple of beers. Colby Lee called long-distance in the middle of one of the games, but Susan shook her head and signaled Ned to say she wasn't home. Until then, I'd never thought she was such a keen sports fan, but she turned back to the TV and seemed engrossed. For supper we had leftover turkey sandwiches. Dr. Tillery picked at his food and sipped a whiskey sour, and I understood why Ashley's father had called the man a Whiskeypalian.

But I was enchanted. The next day, Susan went to a reception for her old piano teacher and Mrs. Tillery took me to Old Salem, a series of restored eighteenth-century houses built by the Moravian settlers on picturesque cobblestone streets. Most had been turned into shops.

Mrs. Tillery bought bayberry candles for her Christmas decorations while I found miniature soaps for Chanuka gifts. Guiltily, I envisioned myself coming downstairs from Susan's pink bedroom on Christmas morning, smelling bayberry and exclaiming over carefully wrapped gifts under the tree. I imagined *being* Susan. Except for Dr. Tillery's drinking, which in my mind fell short of being a drinking *problem,* the family was so uncontroversial, so ordinary, that I was filled with envy. I imagined myself as Susan the child, Susan growing up. I imagined how easy that would be.

Saturday night Susan borrowed her mother's car so we could go see Sidney Poitier in *Lilies of the Field* with three of her girlfriends. When we came into the door afterwards, Colby Lee was on the phone again. Again Susan signaled Ned not to let on she was there.

"I thought you liked him," I said as we started up the stairs.

"It's not that simple."

"Did something happen?"

She sprinted up the steps ahead of me, and I knew not to ask more questions.

In the room, I changed the subject as we started packing. Penny wanted to leave early the next morning to avoid church. I told Susan it had been a wonderful weekend. I told her I hated to go. I told her I loved her bedroom.

Susan looked surprised. "Do you? I haven't slept here for years except with company, but she still keeps it decorated the way it was when I was eight."

"This isn't your room when you're home for the summer?"

"No. That is." She pointed across the hall to what I'd assumed was a spare room, with a blue-green bedspread but no knicknacks. Why would anyone sleep there when they could have . . . this?

"You sleep in the guest room?"

"Sure. Well, actually, *this* is the guest room." She waved toward the flowered wallpaper, the window seat, the dormer windows.

I must have looked stricken.

Susan laughed. "I know. All this time you thought I was pink quilts and big-eyed girls holding kittens. When secretly I was tailored and teal."

I didn't say I'd been puzzled by her choices since the day we met, except the night she wore pink organdy to the Interfraternity Ball.

"I'll tell you a secret," she said. "I always let Mama pick out what I'm going to take to school. Good policy. Gives me leverage on bigger issues like pledging sorority."

I thought she was joking. "You'd be pledging right now if it weren't for Ashley."

"You thought I was a sorority type? Why? Because Penny seemed so shocked when I didn't rush?" She shook her head. "I never liked sororities. Even before."

I was dumbfounded. If my mother had chosen my bedspreads and throw rugs and paintings, and if I'd had to look at them every day instead of shoving them into some closet, emotionally I would have been forever Keane's little girl with the big eyes, sober and obedient. I could never have refused a sorority bid with pink shag under my feet, accusing me of defying tradition. Could never have endured Penny Blankenship's curiosity while reminders of my duties surrounded me twenty-four hours a day. I wondered if Susan's mother had helped her pick out the pink organdy dress she wore to the ball. No matter: Susan was right. She wasn't a pink person. She was spare, teal-colored, strong.

She grinned at what must have been the shock on my

face, and clicked shut the latch on her suitcase. "It's a maturity thing, Beryl. You seventeen-year-olds have no idea."

I lobbed my pillow at her. She caught it and threw it back. "See? A maturity thing." She pulled her suitcase from her bed to the floor, lugged it across the room.

Then she grew serious. "About Colby Lee," she said. "It's no big deal. It's just over."

"So I gathered. I just thought you liked him."

"I liked him. It wasn't a matter of that. It was a matter of—" She paused and drew a breath. "It's not that simple. Okay?"

She walked back to her bed, began to fluff a pillow the way Ashley did. "Daddy's not always the way he was this weekend," she said abruptly. "He doesn't drink a lot unless he's had a bad day. Being a doctor gets frustrating."

This was getting stranger and stranger. "No family is sterling," I told her. "Next vacation you can come to D.C. and witness the Rosinsky family foibles."

"Oh?" She perked up.

"Sure. My mother gives speeches and my father works a million hours a day because he's lousy at business. He used to be an architect until he lost his job and had to buy a dry cleaning store. Miriam had to move in to keep the house from falling apart."

"You're humoring me," she said.

"I'm not. He was investigated by the McCarthy committee. After it was over he got fired. It happened to a lot of people."

She frowned. Maybe she didn't remember McCarthy. Maybe she'd never known about the Hearings. If you were ten at the time and it didn't affect you, why would you?

"The Committee on Un-American Activities," I explained. "They investigated people on suspicion of being Communists. Most of them didn't answer. They took the Fifth Amendment as a matter of principle."

"I thought it was just people from Hollywood."

"No. A lot of people. They couldn't get work in their fields."

"That's terrible."

"It was."

I waited for her to smile but she didn't. She busied herself pulling down the covers. Then she asked, in a strangled, too-loud voice, "Was he one?"

My heart seemed to stop, then made up for it by racing at a frightening gallop. Weren't Southerners supposed to be tactful? I pretended not to understand.

"What?"

"Your father. A Communist."

"Of course not."

But the truth was, I didn't know. I'd always imagined him a socialist like Papa, the sort of man who'd keep a bust of Eugene Debs on display, who'd put his faith in labor unions and help the underdog by designing houses where several families could live. If he'd ever joined the Communist Party, which I doubted, he'd probably done it less out of conviction than to be with a group of friends. Certainly he didn't want to overthrow the government. But I didn't actually *know*.

We got ready for bed quickly, both of us unsettled. Susan turned out the light and was so quiet I thought she'd fallen asleep, but I squiggled endlessly between the too-pink covers. Some things you knew—and you didn't. I couldn't ask if Daddy was a Communist any more than I could have asked why Uncle Abe's fingers had been cut off. Someone would have to volunteer the information. But ten years had passed and no one had. I didn't think they ever would.

19

I didn't realize then that the weeks between Thanksgiving and Christmas on a college campus would be hectic even if my pregnant roommate hadn't been converting religions and planning a wedding or if the surrounding town hadn't been in turmoil, beset by more civil rights demonstrations than it had witnessed since summer. Suddenly, the activists were everywhere, not just in front of Packard's Sandwich Shop but at most of the twenty-six other businesses on a list distributed by CORE that were known to discriminate against Negroes. I looked for David in all the picket lines, but he had disappeared without a word.

No one was sure if President Kennedy's assassination triggered the disruptions or if the time would have been ripe anyway. The Congress On Racial Equality sent out bulletins from its dingy office above a funeral parlor, demanding a public-accommodations law before the holidays and urging

Chapel Hill to be the first totally desegregated town in the state. "Give Freedom for Christmas" was the latest slogan.

In front of Fowler's Food Store, long-haired girls bundled in coats and knee socks carried signs saying "Why Can't Negroes Work Here?" and "Don't Buy Discrimination." The strains of "We Shall Overcome" wafted out even in front of sacred campus hangouts like The Patio and The Shack—a song so beautiful, so powerful, that the segregationists were doubly annoyed to be forced to hear its message. In the not-quite-three weeks before school let out for Christmas, more than a hundred people were arrested, about half of them students. Among them were Marilyn Adler and Emily Moses.

Our housemother, Mrs. West, immediately told Anna Mae to call an emergency dorm meeting to help us deal with this disgrace.

"Girls," Anna Mae said, looking from one to another of us, "what I'm going to tell you isn't pleasant. But I hope it will make you think."

We sat cross-legged on the carpets or curled up on couches and chairs, restless and resentful. It was eleven-fifteen and most of us had tests or papers due the next day. Anna Mae paused to toy with the rollers in her hair. "Not only did Marilyn and Emily participate in an illegal demonstration, but they—"

"There's some question whether it was illegal," I found myself mumbling.

"Not only did they participate in a demonstration," Anna Mae continued. "They also stayed out of the dorm all night without permission.

"The women's Honor Council has no choice, girls. It has to try them, just as it would have to try any of you if you failed to sign out. You know what the penalties can be for that."

We did. Anna Mae sighed. She said she hoped this meeting would serve as fair warning. "I want you to think about what's happened here, even though you're busy. Even though you're studying and trying to finish up before Christmas. Think about whether you want to come back and take your finals in January. Or whether you're willing to put your education in jeopardy, the way some of the residents of this dorm already have. Think about that long and hard."

Although going to the dorm meeting was required, nobody had expected Marilyn and Emily to show up. Certainly Mrs. West hadn't sent anybody to get them. Now, from the back of the crowd, someone raised her hand. Everyone was shocked to see it was Marilyn. She was standing behind the farthest couch, and no one had realized she was there—except Anna Mae, facing the back of the room, who'd pretended not to see her. Anna Mae continued to ignore her now. Marilyn began to walk forward.

"I have something to say." Her voice sounded even smaller than usual, an insipid little girl's voice.

"This is out of order—" Anna Mae began.

"Let her talk," someone said. We looked around for Emily. She'd just emerged through the swinging door that led to the west wing of the dorm.

Marilyn made her way to the front, with Emily just behind her. "It's true Emily and I stayed out overnight without signing out," Marilyn said. "It's also true we didn't have any choice. We were in jail. We wanted to call the dorm, but they wouldn't let us."

A collective gasp filled the room from girls who hadn't known. Marilyn started to say something else, but her voice trailed off and she looked as if she were about to cry. Emily put her hand on Marilyn's shoulder. What happened next startled me as much as it did anybody. I stalked to the front, and before Anna Mae could stop me, I said, "You might not agree with what they're doing, but what happened could happen to anybody. Any one of us could get into a situation where we don't have a choice. You shouldn't have to go before the Honor Council for something you believe in."

From her perch on one of the sofas, Susan gave me a thumbs-up sign. An agreeable murmur filled the room. I looked at Ashley. I thought about what I'd done with David. I turned to Anna Mae. "It's not as if they were out necking with some boy," I said. "And if they were, so what?"

The next day the sun came out and the temperature rose to eighty degrees. Everyone took blankets outside to sunbathe. I lay on my back, staring up through the bare tree branches to white clouds and blue sky. The effect was at once blissful and dizzying. I was by now able to distinguish between the dizziness brought on by my breakup with David and this other, more welcome sensation. After the initial shock of Kennedy's death and David's curt rebuff, I'd been too numb to think. At Susan's I'd been too busy. But after we got back to campus and David didn't call to apologize, I felt once again as if I were tumbling through the empty air of uncertainty. Nothing had been settled. Marilyn told me David had left town, maybe gone to Charlotte to see his folks. No one was sure. No one had seen him.

Instead of feeling liberated, I felt worse. My heart did an erratic dance every time I crossed campus and saw a male on crutches. There were more of them than I'd imagined. If he'd wanted to, David could have called me. I would be reading a book, eating dinner, doing my laundry, when a sudden panicky realization would lick up from my chest into my throat. David was gone. Then, just as suddenly as it had come, the sensation would be gone.

On that warm afternoon on the blanket outside the dorm, I emptied my mind of everything but the sunshine. "In D.C. we never get weather like this in December," I murmured to Susan. My eyes drifted shut, and I was on the edge of sleep. The next thing I knew, she was ramming an elbow into my rib. "Don't you know that guy?" she asked.

230

I sat up and tried to clear my head. It had to be David. Not thinking about him had made him appear. I directed my gaze to where Susan was pointing. He was lumbering up the steps to the dorm, looking noble and haunted. His hair was longer than before, curling around his ears. A beatnik, but handsome. My heart pounded wildly.

"He wasn't actually from my study group," I blurted. "I was seeing him."

"I know," she said.

"Then why didn't you say something?"

"I figured you were the one to bring it up. Which you just did."

I felt glued to the blanket. "I mean, I was seeing him all the time. I was lying about it. Because he was—"

"Hey, I know. There are things I don't talk about, either." She paused. Then she brightened. "Well? Aren't you going to speak to him?"

"I'm not sure . . ."

"Of course you are," she said, and got up and hauled me to my feet.

I caught up with David just as he reached the front door. "When'd you get back in town?" I asked the back of his head. I hoped to startle him, but he turned slowly, unperturbed.

"Yesterday." He scrutinized the fluting on one of the columns. "I thought about calling. I figured if I did, you wouldn't talk to me."

"I probably wouldn't." I realized this was true. He had lost a little weight, and his eyes looked even larger. "We made a big mistake," I said.

In the bright sunshine, his face drained of color. "You mean—?"

Oh, Jesus, I thought. He thinks I'm pregnant. "I don't mean I'm foisting fatherhood on you," I said. "I mean it was stupid."

He took a deep breath, but caught himself before he

sighed. "Listen, the reason I didn't call was because I felt like crap. I had no right to get so angry. To blame you for Ivan. I feel like I took advantage of you."

"There's no 'feel like' about it. You did."

"Yes, but it's not my style. It's not the sort of thing I can—" He fidgeted, which wasn't like him, and I was glad to see it. "It's not something I can take back."

No kidding, I thought. "I didn't die from it," I said.

He looked uncomfortable. "I came over here to—I wanted to apologize. I had no right to say what I did. To think you'd sleep with me because you felt sorry for me."

I didn't say anything. That's just why I *had* slept with him: not out of love, not out of desire. Because I felt sorry for him. Which wasn't something to be proud of.

A breeze drifted through the bare trees, heartbreakingly balmy. We both looked at the girls sprawled on their blankets. David let go of his right hand grip, allowed the crutch to hang free from his arm brace, and lifted his fingers to touch my cheek.

"What if we got something to eat at Harry's later?" The light in his eyes was soft, the way it had been when he talked to Ivan, open to a new beginning. I let his fingers trace the shape of my cheekbone.

Then Marilyn and Emily walked out of the dorm, each holding a sheaf of papers. They saw us and stopped.

"Hey, Beryl, you coming too?" Emily asked.

"Coming where?"

"The meeting about the editorial," she said.

"*The Daily Tar Heel* is doing an editorial saying the Honor Council has no right to prosecute someone who goes to jail on a free-speech issue," David told me. "There's a meeting at the CORE office." His voice was mechanical, a wind-up toy.

Here we go again, I thought.

Marilyn seemed puzzled. "We'll meet you at your car, David," she said. "Come on, Emily."

The two of them walked off.

"You didn't come to apologize. You came to take them to a meeting," I said.

David fooled with the padding on his brace. "I wish you'd come to Harry's later."

"No, thanks." I remembered his calling me a bitch. I was finished with softness.

He shrugged and headed to his car. The tops of the trees swirled in the sunshine. No matter that I didn't even like him; no matter that I wanted it to be over. Even after all this, there was no sense of completion. I was still racing through the air above us, tumbling down and down. I wondered if I was going to turn out like Aunt Gussie.

The sunshine made everyone mellow, as December warmth will. Ashley, who'd driven out to the lake with Paco, came back sunburned. Everyone had color in their cheeks. We sat outdoors till dusk, when the chill crept back into the air. Then we went into the lobby and lingered—more than fifty of us—reluctant to return to our ordinary December lives. We talked to girls we hardly knew, girls we usually avoided. We shared a brief, harmonious sisterhood. Donna Manning from upstairs, one of the regulars who liked to listen to Susan's records, tapped me on the arm and said, "You were right the other night. About the Honor Council trying the colored girl and your friend."

My friend? I supposed she meant Marilyn. I didn't say we hardly knew each other.

"It's true what you said," Penny Blankenship added. "If they wanted to, they could get any one of us for something." She glanced at Ashley, who lowered her gaze. Then, as if to shake off such serious matters, Penny held her arm up to mine to compare the effect of the day's sunshine.

"You get dark in ten seconds," she said. "It takes me weeks."

"Months," Susan corrected. To me she said, "She burns and peels. Burns and peels. By August she's beige."

Emily Moses came through the front door then. "Hey, Emily," Penny called. And without stopping to think, "Wow, Emily, where'd you get your tan?"

Emily froze, eyes big for a second, maybe nonplussed. Then she smiled, wider and wider. "I was born with it," she said.

We all laughed. Penny, too. It was the most amazing thing.

After Thanksgiving, Ashley had come back to school with a wedding planning notebook her mother had given her for listing each task she had to do, and when. She hadn't wanted to have any attendants for the wedding, but her mother talked her into having two cousins as bridesmaids. I never thought I'd be asked to be in the wedding but found it odd that Susan hadn't been, inasmuch as she was kin and had helped Ashley so much.

"You've got it wrong," Susan said when I voiced my opinion. "Even if it weren't for Daddy and Uncle Toby, they'd see me more as a conspirator. You, too."

But although Ashley's mother might not approve of Ashley's choice of a mate or our role in helping the romance along, she was deeply involved in the wedding itself. Ashley was, too. No matter that she was about to make a long-term commitment to a man who was an embarrassment to her family (and she to his), for now the important thing was to plan the correct social occasion. The wedding would be in the church. Then everyone would go to the Carolina Inn for the reception. There would be a decorated wedding cake and nonalcoholic punch.

Instead of going out with Paco every night until curfew, Ashley often sat in the dorm poring over her wedding book, or studying lessons on Catholicism. Even her enthusiasm for the church reminded me of Penny Blankenship's awe of everything related to Chi Omega. I knew Ashley was converting to a religion and not joining a sorority, but the way she acted, it was exactly as if she were pledging.

As the wedding approached, I didn't see David again, but now and then I still felt I was falling. In Graham Memorial, where I spent endless hours studying, the sense of impending doom sometimes overtook me so strongly that I'd have to will myself to concentrate by conjuring up images of Aunt Gussie strapped down to the table where they gave her electric shock. This was a fairly effective technique. I finally learned to hone in on the lesson until the words stubbed out the smolder in my mind and all I could think of was facts. I might be going crazy, but I certainly wasn't going to flunk out of school.

My main worry those last days was not even crash landing; it was going home for Christmas. Mother had said I wouldn't have to sleep in the bed where Bubby Tsippi had died, but I knew I'd insist I didn't mind, and the idea gave me the creeps. Worse, I'd have to make conversation with my family. Natalie and Barry were coming, but only for a weekend. The rest of the time, what would we say? More to the point, what would I say to my mother?

Even before President Kennedy was shot, she'd started dropping me short, personal notes. These were friendly, chatty, conciliatory. Since the night of her surprise visit to Chapel Hill, she hadn't accused me of a thing. A couple of times she'd even phoned the dorm when the rest of the family wasn't around—probably to show she could be persistent enough to get through. I'd wanted her to feel guilty for not knowing where I was my first month here, and apparently she had. Lately she'd made a point of saying she'd take some time off during the holidays while I was home. It was as if she were courting me.

But I was suspicious. Sooner or later she'd start in on me. Why had I stayed at a Southern school? How could I dishonor my father that way? At the very least, why didn't I stand in picket lines? Do something useful? She'd never accept me unconditionally. It wasn't her style. I had to be prepared.

I found myself seizing on topics we could discuss. A few days before class ended, the women's council decided it wouldn't try students who'd spent the night in jail. There was great jubilation in the dorm. Everyone believed that if the system could back down on this, it might back down on anything. People congratulated Marilyn and Emily. Someone even clapped Emily on the shoulder. I would tell my mother that. I would tell her how we'd all laughed when Penny mentioned Emily's suntan. These were the small inklings of progress my mother would appreciate. But the thought of three weeks at home with her loomed.

With my heart full of dread, I wrapped my miniature soaps in blue paper for Chanuka. We would exchange presents when I got there even though the holiday was probably over. Miriam would make potato latkes, fried not in the traditional oil but in *schmaltz*, rendered chicken fat, which always gave me indigestion. There was no avoiding it: three weeks of confrontation. Miriam was none too happy that I wouldn't be coming the minute school let out, that I planned to stay in Chapel Hill an extra night in order to go to the wedding.

"As soon as it's over, you'll come," she insisted.

"There's a reception."

"Come right after it's over, Beryl," my mother urged from the extension. "You haven't been home for three months. A long time. Everyone misses you."

Two days later she sent a ticket for a Trailways bus that departed for Washington immediately after the reception.

236

There was no question now that the wedding would take place. At the last minute, Paco's mother agreed to come. She was flying in just before the ceremony and out the same night. There would be no rehearsal dinner, no joyous get-togethers or other pretenses of support. But at least she would offer her presence.

The dorm closed on Friday. Susan and I spent the night with her friend Jolene on the outskirts of Chapel Hill, while Ashley stayed with her parents at the Carolina Inn. Saturday dawned damp and chilly. I dressed for the wedding and carried a change of clothes in my overnight case. I'd already put most of my luggage in a locker at the Trailways station, to retrieve before I got on the bus. I stuck a wad of Kleenex in my purse, in case I cried. Jolene dropped us off at the church.

Intimidated by the soaring ceilings and starkness of the stone walls, I began to sniff and fidget as soon as the usher guided us to our seats. Ashley's few guests didn't nearly fill up the long wooden benches, and I felt embarrassed for her. Paco's pews were empty except for a few foreign friends who hadn't left for the holiday. Paco's mother was nowhere in sight.

We waited nearly twenty minutes. The organist played the same tune over and over. Someone sneezed. Another coughed. Before long there was general wheezing and snif-fling. Ashley's mother stood at the back, nervously eyeing the door as the congregation's restlessness grew palpable. Finally two Latin-looking women came in, one a grandmotherly type, the other fortyish, slender, and purposeful. Paco's mother, clearly. Everyone gasped.

She was dressed entirely in black. Black crepe dress, tailored so it set off her stylish thinness. Black coat, which she shed and handed to an usher. A veiled Jackie Kennedy pillbox hat perched atop teased Spanish-black hair. Susan nudged me. Paco's mother straightened as we all stared at her, the perfect diplomat's wife, erect and graceful. Her black veil obscured her features so much it was hard to tell if Paco resembled her. But we could see, despite the elaborate gestures of her hands as she greeted Ashley's parents, that she wore a polite, unsmiling expression of strained courtesy.

The organ began once more. Paco's mother leaned heavily on the usher who led her to her seat. She looked as if, weary from deep mourning, she might suddenly decide to faint. Her older companion came down the aisle behind her, on the arm of another usher. She, too, was all in black.

"I think that's what they wear to weddings in South America," Susan whispered.

"I think she has a nerve doing it here," I said. Anyone who worked as a diplomat knew what the customs were in America.

The organist stopped, then started again. I rubbed my nose and wondered if my tissues would last me through the ceremony. A priest came out and stood at the altar in medieval-looking robes, in a slant of unearthly light that came through the stained-glass windows. Paco also stepped out, handsome in his rented tux, followed by his Arabian roommate, his best man.

The procession began: bridesmaids first, then the matron of honor. The music stopped once more, then burst into the strains of "Here Comes the Bride."

Ashley appeared at the end of the aisle, clinging to her father's arm. Her dress was satin with long sleeves, puffed at the top. The neckline was studded with tiny pearls, and a four-foot train trailed her in back. Her mother needn't have worried about Ashley's stomach showing. She had no extra flesh anywhere. More noticeable than her figure was the extraordinary pallor of her face. Every trace of her sunburn was gone, and the pearls that dotted her headpiece were more colorful than her cheeks. It was the groom who was supposed to be pale, wasn't it? Morning sickness, I thought. But lately her nausea had been less. More likely it had dawned on Ashley that this wedding wasn't just a one-day affair, that it meant a commitment she'd be into forever.

At the front of the church, Ashley's father handed her over to Paco, and the bridal couple knelt while the priest mumbled something in Latin. Ashley's father sat down beside her mother, both of them rigid in their seats. The priest went on and on.

A clammy, shadowy feeling swept across me. The Yom Kippur I'd gone out selling flower bulbs as a child, when Mrs. Katz had sent me home because everyone was getting ready for *shul*, I'd had this same cold feeling—a vision of *shul* not as a building and the holiday not as an observance, but each of them as something more, something ominous, where God played by strange, fearful rules I could never understand. The sight of the unfamiliar crucifix made me feel sick, not just in my stopped-up head but all the way to the pit of my stomach, the same helpless feeling I'd had running away from the Katzes' on Yom Kippur Eve.

The priest mumbled, and an altar boy waved a container of incense. Ashley and Paco were still kneeling, crushing their clothes. Some of the guests walked up to the communion railing in the front. Paco's mother stood to follow them but then started sobbing and sank back into the pew. The older woman patted her arm. The priest's voice rose and echoed, louder than before, as if to cover up the weeping.

The sobbing went on, no more to be denied than the despair of the statues, the suffering of Christ on the crucifix. I pressed my hand hard to the bottom of my nose to keep from sneezing. I hated all of it—the images of death, the Stations of the Cross, the mournful expressions cast in stained glass and stone. How much larger they were than the wedding, intentionally so, designed to intimidate and frighten. Why should a religion be based on images of death? Maybe there was wisdom in my parents refusing to go to services.

Paco's mother made a strange, heaving sound. She was

behaving as if her son had died. He might have been in a casket instead of kneeling at the altar in his wedding tux. She actually started to moan. What nerve: this was no death! This was a wedding! A beginning! Paco's mother made it a travesty.

Paco answered the priest in a firm, deep voice, and Ashley spoke in a smaller, shakier one. Paco's mother's moan became a wail. Her companion put an arm around her, but the mother didn't stop. Everyone's eyes were on the two women. The older one led Paco's mother away, not by the side aisle where they would be less conspicuous, but down the center aisle, where a white cloth had been laid for the bridal party.

"What a bitch," Susan said.

"I'll say," I whispered.

Even Ashley and Paco turned to see what was going on. Under her white veil, Ashley's face had a waxy, shiny cast of terror.

The priest spoke again, and the bridal couple turned back to him, heads bowed. How did the woman get away with carrying on like that? Did being religious give her the right?

The noise died down in the back of the church. Ashley and Paco began exchanging rings. Ashley was composed again, but so white she looked insubstantial. So resigned she might have been a shadow. Pretending not to care. Quitting school one semester before graduation. Acting as if Paco's mother wasn't insulting her. How calm could she be?

Finally I heard the phrase, "Man and wife." It was over. The organ began to play. Ashley and Paco rushed down the aisle toward his mother, her sobs now drowned out by the music. Ashley's lips were set in a smile as she passed, but her color was ghostly. I couldn't look at her. When I turned away, I faced not people whose expressions were joyful, here at a wedding, but the wall plaques full of sorrow and pain. Ashley would have the sorrow, too—the morning sickness, the hasty marriage, the unplanned child.

"Christ," I whispered, rising to go.

"Shhh," Susan whispered back. We went out by the side aisle. I felt almost too stiff to walk. Cloud and shadow came in through the stained glass, bluish and wounded, a band of light without heat. When my arm brushed against the cold stone wall, I thought I'd never be warm.

We reached the vestibule before the others, who were still shuffling up the center aisle. The bridal party was organizing itself into a receiving line. Paco's mother stood a little to the side, waiting to be positioned. She wiped her eyes under her veil, dabbed and dabbed with tissues.

I didn't stop walking as I approached her. Didn't veer away. I knocked her hard with my shoulder before I turned, and sent her stumbling toward the wall. She would have caught herself if her hands hadn't been busy wiping her teary eyes. She lost her balance, clutched at the stones, landed in an ungraceful heap on the floor.

"So sorry," I hissed. A gasp rose from the guests behind us. Someone snickered. It seemed only fitting. What right had she to dress in mourning as if the wedding were a death? What kind of God would allow such a thing in His house? It served her right.

Mr. Vance hoisted Paco's mother up. Ashley rushed over to ask if she were all right. Paco's mother nodded and smiled, but there was no acceptance in her face, only unyielding duty and forbearance. As long as the marriage lasted, she would make Ashley miserable.

I rushed from the church and didn't glance back. Who was this God anyway, I wondered, and what did He want?

20

Susan caught up with me as I reached the sidewalk.

"Beryl, wait!" She clicked along on high heels, walking fast. "Are you okay?" she gasped. I finally stopped and faced her.

"No! This whole thing—it just makes me so mad!"

"Me, too."

"And look what I did! What good did it do? None!"

"It was nice to see her go down like that," Susan said. "Nobody saw who bumped her. We were the first ones there."

"That's not the point. The point is, it was an empty gesture. Maybe Ashley's right. Maybe she didn't have any choice. Maybe she had to get married so the Honor Council wouldn't kick her out of school. And have a mother-in-law who sneers at her and a baby a couple months too soon for people who like to keep track of the date. But I hate it. I hate it!"

Susan put her arm around me. She was wearing a forest-green suit and black pumps, and she smelled like her friend Jolene's toilet water. "I hate it, too, Beryl. But Ashley's all right. She really is."

"That's just the problem! She's so—resigned."

"Sometimes there are things you can't change. Sometimes you just—go with it. Even if it's hard."

I wasn't sure if Susan meant Ashley's condition or something else, but before I could ask she nudged my shoulder. "Come on. Come back in. We'll go to the reception."

"I couldn't," I said. "I couldn't face them."

"I told you, nobody saw—"

"Listen. Give Ashley a good-luck kiss for me and tell her I'll see her after Christmas." I waved and fled in the direction of a side door that led to the basement where I'd stashed my overnight case. I changed out of my dress into the warm slacks and sweater I'd brought for traveling, and waited for the wedding guests to leave so I could make my escape unnoticed.

I walked slowly toward town. My bus didn't leave for two hours. I'd get my suitcases from the bus station locker and sit in the waiting room. The air had a frosty, damp, hanging quality. It was only slightly too warm to snow. I wasn't in any hurry. I walked across the deserted campus, onto Franklin Street, past the post office and Harry's. The bus terminal was on West Franklin Street a few blocks away.

In the distance, I was surprised to see picketers in front of Packard's Sandwich Shop. I thought when school let out, they'd take a break. But no—Tripp and Gloria, Laura and Fran, all marched in their accustomed circle—and David, too, the handle of his placard wedged into his arm brace.

After feeling repelled by the pickets for so many months, now I was almost drawn to them—touched by the sight of Gloria after her recent miscarriage, of Laura and Fran loyally marching, of David struggling along on his crutches.

I crossed the street and stood closer, knowing they wouldn't look at me or speak. Even if they did, I'd be out of Chapel Hill in a couple of hours, on my way to another country. With his long hair, David looked nothing like the person I'd met back in September. His clothes were looser, more casual, shabby flannels and jeans. Between that and his crutches he looked younger, more vulnerable, than he'd been in his neat sweaters and chinos.

Although I didn't mean to feel warm toward him, I found myself forgiving him, if not for insulting me after he stripped me of my virginity, at least for being so crabby. After all, he had his reasons. He'd gotten polio while the rest of us escaped, he lived with the consequences every second of his life. Of all the dogs who'd ever been tied up, his was the one who'd managed to hang himself. David was a jerk, granted, but even a jerk couldn't be completely worthless if he was willing to hobble around a picket line on crutches, drawing everyone's eye.

Commotion erupted just as my sentiments threatened to get away from me. Three loud, young men came out of a ladies' shop a few doors down the street, carrying packages and poking each other in the ribs. Anyone could guess they'd been buying Christmas presents for their girlfriends, and were proud of the intimate items they'd chosen. They looked too old to be students, but they were just as rowdy. Walking toward Packard's, they seemed aware of nothing but their private joke until they spied the picketers and stopped. One leaned over and spoke to the others. They all laughed. Then the smallest of the three balled up his package under his arm and resumed walking, wiry and tense, a bit ahead of his friends. He moved close to the circle of picketers, not fast. And just as David passed he stuck out his foot swiftly and smoothly, knocking David's right crutch away from his arm and across the pavement.

No one else saw it. For a second, I couldn't believe it myself.

David lurched forward and flung his hands out to catch himself. He held on to the other crutch as he twisted his body like the athlete he was, and managed to land in a sitting position on his good leg. The right crutch came to a stop a few feet away, and the placard—"Give Freedom for Christmas"— fell to the pavement.

The two men holding the packages laughed. The wiry one, the one who'd tripped David, gave a grin to his companions. David ignored them. Gloria, Tripp, Fran, and Laura kept walking in their perfect circle. On the sidewalk, David sat white-faced and humiliated. Everyone on the street froze and watched. I knew there was nothing that could embarrass him more. He leaned across the concrete, flattened himself out, reaching for his crutch. He moved as if he believed he were alone; he didn't lift his eyes. The picketers didn't even look in his direction.

I couldn't bear it. I didn't believe in passive resistance, never had. Dropping my overnight case, I took two quick steps toward the picket line and snatched up the crutch before David got to it. I thrust it soundly into the stomach of the man who tripped him, then tossed it to David.

The guy grunted. His face contorted; then his eyes focused and he came toward me. I lowered my head and flung myself at him full force. The sky, which moments before had seemed so cold and gray, was suddenly shot through with explosive shards of brightness. Maybe a sign from heaven. I was flying, soaring. I slammed into the man with the same shoulder I'd used on Paco's mother but with ten times the force. He tumbled onto his rear end. I collapsed on top of him—a bumpy landing after all those weeks of falling—and came to a stop in luminous air charged with possibilities.

I didn't feel quite so feisty after I was arrested. At the Chapel Hill jail, a detective fingerprinted me while a policeman asked me questions. Full name, address, age, height, weight. Gloria had been arrested, too, after she pulled me off the man I'd jumped on. We were booked for assault.

"Too bad they didn't arrest David," Gloria said as we rode to the station in the police car. "It would make him feel—you know. Normal."

"Too bad they didn't arrest that jerk who tripped him."

"They couldn't. No witnesses except you. It's bull-hockey, but that's how it is."

She leaned against the sweat-smelling seat of the police car. "David was our spokesman at sit-ins last summer because they'd never take him in. If they arrest somebody on crutches, it doesn't make good press."

"Be serious," I said.

"I am."

At the jail, we were the only prisoners. At least they didn't separate us. They put us in the same cell, a rectangle about the size of someone's bedroom, with gray floors and matching gray walls that were last painted around the turn of the century. A filthy sink and toilet were built into the corner. There was no toilet paper.

Seeing my face, Gloria said, "This isn't so bad. You should see the jail in Hillsboro. It's full of roaches. They make you eat out of old ice trays and plastic bottles."

I sat down on my cot. It was lumpy, and smelled of urine. I wrinkled my nose.

"In Durham they don't even have mattresses," Gloria said. "Just slats."

"Sounds like you've taken the tour."

"Yeah."

"My mother ends up in jail sometimes," I said.

"Stuart told me."

"I can't remember her ever giving a description." As I spoke, I realized how odd this was. She'd been in jail half a dozen times at least, and the only account I'd ever heard was about a prison she'd visited as part of her job.

Gloria tugged at her sweater, which was pressed tight against her breasts. It was a terrible sweater, a Goodwill reject, a yellow-orange crewneck that looked too small. Earlier, the young policeman who'd questioned us had stared at her chest as he wrote down her answers. I wondered when Tripp would show up to bail her out.

There was a window directly above Gloria's cot. We climbed up and looked out at an empty sidewalk under the clouds, with not a person in sight. We got down and sat on our mattresses.

After a while the young policeman came in and gave us brown paper sacks, a bag supper. Each had two hot dogs inside, along with a napkin and packets of mustard.

Gloria took out one of the hot dogs, examined it, and put it back. "I'm not going to eat," she said. "They get the food from Packard's."

"You don't know that for sure," I said, although I'd heard this many times. Besides, I was hungry. All I'd had that day was breakfast.

"It's public record," Gloria said. "Invoices from Packard's for the food for the jail."

"I won't eat, either, then."

"You can," Gloria said. "I'm the one who feels strongly about this. Not you. Don't let me stop you."

"I'm not really hungry," I lied.

We pushed our bags out through the bars of the cell. We didn't talk much. I wondered when I'd be able to make my one phone call. I had to call home, I supposed. I wasn't sure what I'd tell them. In a single day I'd knocked down Ashley's mother-in-law and assaulted David's attacker. Miriam would probably think my healthful trip South had backfired and made me crazier than Aunt Gussie.

Gloria leaned against the cinderblock wall, then slid down to the floor. We both breathed deeply. The scent of the hot dogs was pungent, meaty, delicious. It seemed a strange and intimate time, the two of us alone in the dark jail, inhaling food we weren't going to eat.

"I didn't really think about what I did out there," I mused. "If I had, I wouldn't be here."

She nodded. "Yeah. That happens. Kind of fun, though, wasn't it?"

"Kind of," I agreed without thinking. What was the matter with me? Fun?

"I'm serious, Gloria," I told her. "I wouldn't have done it if I'd thought about it. It was a temporary lapse. A reflex."

"No. You did it to protect David," she said. "I think it was nice."

"Protect him!"

"Sure. What else would you call it?"

"Oh, right," I said sarcastically. "On some deep, instinc-tual level, even though we haven't spoken for weeks—"

"It's not the motive that counts," Gloria said. "The impor-tant thing is, you did it."

She got up and went over to the bags of hot dogs she'd pushed outside the cell. Their mustardy aroma swirled all around us, warming the air. She squinched the tops of the bags tighter, closing them off. "Tripp says we should become vegetarians. I don't think I could. I still get hungry like when I was pregnant."

She sat down again. The smell of the hot dogs was just as strong as before.

"You're still upset about losing the baby, aren't you?" I asked. This was a question I would never have asked, normally, but under the circumstances it didn't seem out of line.

A little frown line formed between her eyebrows. "Yes and no. I thought I wasn't ready for a baby. Now I'm not sure you have to be ready." She looked wistful and resigned.

"Maybe that's what Ashley was thinking."

"What?"

"Ashley. My roommate." It struck me that this might be why Ashley had been so calm these past months as she traveled her bumpy path. She hadn't cared about being ready. She'd always believed that, if you were going to bear the child of the man you loved, you put up with the inconvenience. If that was true, it was a good thing I hadn't told her everything I knew about abortions. Even better that she hadn't seen what I did to her mother-in-law.

Gloria moved her hand to her stomach, as if to remind herself of something. "A baby would have been nice. I mean, we do want children." Her eyes grew glassy. "But not yet."

I saw the wisdom of that. Gloria was too busy for motherhood, going to jail and going on hunger strikes. Maybe she'd miscarried because subconsciously she knew she had something more urgent to do. Maybe my mother had her abortion for the same reason. Maybe Ashley, too, had chosen her path and not just been dropped into it.

My stomach growled, and I felt I had happened on something profound.

I lay back on my cot and thought about food. I was in the dining room at home, the table laden with coffee and sweets. Miriam chewed a piece of sponge cake, and Aunt Gussie mashed hers into shreds with her fork. Bubby Tsippi sat among us, spooning up cottage cheese from a blue bowl. I rushed to stop her.

Then the table was clear, and Miriam was lighting the first candle in a menorah. She passed the candle to Bubby Tsippi, who lit another, then passed it to my mother, who did the same and passed it to me. Beautiful voices sang in the background, but I couldn't make out the words.

"See?" Miriam said to me. "We believe in God. Another name for sense of purpose, is all. For believing in the possibilities of man."

"The possibilities of women, too," said my mother.

I held the candle and hesitated. I felt unworthy. But Bubby Tsippi nodded and urged me on.

The singing grew louder. Voices high and pure. They were not singing a Chanuka song. They were singing "We Shall Overcome."

I opened my eyes and sat up, confused.

"See? I told you the mattress wasn't so bad," Gloria said, her voice tinny. "Otherwise you wouldn't fall asleep."

"I wasn't sleeping," I mumbled. But look! A jail cell. Me! Night had fallen, and the room was full of shadows. The singing grew louder. It was coming from outside. It sounded good.

"I wondered when they'd get here," Gloria said. She leaned against the wall, arms crossed, and looked toward the window that brought in the night.

"Who?"

"Everybody."

She beckoned me over. I shook off my sleepiness and climbed with her onto her mattress. Outside the window, a dozen people stood on the sidewalk. Tripp. David. Some women I didn't know. All singing. Their breath turned to mist in the cold. Streetlights silvered their hair.

We shall overcome . . .

Some . . . day.

The music was a bond of friendship. Of support. We balanced ourselves on Gloria's cot and joined the choir. Later, when the crowd dispersed, I realized it was hours since I'd missed my bus.

A policeman came and took me to make my phone call. Aunt Gussie answered.

"What are you doing there?" I asked. Having a crazy spell?

"I thought you're on the Trailways," she said. "On your way, coming home."

"Not yet," I said. "Is my father home?"

He wasn't. No one was. I left word that I was in jail—probably not for long—and hung up, sure Gussie was too unreliable to convey my message.

The policeman escorted me back to the cell. A few minutes later he opened the door again and brought David and Tripp with him. I'd always thought they took prisoners out to a special visiting room, but maybe not. Tripp held Gloria's hand through the bars, but he spoke to me.

"A bunch of us made an agreement," he said. "If we get arrested, we stay. We don't post bail. As a protest. But we have a bail fund. We can spring you."

"That's okay," I said. "I wouldn't leave Gloria here alone."

"You shouldn't feel you have to stay," he repeated.

"Of course I do, don't be ridiculous." It was the second time that day someone had told me they weren't requiring from me what they required from themselves. Gloria didn't expect me to refuse hot dogs, and Tripp didn't expect me to stay in jail. Who did they think I was?

"You sure?" Tripp asked.

"Yes."

"Well—thanks."

Tripp lifted Gloria's hand to his lips and kissed it. David motioned me to the other side of the cell to give them privacy.

"You didn't need to tackle that guy," he said in a furious whisper when we'd walked as far from Tripp and Gloria as we could. "I was all right, I could have handled it."

"You weren't all right," I whispered back. "You were on the sidewalk. You needed help."

His face was in shadow, but I could see his muscles tighten as he clenched his jaw. "I managed to get up," he said.

"Yes, and you would have gone right back to picketing. You would have let him go."

"So?"

"The guy deserved worse, David. No matter who you are, sometimes you need help." I crossed my arms and turned away from him. "Besides, I didn't do it to help you. I was just mad."

"Oh. Fine. That explains it."

"Don't be such an egomaniac. You weren't the only thing I was upset about."

He looked skeptical, but I didn't care. I told him about the wedding and Paco's mother. I told him how I'd stomped out of the church. Finally he stopped glaring.

"You really knocked her down?"

"It was a reflex," I said.

He smiled, all the muscles in his face relaxing, and then started to laugh.

A door opened at the end of the hall. A shaft of yellow light fell into the corridor. "Time to go, boys," a policeman said.

David's expression grew sober. "When I went away, I was looking for a job," he said. "I'm going to work in a photo lab in Raleigh. I start after New Year's."

"I guess you won't be going to law school," I said.

"I knew in September I wasn't going. I should have told you." He reached through the bar and touched my hand.

"Time to go," the policeman said again.

This time they followed him. David was a dark silhouette moving toward the light. Even though Raleigh was less than thirty miles away, I guessed we wouldn't see each other. Maybe it didn't matter. I wasn't falling anymore. I'd landed back there on Franklin Street, on that redneck grit's soft belly, on soft turf after all, and I wasn't going to die from it. I'd always be glad I'd poked that guy in the stomach.

"David," I called before the door closed behind him. "Good luck."

In the end, the charges were dropped. We were released the next morning. Tripp picked Gloria up and offered me a ride to the station. I said I'd rather walk. I watched Tripp open the door for her, his arm at her curving hip. She was a fertility goddess after all. Next time she'd carry to term, I was sure. I was also certain that, whatever radical political acts she performed afterwards, she'd do them right here at home. I was pleased to think this was possible.

Outside, the morning was crisp and startlingly sunny. The light was different in North Carolina. There was more of it, even in December. My eyes were a long time adjusting.

A familiar car sat at the curb. Mother's. Miriam sat in the passenger seat next to her. Mother got out and waved as she came toward me, her wine-colored lipstick bright and thick, as if she'd been applying it repeatedly while she was waiting. She hugged me hard.

"You all right?"

"Fine."

She held me at arm's length and scrunched up her face to assess me, one jailbird to another. I told her what I'd done.

"You jumped the guy!" she exclaimed. "That's wonderful!" She clapped me on the back—proudly, I thought. "I wouldn't have had the nerve."

"Only because I got mad. Not for some noble reason," I told her. "Not because—"

"Shh," she said. "It's a start. You know why you felt so bad when Bubby Tsippi died? Not because you really did her any harm. But because you thought you should have been paying attention to her and her dishes when your mind was on something else." She paused to take a breath. "I've been guilty of that myself."

"Oh, Mom," I said. And I startled myself by bursting into tears.

She hugged me again. She patted my back. "It's all right, Beryl. What you did yesterday, it's a good thing. You cared about something and you acted. It's a good lesson, Beryl."

Miriam rolled down her window. "So what are you doing, Leah?" she called out. "Making a speech in the middle of the street? Making her cry?" To me she said, "She didn't want you should have to take the bus. We drove all night by machine."

"I'm surprised you got my message." I sniffed and felt better. "Aunt Gussie sounded so—"

"*Ach,* Gussie. Crazy," Miriam said. "She wanted to come, but your mother said no, leave her by Abe. Better Beryl should have the whole back seat."

"You probably didn't get much sleep," Mother explained. She opened the door and motioned me into the back. Then she slid behind the steering wheel.

"I slept a little," I told her.

"Not like sleeping in your own bed."

The bed where Bubby Tsippi had died, I remembered.

"We redecorated," she said as she turned on the ignition. "We got you a new bed. A new dresser."

"You didn't have to."

"Yes, we did. The old furniture was a disgrace. It was time."

We stopped at the bus station for my luggage, then sped down Franklin Street and out of town toward Durham, heading north. As soon as we got onto the highway Miriam handed me a newspaper that must have been in her lap.

"You're famous," my mother said.

"Huh?"

"Look."

I did. It was horrible. There I was, on the front page of the

Chapel Hill Newspaper, flying through the air toward a wiry man who didn't look like he'd be that easy to knock down. Also visible was Gloria, holding her sign: "Integration Now." There was no sign of David.

So. The light I'd been aware of as I leapt toward the man was not, after all, some sign from heaven but the pop of a photographer's flash.

"It says they were downtown taking pictures of the Christmas shoppers," Miriam told me.

I crumpled the newspaper into a ball.

"It's not so serious. School's out. Your friends won't see it," Mother said as she regarded me through the rearview mirror. "It's not like being in the *Washington Post.*" Her last words were soft, but when I caught her eye in the mirror, she winked.

"It wouldn't hurt you, spending one night in jail." Miriam craned her neck in my direction. "When I was your age, I was in jail myself."

"You? In jail?"

"Sure." She shrugged and sniffed, insulted. "You think all I did my whole life was sew dresses? I was in jail for women's suffrage. Mrs. Frank, too. And Mrs. Silverman." These were her friends in the Progressive Women's Club. They were thick of waist and thick of accent, silver-haired and slow.

"Oh, Miriam," I said.

"When you live in Washington, you have no power, even today," Mother interrupted. "You don't vote, you can't—"

Miriam waved her off. "*Zuh den?* Back then was even worse. Women didn't have the vote in Washington or no place else. We didn't have nothing. I could tell you stories."

She paused and waited, expectant. They were wearing me down.

It was five hours home, I thought, more if we ran into traffic. "All right," I said finally. "Tell me stories." I wasn't convinced, probably never would be, but I was listening.

256

Other Titles Available From Spinsters Ink

Spinsters titles are available at your local booksellers or by mail order through Spinsters Ink. A free catalog is available upon request. Please include $2.00 for the first title ordered and 50¢ for every title thereafter. Visa and Mastercard accepted.

Spinsters Ink was founded in 1978 to produce vital books for diverse women's communities. In 1986 we merged with Aunt Lute Books to become Spinsters/Aunt Lute. In 1990, the Aunt Lute Foundation became an independent nonprofit publishing program. In 1992, Spinsters moved to Minnesota.

Spinsters Ink publishes novels and nonfiction works that deal with significant issues in women's lives from a feminist perspective: books that not only name these crucial issues, but—more important—encourage change and growth. We are committed to publishing works by women writing from the periphery: fat women, Jewish women, lesbians, old women, poor women, rural women, women examining classism, women of color, women with disabilities, women who are writing books that help make the best in our lives more possible.

Spinsters Ink
32 E. First St., #330
Duluth, MN 55802-2002
USA

218-727-3222 (phone)   (fax) 218-727-3119
(e-mail) spinsters@aol.com
(website) http://www.lesbian.org/spinsters-ink

Photo by Gray Wells

Ellyn Bache is the author of two other novels: *Safe Passage* (Crown Books, 1988), which was made into a 1995 film starring Susan Sarandon and Sam Shepard, and *Festival in Fire Season* (August House Books, 1992). Her collection of short stories, *The Value of Kindness* (Helicon Nine Editions, 1993) received a Willa Cather Fiction Prize. She has also written a nonfiction book, *Culture Clash,* about sponsoring refugees. Ms. Bache, a native of Washington, D.C., graduated from The University of North Carolina in Chapel Hill in 1964. She lives in Wilmington, N.C.